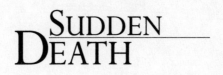

SUDDEN DEATH

SUDDEN DEATH

DAVID ROSENFELT

Published by Warner Books

New York   Boston

Mysterious Press
Warner Books

Time Warner Book Group
1271 Avenue of the Americas, New York, NY 10020
Visit our Web site at www.twbookmark.com.

The Mysterious Press name and logo are registered trademarks of Warner Books.

Printed in the United States of America

First Edition: May 2005

10 9 8 7 6 5 4 3 2 1

Library of Congress Cataloging-in-Publication Data
Rosenfelt, David.
  Sudden death / David Rosenfelt.
    p. cm.
  ISBN 0-89296-783-8
  1. Carpenter, Andy (Fictitious character)—Fiction. 2. Football players—Crimes against—Fiction. 3. Attorney and client—Fiction. 4. Football players—Fiction. 5. New Jersey—Fiction. I. Title.
  PS3618.O838S83 2005
  813'.6—dc22
                                                        2004010698

To Robert Greenwald,
an extraordinary talent, friend,
person, and citizen

Acknowledgments

Okay . . . okay . . . so I didn't do this alone. The point is, I could have . . . I just chose not to. So, a grudging thank you to those who may have provided some slight, unnecessary, almost imperceptible help.

Robin Rue and Sandy Weinberg, agents for life.

Jamie Raab, Les Pockell, Kristen Weber, Susan Richman, Martha Otis, Beth de Guzman, Bob Castillo, and everyone else at Warner. They have been extraordinary partners.

My team of experts, including George Kentris, Kristen Paxos Mecionis, and Susan Brace. They fill in the gaps of my knowledge in the legal and psychological worlds, which is like saying the Atlantic Ocean fills in the gap between Europe and North America.

Those who read early drafts and/or contributed their thoughts and suggestions, including Ross, Heidi, Rick, Lynn, Mike and Sandi Rosenfelt, Sharon, Mitchell, and Amanda Baron, Emily Kim, Al and Nancy Sarnoff, Stacy Alesi, Norman Trell, June Peralta, Stephanie Allen, Scott Ryder, David Devine, and Carol and John Antonaccio.

Debbie Myers, who brightens and informs my life and my work by just being Debbie Myers.

I continue to be grateful to the many people who have e-mailed me feedback on *Open and Shut*, *First Degree*, and *Bury the Lead*. Please do so again at dr27712@aol.com. Thank you.

SUDDEN DEATH

• • • • •

I STEP OFF THE PLANE, and for the first
time in my life, I'm in Los Angeles. I'm not sure why I've
never been here before. I certainly haven't had any preconceived notions about the place, other than the fact that the
people here are insincere, draft-dodging, drug-taking, money-
grubbing, breast-implanting, out-of-touch, pâté-eating, pom-
pous, Lakers-loving, let's-do-lunching, elitist scumbags.

But here I am, open-minded as always.

Walking next to me is Willie Miller, whose own mind is
so wide-open that anything at all is completely free to go in
and out, and often does. I'm not sure how thoughts actually
enter his mind, but the point of exit is definitely his mouth.
"This place ain't so cool," says Willie.

"Willie, it's only the airport." I look over at him and am
surprised to see that he is wearing sunglasses. They seem to
have appeared in the last few seconds, as if he has grown
them. While he doesn't consider the airport "cool," he apparently fears that it might be sunny.

Willie has become a good friend these last couple of
years. He's twenty-eight, ten years my junior, and we met

when I successfully defended him on an appeal of a murder charge for which he had been wrongly convicted. Willie spent seven long years on death row, and his story is the reason we're out here. That and the fact that I had nothing better to do.

We take the escalator down to baggage claim, where a tall blond man wearing a black suit and sunglasses just like Willie's holds up a sign that says "Carpenter." Since my name is Andy Carpenter, I pick up on this almost immediately. "That's us," I say to the man, who is obviously our driver.

"How was your flight?" he asks, an opening conversational gambit I suspect he's used before. I say that it was fine, and then we move smoothly into a chat about the weather while we wait for the bags to come down. I learn that it's sunny today, has been sunny this month, last month, and will be sunny next month and the month after that. It's early June, and there is no chance of rain until December. However, I sense that the driver is a little nervous, because for tomorrow they're predicting a forty percent chance of clouds.

I have just one small suitcase, which I wouldn't have bothered to check had not Willie brought two enormous ones. I make the mistake of trying to lift one of Willie's bags off the carousel; it must weigh four hundred pounds. "Did you bring your rock collection?" I ask, but Willie just shrugs and lifts the bag as if it were filled with pillows.

I've lived in apartments smaller than the limousine that transports us to the hotel. The movie studio is obviously trying to impress us, and so far succeeding quite well. It's only been a week since they called me and expressed a desire to turn my defense of Willie into a feature film, and we are out here to negotiate the possible sale of those rights. It's not something I relish, but Willie and the others involved all coaxed me into it. Had I known we would be flown first-class and whisked around in limos with a bar and TV, it might not have taken quite so much coaxing.

The truth is, none of us need the money we might make from this deal. I inherited twenty-two million dollars from my father, Willie received ten million dollars from a civil suit which we brought after his release, and I split up the million-dollar commission from that suit among everybody else. That "everybody else" consists of my associate, Kevin Randall, my secretary, Edna, and Laurie Collins, who functions in the dual role of private investigator and love of my life.

I would be far more enthusiastic about this trip if Laurie were here, but she decided to fly back to Findlay, Wisconsin, for her fifteenth high school reunion. When I warily mentioned that it would also be a chance for her to see her old boyfriends, she smiled and said, "We've got a lot of catching up to do."

"I'll be spending all my time in LA with nubile young actresses," I countered. "Sex-starved, lawyer-loving, nubile young actresses. The town is full of them." I said this in a pathetic and futile attempt to get her to change her mind and come out here with me. Instead, she said, "You do that." I didn't bother countering with, "I will," since we both know I won't.

So it's just Willie and me that the driver drops off at the Beverly Regent Wilshire Hotel. It's a nice enough place, but based on the nightly rate, the fairly average rooms must have buried treasure in the mattresses. But again, the studio is paying, which is one reason the first thing I do is have a fourteen-dollar can of mixed nuts from the minibar.

Since Willie's release from prison brought him some measure of fame, his life has taken some other dramatic turns. In addition to becoming wealthy, he's gotten married, partnered with me in a dog rescue operation, and become part of the very exclusive New York social scene. He and wife Sondra are out every night with what used to be known as the in crowd, though I am so far "out" that I'm not sure what they're called anymore. He is constantly and unintentionally name-dropping friends in the sports, entertainment, and art worlds, though he comically often has no idea that anyone else has heard of them.

Willie's social reach apparently extends across the country, because he invites me to go "clubbing" tonight with him and a number of his friends. I would rather be clubbed over the head, so I decline and make plans to order room service and watch a baseball game.

First I call Laurie at her hotel in Findlay, but she's out. I hope she's in the process of marveling at how fat and bald all her old boyfriends have gotten. Next I call Kevin Randall, who is watching Tara for me while I'm gone.

Golden retrievers are the greatest living things on this planet, and Tara is the greatest of all golden retrievers, so that makes her fairly special. I hate leaving her, even for a day, but there was no way I was going to put her in a crate in the bottom of a hot airplane.

"Hello?" Kevin answers, his voice raspy.

I put him through about three or four minutes of swearing to me that Tara is doing well, and then I ask him how he's feeling, since his voice maintains that raspy sound. I ask this reluctantly, since Kevin is America's foremost hypochondriac. "I'm okay," he says.

I'd love to leave it at that, but it would ruin his night. "You sure?" I ask.

"Well . . . ," he starts hesitantly, "do you know if humans can catch diseases from dogs?"

"Why? Is Tara sick?"

"I told you she was fine," he says. "We're talking about me now. I seem to have developed a cough." He throws in a couple of hacking noises, just in case I didn't know what he meant by "cough."

"That definitely sounds like kennel cough," I say. "You should curl up and sleep next to a warm oven tonight. And don't have more than a cup of kibble for dinner."

Kevin, who is no dummy, shrewdly figures out that I am going to continue to make fun of him if he pursues this, so he lets me extricate myself from the call. Once I do so, I have dinner and lie down to watch the Dodgers play the Padres. I'm not terribly interested in it, which is why I'm asleep by the third inning.

I wake up at seven and order room service. I get the Assorted Fresh Berries for twenty-one fifty; for that price I would have expected twin Halle Berrys. They also bring an *LA Times* and *Wall Street Journal,* which are probably costing twenty bucks apiece.

The same driver and limo show up at nine in the morning to take Willie and me to the studio. We arrive early for our meeting, so we spend some time walking around the place, looking for stars. I don't see any, unless you count Willie.

We are eventually ushered into the office of Greg Burroughs, president of production at the studio. With him are a roomful of his colleagues, each with a title like "executive vice president" or "senior vice president." There seems to be an endless supply of gloriously titled executives; I wouldn't be surprised if there are three or four "emperors of production." The lowest ranked of the group is just a vice president, so it's probably the pathetic wretch's job to fetch the coffee and donuts.

It turns out that the overflow crowd is there merely as a show of how important we are to them, and everybody but Greg and a senior VP named Eric Anderson soon melts away. Greg is probably in his late thirties, and my guess is, he has ten years on Eric.

"Eric will be the production executive on this project," Greg informs. "He shares my passion for it." Eric nods earnestly, confirming that passion, as if we had any doubt.

Willie's been uncharacteristically quiet, but he decides to focus in on that which is important. "Who's gonna play me?"

Greg smiles. "Who do you have in mind?"

"Denzel Washington," says Willie without any hesitation. He's obviously given it some thought.

"I can see that." Greg nods, then looks at Eric, whose identical nod indicates that he, too, can see it. "The thing is, Will, we don't start to deal with casting until we have a script and director in place. But it's a really good thought."

Eric directs a question at "Will." "I hope you don't mind my asking, but do you have a mother?"

Willie shakes his head. "Nah. Used to."

"Why?" asks Greg of Eric, barely containing his curiosity.

"Well," Eric says, looking around the room and then back at Willie, "I hope I'm not talking out of turn, and this is just me speaking off the top of my head, but I was thinking it would be really great if you had a mother."

"Interesting," says Greg, as if this is the first time he has heard this idea. My sense is that Eric wouldn't say "good morning" without first clearing it with Greg, even if it's just "off the top" of his head.

"Well, it ain't that interesting to me," says Willie. "My mother took off when I was three and left me in a bus station. I ain't got no family."

Eric nods. "I understand, and again, I'm just thinking out

loud off the top of my head, but I'm talking about for the sake of the story. If your mother was there, supporting you the whole time you were in prison, believing in you . . ."

Willie is starting to get annoyed, which in itself does not qualify as a rare occurrence. "Yeah, she could have baked me fucking cupcakes. And we could have had a party in the prison. Mom and Dad could have invited all my fucking invisible aunts and uncles and cousins."

I intervene, partially because I'm concerned that Willie might throw Greg and Eric out the fifth-story window and they might bounce off the top of their heads. It would also necessitate getting two other passionate executives in here, thereby prolonging this meeting. The other reason I jump in is that they are alluding to an area in which I have a real concern, which is taking dramatic license and changing the characters and events. I've heard about the extraordinary liberties Hollywood can take with "true" stories, and I don't want to wind up being portrayed as the lead lawyer of the transvestite wing of Hamas.

We hash this out for a while, and they assure me that the contract will address my concerns. We agree on a price, and they tell me that a writer will be assigned and will want to go back East to meet and get to know all of us.

I stand up. "So that's it?"

Eric smiles and shakes my hand. "That's it. Let's make a movie."

• • • • •

THE FLIGHT HOME is boring and uneventful, which I view as a major positive when it comes to airplane flights. The movie doesn't appeal to me, so I don't put on the headphones. I then spend the next two hours involuntarily trying to lip-read everything the characters are saying. Unfortunately, the movie is *Dr. Dolittle 2,* and my mouse-lipreading skills are not that well developed.

Willie, for his part, uses the time to refine his casting choices. On further reflection he now considers Denzel too old and is leaning toward Will Smith or Ben Affleck, though he has some doubts that Ben could effectively play a black guy. I suggest that as soon as he gets home he call Greg and Eric to discuss it.

Moments after we touch the ground, a flight attendant comes over and leans down to speak with me. "Mr. Carpenter?" she asks.

I get a brief flash of worry. Has something happened while we were in the air? "Yes?"

"There will be someone waiting at the gate to meet you. You have an urgent phone call."

"Who is it?" I ask.

"I'm sorry, I really don't know. But I'm sure everything is fine."

I would take more comfort from her assurances if she knew what the call was about. I fluctuate between intense worry and panic the entire time we taxi to the gate, which seems to take about four hours.

As soon as the plane comes to a halt, Willie and I jump out of our seats and are the first people off the plane. Somebody who works for airline security is there to meet us, and he leads us to one of those motorized carts. We all jump on and are whisked away.

"Do you know what's going on?" I ask.

The security guy shrugs slightly. "I'm not sure. I think it's about that football player."

Before I have a chance to ask what the hell he could possibly be talking about, we arrive at an airport security office. I'm ushered inside, telling the officers that it's okay for Willie to come in with me. We're led into a back office, where another security guy stands holding a telephone, which he hands to me.

"Hello?" I say into the phone, dreading what I might hear on the other end.

"It took you long enough." The voice is that of Lieutenant Pete Stanton, my closest and only friend in the Paterson Police Department.

I'm somewhat relieved already; Pete wouldn't have started the conversation that way if he had something terrible to tell me. "What the hell is going on?" I ask.

"Kenny Schilling wants to talk to you. And only you. So you'd better get your ass out here."

If possible, my level of confusion goes up a notch. Kenny Schilling is a running back for the Giants, a third-round pick a few years ago who is just blossoming into a star. I've never met the man, though I know Willie counts him as one of his four or five million social friends. "Kenny Schilling?" I ask. "Why would he want to talk to me?"

"Where the hell have you been?" Pete asks.

Annoyance is overtaking my worry; there is simply nothing concerning Kenny Schilling that could represent a disaster in my own life. "I've been on a plane, Pete. I just flew in from Fantasyland. Now, tell me what the hell is going on."

"It looks like Schilling killed Troy Preston. Right now he's holed up in his house with enough firepower to supply the 3rd Infantry, and every cop in New Jersey outside waiting to blow his head off. Except me. I'm on the phone, 'cause I made the mistake of saying I knew you."

"Why does he want me?" I ask. "How would he even know my name?"

"He didn't. He asked for the hot-shit lawyer that's friends with Willie Miller."

An airport security car is waiting to take us to Upper Saddle River, which is where they tell us Kenny Schilling lives, and they assure us that our bags will be taken care of. "My bag's the one you can lift," I say.

Once in the car, I turn on the radio to learn more about the situation, and discover that it is all anyone is talking about.

Troy Preston, a wide receiver for the Jets, did not show up for scheduled rehab on an injured knee yesterday and did not call in an explanation to the team. This was apparently uncharacteristic, and when he could not be found or contacted, the police were called in. Somehow Kenny

Schilling was soon identified as a person who might have knowledge concerning the disappearance, and the police went out to his house to talk to him.

The unconfirmed report is that Schilling brandished a gun, fired a shot (which missed), and turned his house into a fortress. Schilling has refused to talk to the cops, except to ask for me. The media are already referring to me as his attorney, a logical, though totally incorrect, assumption.

This shows signs of being a really long day.

Upper Saddle River is about as pretty a New York suburb as you are going to find in New Jersey. Located off Route 17, it's an affluent, beautifully wooded community dotted with expensive but not pretentious homes. A number of wealthy athletes, especially on those teams that play in New Jersey like the Giants and Jets, have gravitated to it. As we enter its peaceful serenity, it's easy to understand why.

Unfortunately, that serenity disappears as we near Kenny Schilling's house. The street looks like it is hosting a SWAT team convention, and it's hard to believe that there could be a police car anywhere else in New Jersey. Every car seems to have gun-toting officers crouched behind it; it took less firepower to bring down Saddam Hussein. Kenny Schilling is a threat that they are taking very seriously.

Willie and I are brought into a trailer, where State Police Captain Roger Dessens waits for us. He dispenses with the greetings and pleasantries and immediately brings me up-to-date, though his briefing includes little more than I heard in radio reports. Schilling is a suspect in Preston's disappearance and possible murder, and his actions are certainly consistent with guilt. Innocent people don't ordinarily barricade themselves in their homes and fire at police.

"You ready?" Dessens asks, but doesn't wait for a reply. He picks up the phone and dials a number. After a few moments he talks into the phone. "Okay, Kenny, Carpenter is right here with me."

He hands me the phone, and I cleverly say, "Hello?"

A clearly agitated voice comes through the phone. "Carpenter?"

"Yes."

"How do I know it's you?"

It's a reasonable question. "Hold on," I say, and signal to Willie to come over. I hand him the phone. "He isn't sure it's me."

Willie talks into the phone. "Hey, Schill . . . what's happenin'?" He says this as if they just met at a bar and the biggest decision confronting them is whether to have Coors or a Bud.

I can't hear "Schill's" view of what might be "happenin'," but after a few moments Willie is talking again. "Yeah, it's Andy. I'm right here with him. He's cool. He'll get you out of this bullshit in no time."

Looking out over the army of cops assembled to deal with "this bullshit," I've got a feeling Willie's assessment might be a tad on the wildly optimistic side. Willie hands the phone back to me, and Schilling tells me that he wants me to come into his house. "I need to talk to you."

I have absolutely no inclination to physically enter this confrontation by going into his house. "We're talking now," I say.

He is insistent. "I need to talk to you in here."

"I understand you have some guns," I say.

"I got one gun" is how he corrects me. "But don't worry, man, I ain't gonna shoot you."

"I'll get back to you," I say, then hang up and tell Captain Dessens about Schilling's request.

"Good," he says, standing up. "Let's get this thing moving."

"What thing?" I ask. "You think I'm going in there? Why would I possibly go in there?"

Dessens seems unperturbed. "You want a live client or a dead one?"

"He's not my client. Just now was the first time I've ever spoken to him. He didn't even know it was me."

"On the other hand, he's got a lot of money to pay your bills, Counselor." He says "Counselor" with the same respect he might have said "Fuehrer."

Dessens is really pissing me off; I don't need this aggravation. "On the other hand, you're an asshole," I say.

"So you're not going?" Dessens asks. The smirk on his face seems to say that he knows I'm a coward and I'm just looking for an excuse to stay out of danger. He's both arrogant and correct.

Willie comes over to me and talks softly. "Schill's good people, Andy. They got the wrong guy."

I'm instantly sorry I didn't leave Willie at the airport. Now if I don't go in, I'm not just letting down a stranger accused of murder, I'm letting down a friend. "Okay," I say to Dessens, "but while I'm out there, everybody has their guns on safety."

Dessens shakes his head. "Can't do it, but I'll have them pointed down."

I nod. "And I get a bulletproof vest."

Dessens agrees to the vest, and they have one on me in seconds. He and I work out a signal for me to come out of the house with Schilling without some trigger-happy, Jets-fan officer taking a shot at us.

Willie offers to come in with me, but Dessens refuses. Within five minutes I'm walking across the street toward a quite beautiful ranch-style home, complete with manicured lawn and circular driveway. I can see a swimming pool behind the house to the right side, but since I didn't bring my bathing suit, I probably won't be able to take advantage of it. Besides, I don't think this bulletproof vest would make a good flotation device.

As I walk, I notice that the street has gotten totally, eerily silent. I'm sure that every eye is on me, waiting to storm the house if Schilling blows my unprotected head off. "The tension was so thick you could cut it with a knife" suddenly doesn't seem like a cliché anymore.

Four hours ago my biggest problem was how to ask the first-class flight attendant for a vodkaless Bloody Mary without using the embarrassing term "Virgin Mary," and now I've got half a million sharpshooters just waiting for me to trigger a firefight. I'm sure there are also television cameras trained on me, and I can only hope I don't piss in my pants on national television.

As I step onto the porch, I see that the door is partially open. I take a step inside, but I don't see anything. Schilling's voice tells me to "Come in and close the door behind you," which is what I do.

The first thing I'm struck by is how sparsely furnished the place is and how absent the touches of home. There are a number of large unopened cardboard boxes, and my sense is that Schilling must have only recently moved in. This makes sense, since I saw on ESPN a few weeks ago that the Giants just signed him to a fourteen-million, three-year deal, a reward for his taking over the starting running back job late last season.

Schilling sits on the floor in the far corner of the room, pointing a handgun at me. He is a twenty-five-year-old African-American, six three, two hundred thirty pounds, with Ali-like charismatic good looks. Yet now he seems exhausted and defeated, as if his next move might be to turn the gun on himself. When I saw him on ESPN, he was thanking his wife, teammates, and God for helping him achieve his success, but he doesn't look too thankful right now. "How many are out there?" he asks.

Why? Is he so delusional as to think he can shoot his way out? "Enough to invade North Korea," I say.

He sags slightly, as if this is the final confirmation that his situation is hopeless. I suddenly feel a surge of pity for him, which is not the normal feeling I have for an accused killer pointing a gun at me. "What's going on here, Kenny?"

He makes a slight head motion toward a hallway. "Look in there. Second door on the left."

I head down the hall as instructed and enter what looks like a guest bedroom. There are five or six regular-size moving cartons, three of which have been opened. I'm not sure what it is I'm supposed to be looking for, so I take a few moments to look around.

I see a stain under the door to the closet, and a feeling of dread comes over me. I reluctantly open the door and look inside. What I see is a torso, folded over with a large red stain on its back. I don't need Al Michaels to tell me that this is Troy Preston, wide receiver for the Jets. And I don't need anybody to tell me that he is dead.

I walk back into the living room, where Kenny hasn't moved. "I didn't do it," he says.

"Do you know who did?"

He just shakes his head. "What the hell am I gonna do?"

I sit down on the floor next to him. "Look," I say, "I'm going to have a million questions for you, and then we're going to have to figure out the best way to help you. But right now we have to deal with *them*." I point toward the street, in case he didn't know I was talking about the police. "This is not the way to handle it."

"I don't see no other way."

I shake my head. "You know better than that. You asked for me . . . I'm a lawyer. If you were going to go down fighting, you'd have asked for a priest."

He wears the fear on his face like a mask. "They'll kill me."

"No. You'll be treated well. They wouldn't try anything . . . there's media all over this. We're going to walk out together, and you'll be taken into custody. It'll take some time to process you into the system, and I probably won't see you until tomorrow morning. Until then you are to talk to no one—not the police, not the guy in the next cell, no one. Do you understand?"

He nods uncertainly. "Are you going to help me?"

"I'm going to help you." It's not really a lie; I certainly haven't decided to take this case, but for the time being I will get him through the opening phase. If I decide not to represent him, which basically means if I believe he's guilty, I'll help him get another attorney.

"They won't let me talk to my wife."

He seems to be trying to delay the inevitable surrender. "Where is she?" I ask.

"In Seattle, at her mother's. They said she's flying back. They won't let me talk to her."

"You'll talk to her, but not right now. Now it's time to end this." I say it as firmly as I can, and he nods in resignation and stands up.

I walk outside first, as previously planned, and make a motion to Dessens to indicate that Kenny is following me, without his gun. It goes smoothly and professionally, and within a few minutes Kenny has been read his rights and is on the way downtown.

He's scared, and he should be. No matter how this turns out, life as he knows it is over.

• • • • •

I PICK UP TARA at Kevin's house. She seems a little miffed that I had abandoned her but grudgingly accepts my peace offering of a biscuit. As a further way of getting on her good side, I tell her that I'll recommend she be allowed to play herself in the movie.

Kevin has followed the day's events on television, and we make plans to meet in the office at eight A.M. I'm starting to get used to high-profile cases; they have a life of their own, and it's vitally important to get on top of them immediately. And if one star football player goes on trial for murdering another, it's going to make my previous cases look like tiffs in small-claims court.

As I enter my house, I'm struck by the now familiar feeling of comfort that envelops me. Two years ago, after my father's death, I moved back to Paterson, New Jersey, to live in the house in which I grew up. Except for rescuing and adopting Tara from the animal shelter, coming back to this house is the single best thing I've ever done. I've hardly changed the interior at all; the house was already perfectly furnished with memories and emotions that only I can see and feel.

I've barely had time to put a frozen pizza in the oven when Laurie calls from Findlay. Such was the intensity of today's events that I haven't thought about her in hours.

"Are you okay?" she asks. "I saw what happened on television. I've been trying you all day on your cell phone."

I left my cell phone in my suitcase, which the airline has delivered and is in the living room. "I'm fine. But we may have ourselves a client."

"Is it true the victim's body was in his house?" she asks.

"In the closet," I confirm.

"Sounds rather incriminating."

"Which is why you have to come home and uncover the kind of evidence that will let me display my courtroom brilliance."

"I'll be back tomorrow," she says. "I've missed you terribly."

I let the words roll gently over me, sort of like a verbal massage. I know she loves me, but I have an embarrassing need for reassurance. At least it would be embarrassing if I were to reveal it to her. Which I won't. Ever.

"Have you had fun?" I ask.

"It's been an amazing experience, Andy. These are people I haven't seen or thought about in more than fifteen years. And in five minutes all the memories came back . . . I even recognized their mannerisms. It makes me wonder why I cut off from them . . . why we never stayed in touch."

Laurie's father was a police officer in Findlay but decided to leave for a higher-paying job back East in Paterson, which qualified as the "big city." He died five years ago, and I never got to meet him, but Laurie tells me he felt the move was the biggest mistake he ever made. I don't recall her ever telling me if she shares that view.

We talk some more about reconnecting with old friends; she knows I completely understand because of my experience in moving back to Paterson. "The Internet is the way to stay in touch," I say. "E-mailing makes it easy, and there are no pregnant pauses in the conversation."

She doesn't seem convinced, in fact seems vaguely troubled. I could ask her about this honestly and directly, but that would require too great a change in style. So instead, I change the subject. "If we take this case, we won't be able to go away." We had talked about a vacation.

"That's okay," she says, and again I hear the tone of voice that I don't recognize as belonging to Laurie. It's a halfhearted statement in a mostly halfhearted conversation. I'm not sure why, and I'm certainly not sure if I want to find out.

I get up really early in the morning to take Tara for a long walk. She attacks the route eagerly—tail-wagging and nose-sniffing every step of the way. We've gone this way a thousand times, yet each time she takes fresh delight in the sights and smells. Tara is not a "been there, done that" type of dog, and it's a trait I admire and envy.

As I get dressed to go to the office, I catch up on what the media are saying about the Schilling case. There are reports that Schilling and Preston were out together the night Preston disappeared and that witnesses claim the last time Preston was seen was when Schilling gave him a ride home.

The striking part of the media coverage is not the information that is revealed, but the overwhelming nature of the effort to reveal it. I have 240 channels on my cable system, and it seems as if 230 of them are all over this case. One of the cable networks has already given a name to it, and their reports are emblazoned with the words "Murder in the Back-field" scrawled across the screen. They seem unconcerned with the fact that the victim was a wide receiver.

As has become standard operating procedure, guilt seems to be widely assumed, especially in light of the way Schilling was taken into custody. His were not the actions of the innocent, and if we ever go to trial, that is going to be a major hill to climb. The fact that a national television audience watched as he fended off police with a gun only makes the hill that much steeper.

Kevin and I don't have much to talk about, and we just compare notes on what we've learned from the media. I've got a ten o'clock appointment at the jail to meet with Schilling, and Kevin plans to use the time to learn what the prosecution is planning in terms of arraignment. Kevin knows my feelings about defending guilty clients, feelings that he shares, and he's relieved when I tell him that I've made no decision on whether to take on Schilling as a client.

We both leave at nine-forty-five, which is when Edna is arriving. I've always felt that a secretary should arrive very early and have the office up and running by the time everyone else arrives. Unfortunately, Edna has always felt pretty much the opposite, so basically, she comes in whenever she wants. Though she is one of the financial beneficiaries of the commission from the Willie Miller case, I can honestly say that the money hasn't changed her. She's worked for me for five years and is just as unproductive today as before she was rich.

I briefly tell her what is going on; she's heard absolutely nothing about Schilling or the murder. Never let it be said that Edna has her finger anywhere near the public pulse.

Schilling is being held at County Jail, which is why an

entire media city has set itself up outside. Having become all too familiar with this process, I've learned about a back entrance which allows me to avoid the crush, and I make use of it this time.

Guarding the door is Luther Hendricks, a court security officer who carries a calendar with him so he can count the days until retirement. "You sure stepped in shit this time," he says as he lets me in. I know he's talking about this case, so I don't even bother to check my shoes.

Nothing moves quickly within a prison bureaucracy, and the high-profile nature of this case doesn't change that. It takes forty-five minutes for me to be brought back to the room where I will see Kenny Schilling and then another twenty minutes waiting for him to arrive.

He's brought in cuffed and dressed in prison drab. I had thought he looked bad huddled in the corner of his living room yesterday, but compared to this, he actually appeared triumphant. It looks as if fear and despair are waging a pitched battle to take over his face. The process of losing one's freedom, even overnight, can be devastating and humiliating. For somebody like Kenny, it's often much worse, because he's fallen from such a high perch.

"How are you doing, Kenny?" is my clever opening. "Are they treating you okay?"

"They ain't beating me, if that's what you mean. They tried to talk to me, but I said no."

"Good."

"They took some blood out of my arm. They said they had the right. And I didn't care, because all they're gonna find is blood. I don't take no drugs or anything."

They actually don't have that right, unless they had probable cause to believe that drug usage had something to do with the murder. I have heard nothing about any suspicions that drugs were involved in this case, but then again, I know almost nothing about this case. "You're sure you've never taken any kind of drugs?" I ask.

He shakes his head firmly. "No way; I just told you that." Then, "Man, you gotta get me out of here. I got money . . . whatever it takes. I just can't stay in here."

I explain that we won't know the likelihood of bail until the district attorney files charges, but that those charges are likely to be severe, and bail will be very difficult. I'm not sure he really hears me or understands what I'm saying; he needs to cling to a hope that this is all going to blow over and he'll be back signing autographs instead of giving fingerprints.

I ask him to tell me everything he knows about the night that Preston disappeared. "I didn't kill him," he says. "I swear to God."

I nod. "Good. That covers what you didn't do. Now let's focus on what you did do. How well did you know him?"

He shrugs. "Pretty well. I mean, we weren't best friends or anything—he played for the Jets. But in the off-season a lot of guys hung out . . ."

"So you hung out with him that night?" I ask.

He shrugs. "Not just him . . . a whole bunch of people. We went to the Crows Nest. No big deal. We probably did that three or four times a week."

"How many people were there that night? With you and Troy."

"Maybe fifteen."

I take him through the events of the night, which mainly consisted of drinking beer, talking football, and occasionally leering at women. I never realized how much I had in common with star football players. "How long did you stay there?" I ask.

"I was real tired, so we left about twelve-thirty."

"We?"

He nods. "I gave Troy a ride home."

This is not good and confirms the media reports. The last time the victim was seen, it was by fifteen people, who watched him leave with my client. "Was that an unusual thing for you to do?"

He shakes his head. "No, he lived about two blocks from me. And I don't drink that much, so he'd leave his car at the bar, and I guess he'd pick it up in the morning."

"So he lived in Upper Saddle River?" I ask.

Kenny shakes his head and explains that Preston lived in an apartment in East Rutherford. Kenny did as well; he and his wife had only recently purchased the house in Upper Saddle River and hadn't fully moved in yet. This explains the boxes spread around the house.

Kenny claims to have spent the fateful night in his East Rutherford apartment, alone. "I dropped Troy off and went home. That's the last time I saw him."

"Why did the police come to your house in Upper Saddle River?" I'll learn all this in discovery, but it's helpful to hear my client's version first.

"The next morning my car was gone. I parked it on the street, and I figured it was stolen. Which it was. I reported it to the police. I hadn't even heard about Troy being missing yet. Then yesterday I got a rental car and went up to the new house. I was unpacking boxes when I saw some blood on the floor. Then I found his body in that closet. I was about to call the cops, but before I could, they showed up at my door with guns. I freaked and wouldn't let them in."

"And took a shot at them," I point out.

"They pulled out guns first . . . I wasn't even sure they were cops. They could have been the guys that killed Troy.

Even when I figured out who they were, I was afraid they'd come in shooting. Hey, man . . . I wasn't trying to hit them. I just figured if they found the body like that, they'd think I did it. Which they did." He sees the look on my face and moans. "Man, I know it was stupid. I just freaked, that's all."

Kenny doesn't know what brought the police to the Upper Saddle River home, but he believed from their attitude that they were there to arrest him. I'll find that out soon enough, so I use our remaining time to ask him about his relationship with Preston.

"I met him when we were in high school," he says. "One of those sports magazines did an all-American high school team, and they brought everybody to New York and put us up in a hotel for the weekend. I think he was from Pennsylvania or Ohio or something . . ."

"But you've never had an argument with him? There is no motive that the prosecution might come up with for your killing him?"

He shakes his head vigorously, the most animated I've seen him. "No way, man. You gotta believe me. Why would I kill him? It don't make any sense."

The guard comes to take him back to his cell, and I see a quick flash of shock in Kenny's eyes, as if he thought this meeting could last forever. I tell him that I will get to work finding out whatever I can and that the next time I will see him is at the arraignment.

For now I'm far from sure I believe in his innocence. But I'm not sure that I don't.

• • • • •

LAURIE'S FLIGHT IS more than an hour late because of heavy thunderstorms in the area. They are my favorite kind of storms, the ones where the skies get pitch-black in late afternoon on a hot summer day, and then the water comes bursting out, bouncing off the street as it lands. Eat your heart out, Los Angeles.

I stand with a bunch of people in the Newark Airport baggage claim waiting for the passengers. Laurie walks in the middle of a group of about twenty; she couldn't stand out more clearly if she were wearing a halo. I have an urge to nudge the guy next to me and say, "I don't know who you're waiting for, loser, but that one is mine." It's an urge I stifle.

I'm not big on airport arrival hugs, but Laurie gives me a big one, and I accept it graciously. I ask, "How was your flight?"—a witty line I picked up from our LA driver. Laurie shares my general disdain for chitchat, so by the time we're in the car, she's questioning me about the recent events.

"Are you going to take the case?" This is the key question for her, since as my main investigator it will determine how she spends the next few months of her life.

"I don't know; I haven't heard the evidence yet."

"I'm not saying he's guilty," she says, "but they wouldn't go after a high-profile guy like that unless they felt they had a strong case. And he didn't help himself by turning his house into the Alamo."

What she's saying is certainly true. On the other hand, "Willie says he's innocent."

"Willie might be slightly biased," she points out. She's referring to both the fact that Schilling is his friend and also the fact that Willie himself is a walking example of a law enforcement mistake. As a wrongly convicted man Willie has less than full confidence in the justice system.

Laurie has other questions, and almost on cue, Kevin calls me on my cell phone with some of the answers. None of it is good. At the arraignment on Monday morning Schilling is to be charged with first-degree murder. To make matters worse, Dylan Campbell has been assigned to prosecute the case. Dylan is difficult and obnoxious, which would be okay if he weren't also tough and smart.

And Dylan will have a more personal incentive to win. Last year Laurie was herself on trial for the murder of a Paterson Police lieutenant, her boss in the days that she was on the force. I defended her and won her acquittal, despite Dylan's vigorous prosecution. It was a high-profile trial, and I have no doubt he's been lying in wait to kick my ass on another case.

Dylan refused to give Kevin a preview of their evidence, despite the fact that they will have to turn it over in discovery early next week. It is a confirmation of how contentious this case will be, which on one level makes me more eager to tackle it. I would take great pleasure in beating Dylan again, but it would be nice to know if I have a shred of evidence to utilize.

Laurie doesn't even want to stop off at her place; she wants to come home with me. The way we've structured our living arrangements is to have our own homes while staying together Monday, Wednesday, Friday, and Sunday nights. It's flexible, but since today is Friday, I'm glad we're not exercising that flexibility tonight.

Camped out in front of my house when we pull up are half a dozen media types, with two camera trucks. The thirst for news on this case is going to be unquenchable, and Schilling's lawyer will be a permanent source. Since I am that lawyer, at least for now, I've got to get used to it and learn to use it to my advantage.

I pull the car into the garage, and Laurie goes inside while I go outside to speak to the press. I've got nothing whatsoever to tell them, especially since I don't yet know the facts of the case. The last thing I want is to blow my future credibility by saying something that turns out to be wrong.

"Listen," I say, "I just came out to tell you that I have no comment. And I thought you'd want to hear that in time to change the front-page headline."

Karen Spivey, a reporter who's covered the court beat far longer than I, is the only one of the group to laugh. "Thanks, Andy. We can always count on you."

"Glad I can help. And you're welcome to sit out here as long as you like, but I'm going to be in there sleeping."

They take that as a signal that they can safely leave without missing any breaking news, and pack up to leave. I go inside, and Laurie and I are in bed within fifteen minutes, including the five minutes she spends petting Tara. Laurie turns on CNN, which would not have been my first choice.

SEX would have been my first choice. But Laurie didn't get to follow the news much the last few days, and she apparently wants to let Larry King bring her up-to-date on what's happening in the world.

Ol' Larry proves to be quite the aphrodisiac, because within ten minutes the TV is off and Laurie and I are making love. We've only been together for two years, and maybe there will come a time when I take our physical relationship for granted, but I can't imagine when.

I'm just about to doze off when she says, "I really love you, Andy. It's important to me that you know that."

Something about the way she says it worries me, but I can't figure out why. It's the same feeling I had when I talked to her on the phone, and I briefly consider whether to reveal my concern. "I love you too" is what winds up coming out. I am Andy, master conversationalist.

Kevin phones the next morning to suggest that he come to the house to discuss our plans for the case. It's Saturday, so he says it's more comfortable than going to the office. He doesn't mention that this will also provide him with an opportunity to eat Laurie's French toast and to act surprised when she offers to make it.

While he is inhaling his breakfast, we do little more than acknowledge the fact that there is nothing we can effectively do until the arraignment. Laurie sits in on our conversation, a tacit acceptance of the job as investigator for our team.

We turn on the television, since that seems to be our main source of news, and receive another jolt. An anonymous source within the prosecution has leaked the fact that Kenny failed the drug test administered after his arrest. If this is true, and it probably is, it would mean that Kenny lied to me, not a good way to start a lawyer-almost-client relationship.

I'm torn about whether I want to handle this case at all. On its face it seems a near-certain loser, mainly because there is a very substantial chance Kenny is guilty. My financial and professional situation is such that I have little stomach for securing the release of people who shoot other people and stuff them in closets.

On the other hand, I don't know that Kenny is guilty, and this case represents a chance to get back into the action. Ever since the Willie Miller trial, I have been very selective in picking my clients, with the result being a lot of downtime. It's been three months since I've been in a courtroom, and I can feel the juices starting to flow. The fact that I could be taking on Dylan is an added, competitive benefit.

Once Kevin leaves, Tara and I take a ride over to the building that houses the Tara Foundation, the dog rescue operation that Willie and I run. More accurately, Willie and I finance it, and Willie and his wife, Sondra, run it. It's a labor of love for them, and I've loved helping them rescue and place over six hundred dogs in our first year.

As we enter, Willie and Sondra are behind the desk while a young couple gets to know one of the dogs, a large yellow Lab mix named Ben. They are sitting on the floor and playing with him, unknowingly making a good impression on Willie, Sondra, and me in the process. As a general rule, people who get on the floor with dogs provide them with good homes.

I overhear Sondra talking to Willie before they see me. "Samuel Jackson?" she says. "Are you out of your mind?"

Apparently, Willie is nearing a final casting decision. Sondra sees me and tries to enlist me in her cause. "Andy, tell him that Samuel Jackson is old enough to be his father."

"Samuel Jackson is old enough to be your father," I say as instructed.

"Then what about Danny Glover?" Willie persists.

"Damn," says Sondra. "Danny Glover is old enough to be Samuel Jackson's father."

Willie is getting frustrated, so he turns to me. "You got any ideas?"

I nod. "Sidney Poitier."

"Who's he?" asks Willie, and Sondra shares his baffled expression.

"A new guy," I say. "But he has potential."

I go off to pet the dogs that have not yet been adopted, and then Tara and I head home. Starting Monday, I'm going to be totally focused on the Schilling case, and until then I'm going to be totally focused on the NBA play-offs.

Between now and tomorrow there are six games, culminating in the Knicks-Pacers game tomorrow night. All the games have betting lines and are therefore totally watchable. I have gotten so used to betting on these games that sometimes I wonder if I'm actually a basketball fan anymore. Would I be watching if I couldn't wager? I'm confident I'd watch the Knicks, but would I care if Detroit beats Orlando? I'm not sure why, but these are somewhat disconcerting issues to contemplate.

The flip side is even more worrisome. If I could gamble on other events, currently exempt, would I automatically become a fan of those events? If I could wager on ballet, would I be pulling for the team in green tutus? And what about opera? If I could bet that the fat lady would sing before the fat guy, would I become an opera buff?

I've got to get control of myself and erase these self-doubts. The last thing I ever want to do is ask my bookie if he has a wagering line on the Joffrey or an over/under on how many haircuts will be given by the barber of Seville.

Tara is a help to me at times like this. She gets me to

focus on that which is important: the beer, the potato chips, the dog biscuits, and the couch. I've taught her to fetch the remote control, and her soft golden retriever mouth never damages it.

Laurie's having dinner with some of her girlfriends tonight and then coming over tomorrow to spend the day. She doesn't seem to be acting strangely anymore, and I would spend time reflecting on how pleased I am by that if I didn't have to watch these games . . .

• • • • •

LAURIE COMES INTO the room carry-
ing a blanket. That's not what's worrying me. What's worrying me is that she also has two pillows. I have to assume
that she intends for my head to be occupying one of them,
which is a problem, because it's Sunday evening and I
have other plans for my head. At least for the next two
hours.

"Let's go," she says, instantly confirming my fears.

"Go where?"

"Outside. It starts in less than half an hour." I think she
can tell from my blank expression that I have no idea what
she is talking about, so she explains. "The *eclipse,* Andy. Remember?"

I do remember, at least partly. I remember that Laurie
had said an eclipse was coming and that it would be really
nice if we could lie outside and watch it together. Unfortunately, it never entered my mind that God would have
scheduled an eclipse at the same time the Knicks were in
their first play-off game in four years.

My mind races for a solution; there must be something it

can instruct my mouth to say to get me off this literally astronomical hook. "Now? The eclipse is now?" Suffice it to say, I was hoping to come up with something stronger.

"Eight-thirty-one," she says, since eclipses are really precise things.

"Just about the beginning of the second quarter," I say. "Talk about your coincidences."

"Andy, if you'd rather watch the basketball game . . ." She doesn't finish the sentence, but based on her tone, an appropriate finish would be, "then you can kiss my ass."

"No, it's not that," I lie. "It's just that it's a play-off game, and it's the Knicks. How often does that happen?"

"The next eclipse won't happen for over four hundred years," she counters.

I shake my head. "That's what they say, but don't believe it. They always announce that the next one won't come until 2612, so everybody goes out to see it, but then there's another one two weeks later. The whole thing is a scam."

"Who's doing the scamming?" she asks, a slight gleam in her eye, which could mean that she's either secretly finding this amusing or planning to kill me.

"I'm not sure," I say. "It could be the telescope industry, or maybe blanket and pillow manufacturers. But take it from me, these people are not to be trusted."

"I've got an idea," she says. "Why don't you tape it?"

"Great!" I say enthusiastically. "I didn't even know you could tape an eclipse."

Her expression turns serious; banter time is over. "Andy, we need to talk."

Maybe there's a more ominous phrase in the English language than "We need to talk." Perhaps "Michael Corleone says hello." Or maybe "I'm afraid the test results are back."

But right now what Laurie just said is enough to send spasms of panic through my gut.

I could be overreacting. Maybe it's not so bad. "We need to talk." That's what people do, they talk, right? But the thing is, a talk is like a drink. It's fine unless you *need* to have it. Then it's a major problem. And I've got a feeling Laurie is going to play the U.S. Air Force to my Republican Guard and drop a cluster bomb in the middle of my life.

I take a pillow from Laurie and follow her outside. Tara trails along; she clearly considers this "talk" potentially more entertaining than the Knicks game. We don't say anything as we align the blanket and pillows to view the stupid eclipse. I'm so intent on what is about to be said that if the sun and moon collided, I wouldn't notice.

"The sky's clear; we should be able to see it really well," she says.

Is she going to chitchat first? I swallow the watermelon in my throat. "What is it you wanted to talk about?" I ask.

"Andy . . ." is how she starts, which is already a bad sign. I'm the only other person here, so if she feels she has to specify whom she's talking to, it must mean that what she has to say is very significant. "Andy, you know that my father and mother split up when I was fifteen."

I wait without speaking, partially because I am aware of her parents' divorce, but mainly because I want this to go as fast as possible.

"My father got custody simply because my mother didn't contest it. She no longer wanted a family—I don't know and it doesn't really matter why—and he made it easy for her. He found a job here and took me with him. One day I was living in Findlay, and the next day I wasn't. I literally never even said goodbye to my friends."

She takes a deep breath. "And I never went back. Not

once. Not even a phone call. My mother died five years ago without me seeing or talking to her. That's how she wanted it, and it was fine with me."

With her voice cracking as she says this, it doesn't take a keenly analytical mind to know that it wasn't really fine with her.

She goes on. "In the process I cut off from my friends, my boyfriend at the time, everybody. I'm sure they must have heard where I had gone, but they wouldn't have had any way to contact me, and I certainly never contacted them. I never even considered it."

"Until this weekend" is my first verbal contribution.

She nods. "Until this weekend. I've been nervous about going back, but when I saw how it was for you to get back into this house . . . I know it's different because you never left this area . . . but it gave me extra motivation.

"And it was wonderful," she continues. "Better than I could have imagined. Not just seeing my old friends, though that was great. It was about going home, about reconnecting with how I became who I am. I even met three cousins I never knew. I have family, Andy."

"That's great," I say.

"I was stunned by the impact the whole thing had on me, Andy. When I drove past my grammar school, I started to cry."

That impact and the resulting emotions are clear as a bell, and it makes me feel for her. For a moment I even stop thinking about myself and how whatever is going to be said will affect me. But only for a moment.

"I had a boyfriend named Sandy. Sandy Walsh."

"Uh-oh," I say involuntarily.

"He's a businessman and sort of an unelected consultant to the town."

"Married?"

"A less significant question would be hard to imagine," Laurie says, "but no, he's not married."

I simply cannot stand the suspense anymore. "Laurie," I say, "I'm a little nervous about where this is going, and you know how anxious I am to watch the eclipse, so can you get to the bottom line?"

She nods. "Sandy talked to the city manager, and they offered me a job. They've been aware of my career; I'm like a mini–hometown hero. A captain's position is going to be opening up on the police force, and Chief Helling is approaching retirement age. If all goes well, I could be chief of police within two years. It's not a huge department, but there are twelve officers, and they do real police work."

Kaboom.

"You're moving back to Findlay?" I ask.

"Right now all I'm doing is talking to you about it. The captain's slot won't open for at least three months, so Sandy is giving me plenty of time. He knows what a big decision this is."

"That Sandy's a sensitive guy," I marvel.

"Andy, please don't react this way. I'm talking to you because I trust you and I love you."

Her words function as a temporary petulance-remover. "I'm sorry, I'll try to be understanding, and a person for you to talk to, but I just don't want you to leave. We can talk for the next twelve years, and I still won't want you to leave."

"You know how much I've wanted to get back into police work," she says, "and in a position like that, I could really make a difference."

Laurie was working for the Paterson Police Department when she told what she knew about the crooked lieutenant she was working for. When the issue was whitewashed, she left in protest. Her family has been in police work for gen-erations, and she's never felt fully comfortable with leaving. "You make a difference *here*, Laurie."

"Thank you, but this is different. And you could be the best attorney in Findlay," she says. Her smile says she's kid-ding, but only slightly. "I had forgotten what an amazingly wonderful place it is to live."

"So you want me to move to Findlay?" I ask, my voice betraying more incredulousness than I would have liked, but less than I feel. "Is good old Sandy offering me the town justice of the peace job? Great! You arrest the jaywalkers, and I'll put 'em away for good. And then on Saturday nights we can get all dressed up, head down to the bakery, and watch the new bread-slicing machine."

"Andy, please. I'm not saying you should move. I'm not even saying I should move. I'm just putting everything on the table." She looks up from this grass table just as the eclipse is starting. "God, that's spectacular," she says.

"Yippee-skippee," I say. "Now I can't wait for 2612."

• • • • •

THREE SECONDS AFTER I wake up I
have that awful feeling. It's the one where you've forgotten
something really bad while you were asleep, and the sudden remembrance of it in the morning is like experiencing
it fresh all over again. Why doesn't that happen with good
things?

Laurie may leave. That is a simple fact; I can't change it.
Or if I can change it, I don't know how, which is almost as
bad.

A number of months ago we talked about marriage. She
didn't feel she needed it, but loved me and was willing to
marry if it was important to me. I didn't force the issue, but
what if I had? How would it impact on this situation, on her
decision? Would she even consider leaving her husband behind?

But we're not married, and I'm not her husband, so what
the hell is the difference?

I know it's immature, but the chances of my taking on
Kenny Schilling's case just went up very substantially. I need

something else to think about, and the total focus and intensity of a murder case and trial are a perfect diversion.

I can feel this diversion start to take effect as I arrive at the courthouse for the arraignment. The streets surrounding the place are mobbed with press, and this will not change for the duration of the case. Clearly, the public view is that Kenny is guilty. This is true not because he is widely disliked; in fact, he's been a fairly popular player. The fact is that the public always assumes that if someone is charged with a crime, then he or she is guilty. While our system purports to have a presumption of innocence, the public has a presumption of guilt. Unfortunately, the public makes up the jury.

I have to confess that this sentiment against Kenny also contributes to my desire to represent him. Great basketball players like Michael Jordan, Larry Bird, and Kobe Bryant have always said that what they love most is winning on the road, against the odds in hostile environments. I can't shoot a jump shot into the Passaic River, but I know what they mean. It's not something I'm necessarily proud of, but the legal "game" is more fun, more challenging, when I'm expected to lose.

Kevin and I meet with Kenny in an anteroom before the arraignment. He's more composed than he was in the jail, more anxious to know what he can do to help in his own defense. I tell him to write down everything he can remember about his relationship with Troy Preston, whether or not he thinks a particular detail is important.

I describe what will take place during the arraignment. It's basically a formality and one in which Kenny's only role will be to plead. The rest will be up to me, although in truth my role is limited as well. This is the prosecution's day, and Dylan will try to make as much of it as possible.

The judge who has been assigned is Susan Timmerman, who coincidentally presided over the arraignment the last time Dylan and I tangled. She is a fair, deliberate jurist who can handle sessions like today's in her sleep. I would be quite content if she is assigned the actual trial, but that will be decided by lottery sometime down the road.

Dylan does not come over to exchange pleasantries before the session begins, and seems to avoid eye contact as well. I say "seems to" because not being an eye-contacter myself, I can't be sure. I'm not even positive what eye contact is, but Laurie says you know it when you see it. Of course, it's hard for me to see it, because I don't do it.

The gallery is packed, and Kenny's wife, Tanya, sits right behind us, a seat I assume and hope she'll be in every day of the trial. I also see a few of Kenny's teammates in the third row. That's good; their abandoning him would be a major negative in the eyes of the public. And as I said, twelve members of that public are going to be the jurors in this case.

Dylan presents the charges, and I can see Kenny flinch slightly when he hears them. The State of New Jersey is charging Kenny Schilling with murder in the first degree, as well as an assortment of lesser offenses. They are also alleging special circumstances, which is New Jersey's subtle way of saying that if it prevails, it will pay someone to stick a syringe in Kenny's arm and kill him.

There is a slight tremor in Kenny's voice when he proclaims himself not guilty, and I can't say I blame him. If I were charged with a crime like this, I'd probably croak like a frog. Kenny is used to being applauded and revered. New Jersey is calling him a brutal murderer, and the worst thing that's been said about him before this is that he has a tendency to fumble more than he should.

Judge Timmerman informs us that a trial judge will be assigned next week, then asks if we have anything we need to bring up.

I rise. "There is the matter of discovery, Your Honor. We've discovered that the prosecutor does not seem to believe in it. They have not turned over a single document to us."

Dylan rises to his feet, a wounded expression on his face. "Your Honor, the defense will receive what they are due in a timely manner. The arrest took place on Friday, and this is Monday morning."

I respond quickly. "Since I had no evidence to examine, Your Honor, I spent some time over the weekend looking at the rules of discovery, and it quite clearly states that the prosecution must turn over documents as they receive them, even if, God forbid, it interferes with their weekend. I might add that they were able to find the time during that same weekend to provide information to the media. Perhaps if I had a press pass, I would have a better chance of getting the information the discovery statute requires."

Judge Timmerman turns to Dylan. "I must say I was concerned by the amount of information available in the media."

Dylan is embarrassed, a state I would like to keep him in as much as possible. "I do not countenance leaks to the press, Your Honor, and I am doing all I can to prevent it."

I decide to push it and agitate Dylan even more. "May we inquire what that is, Your Honor?"

Judge Timmerman asks, "What are you talking about?"

"Well, Mr. Campbell has just said that he is doing all he can to prevent leaks. Since he's obviously failed, I would like to know exactly what affirmative steps he's taken. Perhaps you and I can give him some advice and make him better at it in the process."

Dylan blows his top on cue, ranting and raving about his own trustworthiness and his outrage at my attacking it. Judge Timmerman calms the situation down, then instructs Dylan to start providing discovery materials today.

"Is there anything else we need to discuss?" she asks, clearly hoping that the answer will be no. I could come up with other diversions, but that's all they would be, and they really wouldn't divert. The fact is, I could strip naked, jump on the defense table, and sing "Mammy," and it wouldn't be the lead story on the news tonight. The lead will be that Kenny Schilling, star running back for the Giants, is facing the death penalty.

It takes me twenty minutes to get through the assembled press outside the courthouse. I've changed my standard "No comment" to an even more eloquent and memorable "We're completely confident we will prevail at trial."

Winston Churchill, eat your heart out.

• • • • •

THE FIRST MESSAGE on my call sheet

when I get back to the office is from Walter Simmons of the New York Giants. I have to look twice at the sheet before I can believe it. The New York Giants are calling me, Andy Carpenter.

I have been waiting for this call since I was seven years old. But is it too late? I'm almost forty; can I still break tackles like I used to? How will I handle the rigors of two-a-day practices? Can I still run the down-and-out, or is my body down-and-out? All I can do is give it a hundred and ten percent, and maybe, just maybe, I can lead my beloved Giants to victory and . . .

There's just one problem. I've never heard of Walter Simmons. If he were involved with the football side of the operation, I would know the name. I can feel the air go out of my balloon; the love handles resting on my hips are actually starting to deflate.

I call Simmons back, and my worst fears are confirmed: He is the Giants' vice president of legal affairs. "I'd like to talk to you about this matter with Kenny Schilling," he says.

"You mean the matter in which he is on trial for his life?"

He doesn't react to my sarcasm. "That's the very one."

He wants to meet in his office at Giants Stadium, but I'm pretty busy, so I tell him he can come to me. He doesn't really want to, and I must admit that the prospect wouldn't thrill me either, since my office doesn't inspire much in the way of respect and awe. It's a three-room dump in a second-floor walk-up over a fruit stand. Everybody tells me I need to upgrade our office space, which is probably why I don't.

Simmons and I wrangle over the meeting location for a brief while until I come up with the perfect solution.

We can meet at Giants Stadium. On the fifty-yard line.

My drive to the stadium takes about twenty-five minutes, and a security guard is in the empty parking lot to greet me. He takes me in through the players' entrance, which allows me another three or four minutes of solid fantasizing. Before I know it, I'm on the field, walking toward the fifty-yard line. A man who must be Walter Simmons, dressed in a suit and tie, walks from the other sideline to meet me at midfield. It's as if we're coming out for the coin toss.

A group of players is on the field, in sweat suits without pads. They're throwing some balls around, jogging, doing minor calisthenics. A placekicker booms field goals from the forty-yard line. These are no doubt voluntary off-season workouts; the serious stuff is a good month away.

Of all the people on the field, Walter Simmons is the only one I could outrun. He looks to be in his early sixties, with a healthy paunch that indicates he's probably first on line for the pregame meal. He's got a smile on his face as he watches me react to these surroundings.

"Not bad, huh?" he asks. "I come down here fairly often. It brings me back to my youth."

"Were you a football player?"

He grins again. "I can't remember. At my age, after lying about my athletic exploits for so many years, I'm not sure what's true and what isn't. But I certainly never played in a place like this."

One player on the field overthrows another, and the next thing I know there is a football at my feet. I pick it up to throw it, glancing toward the sidelines just in case a coach is watching. This could be my chance.

I rear back and throw the ball as far as I can. It is the kind of effort for which the term "wounded duck" was coined. Perhaps even more accurately, it flops around in the air like an exhausted fish on the end of a hook, then falls unceremoniously to the ground fifteen yards in front of the intended receiver. Neither Simmons nor the receiver laughs at me, but I still want to dig a hole in the end zone and lie down next to Jimmy Hoffa.

"That's what happens when I don't warm up," I say.

"How long would it take you to get warm?"

I shrug. "I should be ready about the time of the next eclipse. What's on your mind?"

What's on his mind of course is Kenny Schilling. The Giants are in the uncomfortable position of having given him a huge contract, one befitting a star, two weeks before he is arrested for murder. Not exactly a PR man's dream.

But Simmons says that the Giants are standing behind him, financially and otherwise, and are in fact paying his salary while he deals with the accusations. "He's a terrific person and has never given us a day of trouble since we drafted him."

"And he can run the forty in 4.35," I point out.

He nods at the truthfulness of that statement. "Of course.

We're a football team. If he was built like me or threw the ball like you, we wouldn't be having this conversation."

"I'm still not sure why we are having it," I say.

"Because we can be helpful to you," he says. "The league and the Giants have substantial security operations. We might possibly have better access to certain people than you would. We are prepared to do whatever we can, within reason, of course."

"And in return?" I ask.

"We would like a heads-up if things are going to break in such a way that the organization will be embarrassed."

"While respecting lawyer-client confidentiality." He's a lawyer; he knows I'm not going to reveal more than is proper.

"Of course."

We shake hands on the deal, which I am willing to do since I've given up absolutely nothing and gotten something in return. I decide to test him right away. "Can you get me a list of the players Kenny was closest to?"

"I'll have our people get started on it. We'll also put out the word that they should talk to you, but of course, we can't force them."

I push it a little further. "Actually, you do a lot of personal research on players before you draft them, right?"

"You'd be amazed how much."

"Then I'd like everything you have on Kenny."

"No problem," he says.

I'm starting to like this feeling of power. "Any chance you can get the information the Jets have on Troy Preston?"

"I'll try. I think that information might be helpful. I don't know the specifics, but I believe Preston was a problem."

I press him for more information, but he professes not to have any. I thank him for his time, then turn with a flourish and trot to the sidelines, imagining the crowd roaring in appreciation of my spectacular touchdown pass.

I've got a really strong imagination.

When I get back to the office, Tanya Schilling, Kenny's wife, is waiting for me. I had asked Edna to set up an appointment with her, but I characteristically forgot about it.

Tanya is a strikingly beautiful young woman and one who radiates a strength that belies her diminutive size. "Mr. Carpenter, I know you hear this from every client you've ever had, but I'm going to say it anyway. Kenny is innocent. He simply could not have done this."

I know that she is telling me the truth as she sees it, but that doesn't make it the truth. "He's got an uphill struggle," I say.

She nods. "Let me tell you a story about Kenny. When he was eight years old, he woke up one morning in his apartment and found the police there. His mother had reached under her bed and was bitten during the night by a neighbor's pet snake. It had gotten loose and somehow made it into the Schillings' apartment. The police asked her why she didn't call them during the night when it happened, and she said it was because in the dark she assumed she had been bitten by a rat. That's the kind of neighborhood Kenny grew up in. So uphill struggles don't scare him; they're the story of his life."

"That is indescribably awful," I say, "but this may be tougher."

She nods. "But he'll come out on top. Usually, he does it on his own; sometimes we do it together. This time we need you to help us."

I ask her some questions about Kenny and his relationship with Troy Preston but get basically the same answers that Kenny gave me. By the time Tanya leaves, I'm very impressed by her, and by extension impressed that Kenny was able to get her to marry him.

Laurie arrives a few minutes later, and once again I get a mini–electric jolt of remembrance that she may be leaving. We've agreed not to discuss it for a while, but rather to sit with it and let our feelings settle. Patient introspection is not my strong point, so my approach is to let work push everything else in my head out of the way. Seeing Laurie makes that very difficult.

Laurie is here to discuss the case and find out what I want her investigation to cover. In these early stages I'm interested in three basic things. The first is Troy Preston, especially after Simmons's comment at Giants Stadium. The second is Kenny Schilling; it is absolutely imperative to know who the client is, warts and all, before he can be properly defended. The third is the relationship between the two men, and whether or not there is anything there that Dylan can claim to be a motive for murder.

Kevin comes in just as the first discovery documents arrive. They're mostly police reports, detailing the actions of the officers on the scene when Kenny turned Upper Saddle River into the O.K. Corral. The reports are devastating but not surprising; we already knew how Kenny acted under that pressure.

Just as bad are the reports concerning the disappearance of Troy Preston. Preston was seen leaving the bar with Kenny, which we knew. What we didn't know is that Kenny's car was found abandoned in the woods just across the Jersey border in New York State, not far from Upper Saddle River. Worse yet, there were no fingerprints in the car other than Kenny's and Preston's, and Preston left behind another calling card: specks of his blood.

To complete the trifecta, Kenny's blood tested positive

for the stimulant Rohypnol, and Preston's did as well. Dylan and the police obviously believe that the drugs are tied into the motive for the killing, but that belief is not, and does not have to be, detailed in these reports. I make a note to myself to find out everything I can about the drug and to confront my client with the evidence that he lied to me about taking it.

It's strange that I've begun to think of Kenny as my client on a more permanent basis. Catching him in this lie about the drugs might have disqualified him at this stage, and I would have helped him secure other counsel. But I seem to want to continue, be it because of the diversion from my worries about Laurie or because of my competitive nature vis-à-vis Dylan.

This analysis of my decision to keep Kenny as a client is typical of my version of introspection, which consists of thinking about myself in the third person. It's as if I'm saying, "I wonder why he's thinking like that" or "I wonder why he did that." The "he" in these sentences is me.

I generally don't do even this pathetic introspection for very long. If it becomes too painful, if I discover too much about myself, I shrug and say, "That's *his* problem," and move on.

• • • • •

SOMEHOW during the night, I come up with a brilliant theory. And unlike most ideas that come in dreams, this one holds up in the light of morning.

That's the good news. The bad news is that the theory has nothing to do with the Schilling case. It has to do with football.

My fantasy on the Giants Stadium field yesterday centered on my making the team as a running back or wide receiver, and even my delusional mind knows that is impossible.

I'm going to make it as a placekicker.

Think about this. There are at least two dozen behemoths on every pro roster, weighing in excess of three hundred pounds and able to bench-press Argentina. Yet the kicker is always a little guy, about the size of a late night snack for a defensive lineman.

This leads me to the inescapable conclusion that strength is not a significant factor in placekicking. If it were, then the strongest guys, and not the weakest, would be doing it. What must be necessary to succeed is technique, which the little guys have taken the time to master. There must be a trick to the leg swing, or the body-lean into the ball, or something.

Now, as far as I can tell, there is no reason a thirty-nine-year-old lawyer can't learn the technique. I'm a smart guy; I'll get somebody to teach me, and I'll practice until I've got it down pat. I don't know if the Gramatica brothers can learn torts, but I sure as hell can master a leg sweep.

So now I've got a plan. I get Kenny acquitted, and the very grateful Giants offer me a tryout before next season, which gives me months to learn the technique. I become a football hero, and Laurie stays and becomes head cheer-leader. The only flaw in that plan is the "Kenny acquitted" part, since I have no idea how the hell to do that.

I get to the office at nine o'clock, a little late for me, but a little early for the shock I receive. Edna is already in and brewing coffee. Eclipses happen with considerably greater frequency than Edna getting in before ten, and I didn't know she knew where the coffeemaker was.

A casually dressed man of about twenty-five sits across from Edna, and they have a *New York Times* open on the table between them. She seems to be lecturing him on the intricacies of crossword puzzle solving, a speech she is uniquely qualified to give. Edna is to crossword puzzles what Gretzky was to hockey, alone on a level above all pos-sible competition.

Edna finally notices that I've come in, and she reluctantly pauses in her tutorial to introduce the stranger as Adam Strickland. He's the writer the studio sent to get to know us and see how we operate so that he can write the screenplay more effectively and accurately. I had forgotten he was even coming, and now very sorry that he did. One thing I don't need now is a distraction from the case.

Adam apologizes for coming on such short notice, though he did call yesterday afternoon. I wasn't in, but Edna took the call, hence her early arrival.

I invite Adam back into my office. As he gets up, Edna asks, "Do you want me to type up a summary of what we talked about?"

He shakes his head. "I don't think so. I've got it." He smiles and holds up the pad on which he's been taking notes.

Edna lowers her voice slightly, wary of my overhearing, which I do anyway. "The point is, it's never been done."

Adam nods in agreement. "It's *Rocky* with a pencil. Thanks for the coffee."

Edna smiles, confident that she's gotten her message through. On the way back to my office I stop and get my own coffee. "*Rocky* with a pencil?" I ask.

"Right," he says. "Edna was pitching me an idea for a script. It's about a young girl who grows up with a dream to be the best crossword puzzle player in America. Winds up winning the national title and representing America against the Russian champion in the Olympics."

"I didn't know crossword puzzling was an Olympic sport," I say.

He nods. "She knows the idea needs a little work."

I take a sip of Edna's coffee, which is not the greatest way to start the day. It tastes like kerosene, though I doubt kerosene is this lumpy. "Your coming at this time may be a little awkward," I say.

"Because of the Schilling case?" he asks.

"Yes. I assume you want to observe us, but everything you'd observe would be protected by client privilege. Which means you aren't allowed to hear it."

"I thought you'd say that. I may have come up with a solution."

"I can't imagine how you could," I say.

"A close friend of mine is a lawyer, and I talked to him about it. Here's the plan: You have people that work here that aren't lawyers, right? Like Edna, or maybe outside investigators. They are bound by the privilege because they work for you, right?"

"Right," I say, immediately seeing where he's going.

"So hire me. Pay me a dollar to be your investigator. I'll be covered by the privilege, and I'll sign a confidentiality pledge that only you or your client can release me from."

Surprisingly, the idea is a good one, at least legally. But it's not good enough to make me want to do it. I just don't need someone hanging around during the intensity of a murder trial. On the other hand, I signed a contract and committed to this project, so I have an obligation.

"I have my doubts," I say. "But I'll talk to my client."

"It would really mean a lot to me," he says. "The Schilling case is real drama, you know? And depending on how it comes out, it's a movie that can get made."

"What about the Willie Miller case?" I ask. "Isn't that a movie that will get made?"

He smiles. "I wish, but no way. It's jerk-off time."

He's lost me. "Excuse me? Why is the studio buying it if they don't plan to make it? Why would they pay you to write it?"

"You're not going to like this, but think of movie production as a long pipeline," he says. "Executives, some smart, some idiots, feed projects into the pipeline because they've been told the pipe is supposed to be filled. And that's their job: They're pipe fillers."

"So?" is my probing question.

"So the problem is that the other end of the pipe leads to the sewer, which is where ninety-nine percent of the projects wind up."

"But the theaters are filled with movies," I point out.

He nods. "Right. Because every once in a while a big-shot producer or director or star punches a hole in the pipe and pulls out a project before it can get to the sewer. But once they do, they patch it back up so nothing else leaks out."

"Have you ever had a movie made?"

He shakes his head. "Not even close. But the Schilling case could stay out of the sewer. It's *Pride of the Yankees* meets *In Cold Blood*."

"Do you always talk like that?"

"Pretty much. I've loved movies since I was a little kid, and there's a movie that has dealt with just about every situation ever."

"Except international crossword puzzle tournaments."

He smiles. *"Searching for Edna Fischer."*

I like this guy. He inhabits another world that coexists on the same planet as mine, but he seems to be honest, enthusiastic, and probably smart. "I'll talk to Kenny. Can you give me a couple of days?"

He's fine with that and leaves his number at the Manhattan hotel where he's staying. "I love New York, and the studio's paying, so take your time."

"I recommend the mixed nuts from the minibar," I say. "Only fourteen dollars, but there's plenty of cashews."

Adam leaves, and I open an envelope on my desk with the New York Giants' logo on it. It's a letter from Walter Simmons, confirming our discussion and telling me that the reams of information that the team has on Kenny will be sent shortly. He also lists Kenny's closest friends on the team and assures me that they have been contacted and urged to cooperate.

Laurie's out learning what she can about Troy Preston, so even though investigating is not my strong suit, I might as well start on this list. The first name on it isn't even a player. It's Bobby Pollard, one of the team's trainers. Simmons has helpfully provided me with phone numbers and addresses, and Pollard's wife, Teri, answers on the first ring.

I explain who I am, and she says that Bobby should be home soon and that she'll call him and tell him I'm coming over. He's distraught over what has happened to Kenny, and she's sure he'd love to be able to help. We agree that I'll be there in thirty minutes. This investigating stuff is not so tough after all.

The Pollards live in Fair Lawn, a nice little town adjacent to Paterson. Its size and location are such that it is really a suburb of Paterson, but the people of Fair Lawn would tend to strangle anyone who made such a reference. All northern New Jersey residents consider themselves connected to New York City, and certainly not to Paterson. This is despite the fact that Fair Lawn is heavily populated with former Patersonians, who escaped in a mass exodus in the sixties and seventies.

Teri Pollard is standing on the front porch of their modest home when I pull up. Her presence is the only thing that distinguishes this house from the others on the street, and as distinguishing features go, it's a good one. Teri is very attractive in a comfortable, homespun way. I seem to be noticing attractive women more these days; am I getting in practice for a post-Laurie bachelor life?

Teri is also wearing a nurse's uniform. "You're a nurse?" I ask, checking to see if my deductive skills are working properly.

"Yes. Part-time. Most of the time I spend with Bobby."

Teri's smile matches the rest of her, and she invites me into the den. "Would you like something to drink? We have coffee, tea, soda, orange juice, grapefruit juice, and lemonade."

"I'll have a grande decaf cappuccino." When Kramer said it to Elaine's shrink on *Seinfeld,* it was funny, but Teri doesn't react. I settle for coffee, and she goes off to get it, leaving me with nothing to do but look around the room.

It is definitely a football player's room, and since Teri doesn't look like the linebacker type, I assume that this is where Bobby sits and relives some past gridiron glories. The football pictures all show a young man in a high school uniform, so Bobby may have never made it to college ball. It's surprising, because he appears to be a very large, very powerful young man, and just based on this room, it's doubtful that his dedication to the sport waned.

There are a number of pictures of Bobby with Kenny Schilling, many in football uniform. All but one have them in "Passaic High" uniforms; in the exception their jerseys say "Inside Football" across the front. The pictures also reveal Bobby to be African-American, whereas Teri is white. I do a quick mental calculation and decide that they are young enough not to have encountered too much societal resistance to their union, though I'm sure some still exists.

Teri comes back with the coffee and sees me looking at the pictures. "Bobby was a great player," she says, and then smiles sheepishly. "Not that I would necessarily know a great football player if I saw one, but everybody says he was terrific. The fact that he never played in the NFL with Kenny is something he hasn't fully gotten over, though he'd never admit it."

At that moment the door opens and Bobby comes in. He

brings with him the solution to the mystery of why he gave up football, why he never played in the NFL. Bobby, powerful arms propelling his large frame, sits in a wheelchair. I have no idea what put him there, or when it happened, but the sight of him is an instantly saddening story of shattered dreams. It is also an explanation of why Teri is not a full-time nurse; Bobby must need some help getting around.

"Mr. Carpenter?" he asks, though I suppose Teri has already answered that question for him.

"Andy," I say, and wait until he offers his hand before I walk over and shake it. His grip is powerful, his biceps enormous, and my mind processes the fact that this wheelchair-bound invalid could twist me into a pretzel. "Walter Simmons from the Giants gave me your name. He said you might be willing to talk to me about Kenny."

"Kenny's my best friend. I'll help in any way I can."

"I take it you don't think he's guilty."

"No fucking way."

Teri seems to cringe slightly from the language and excuses herself so that we can talk. As soon as she does, Bobby launches into a spirited defense of Kenny, whom he ranks as sort of a male, football-playing Mother Teresa.

"He's the reason I have my job," says Bobby. "He told the Giants that if they didn't hire me, he'd become a free agent and move to a team that would. He wouldn't back down, so they did."

I doubt that the story is quite how Bobby describes it but it's probably how he believes it. "How long have you known him?"

"Sophomore year in high school. That's when I moved to Passaic and we met on the football field. I was the right guard. He ran right behind my ass for over a thousand yards that year and two thousand each of the next two. Still holds the Jersey state record. Kenny and I were both named high school all-Americans."

Bobby and Teri were both at the bar the night that Preston was killed, and Bobby admits with reluctance that he saw Preston and Kenny leave together. He completely rejects any possibility that Kenny is the killer. "And I told that to the police," he says. "I don't think they wanted to hear it."

The conversation moves back to Bobby's own football career, mainly because that's where he moves it. My guess is that pretty much every conversation he has moves to the same place. He talks about how he was going to attend Ohio State on a full football scholarship. That all came to an end when he was injured in a car crash.

"It happened in Spain," he says. "I was taking a few weeks to travel through Europe. I was on one of those winding roads, and my car went over the edge. I haven't been out of this chair since. If it happened here, with American doctors . . . who knows if it would have been different, you know?"

I don't know what to say, so I don't say anything. Everything Bobby ever wanted disappeared when his car went a few inches off the side of the road. I can almost feel the disappointment in the air, weighing on him.

I'm relieved when the door opens and Teri comes in, still wearing her nurse's uniform. She also has with her a young boy, whom she introduces as Jason, their seven-year-old son. Jason seems tall for his age and has none of his father's offensive lineman bulk. He's either going to be a wide receiver when he grows up or, if he takes after his mother, a nurse.

"I'm off to work, Bobby," Teri says. "Don't let Jason stay up too late."

He smiles. "What do you mean? I thought we'd go out

drinking tonight." He taps Jason lightly in the ribs. "Right, big guy?" Jason taps him right back and mimics his "Right, big guy." There seems to be an easy relationship between father and son.

Teri says goodbye to me and leaves. Once she's out of the house, Bobby says, "She works like crazy and takes care of me and Jason. She's unbelievable."

"Can you drive?" I ask.

He nods. "Yup. They make hand controls for cars. But it's still a hell of a lot easier when she's with me. The team lets her come on road trips."

Jason asks Bobby to read him a story, and I take advantage of the interruption to say my goodbyes.

I drive back home, no more enlightened about the facts of the case, but liking my client a little more. He has taken good care of this one friend, and on some level it makes it harder for me to believe he killed another one.

• • • • •

LAURIE MAKES MY favorite for dinner, pasta whatever. She seems to add anything lying around into the sauce, and somehow it turns out terrifically. The best part is, she never tells me the ingredients, since if I knew how healthful they were, I probably wouldn't eat them.

We have an agreement that we never discuss business at home, but while we're on a case, we break the agreement pretty much every night. Tonight is no exception, and during dinner she tells me about her initial efforts to investigate the life of Troy Preston.

Mostly working with her own contacts, the picture she's getting of Preston is not a positive one. Word has it that he failed an NFL drug test last season. NFL policy is to put the failed player on probation and mandate counseling. The infraction remains secret until the second offense, at which point there is a four-week suspension. The prosecution's postmortem blood test on Preston indicated that he would have failed another test had one been scheduled any time soon. That's not something he needs to worry about now.

The Jets, according to Laurie's sources, were very worried about Preston and felt that drug use was responsible for his mediocre performance last season. He was never more than an adequate reserve anyway, and with his knee injury he was in danger of being cut from the squad this year.

After dinner we go into the living room, put on an Eagles CD, open a bottle of chardonnay, and read. I had run a Lexis-Nexis search on Kenny, which through the miracle of computers allows me to access pretty much everything that has been written about him. Edna has pared it down to everything not related to game performances, leaving me with a thick book of material to go through.

Laurie reads a mystery, one of probably a hundred she reads every year. It surprises me, because solving mysteries is what she does for a living. I'm a lawyer, and trust me, when I have spare time, you won't catch me reading *The Alan Dershowitz Story*.

Tara takes her spot on the couch between us. Music seems to put her in a mellow mood, which Laurie and I augment by simultaneously petting her. My assigned zone is the top of her head, while Laurie focuses on scratching Tara's stomach.

Laurie and I haven't discussed her possible move back to Findlay since the night of that stupid eclipse. I keep forming sentences to address it, but none of them sound right while taking the route to my mouth, so I don't let them out.

"This is so nice," Laurie says with total accuracy.

I need to let her feel how nice this is without saying anything about the possibility of her leaving and ruining it. I have to let her deal with this on her own; my advocating a position is not going to help. "It is nice," I agree. "Completely nice. Totally nice. As long as you and I and Tara live here in New Jersey, we will have this permanent niceness." In case you haven't noticed by now, I'm an idiot.

"Andy . . . ," she says in a gentle admonishment. Then, "I do love you, you know."

"I know," I lie, since that is no longer something I know. I've pretty much broken it down to a simple proposition: If she stays, she loves me; if she leaves, she doesn't.

Usually, we have CNN on as background noise, but lately, we're unable to do that because their policy seems to be "all Kenny Schilling, all the time." Nobody on these shows has any knowledge whatsoever about the case, but that doesn't stop them from predicting a conviction.

I get up and walk around the house, bringing my wine-glass with me. I grew up in this house, then lived in two apartments and two houses before coming back here. I could barely describe anything about those other places, yet I know every square inch of this house. Even when I wasn't living here, it was completely vivid in my mind.

No matter what I look at, the memories come flooding back. Wiffle ball games, playing gin with my father, stoop-ball, trying a puff of a cigarette in the basement, eating my mother's cinnamon cake, having the Silvers, our next-door neighbors, over to watch baseball games on TV . . . my history was played out here. I left it behind me once, and I won't do so again.

I am painfully aware that Laurie's history is in Findlay. Not in a house, maybe, and I'm sure that her memories aren't as relentlessly pleasant as are mine. But it is where she became who she is, and she's being drawn back to it. I understand it all too well.

I need to stop thinking about it. She will make her decision, one way or the other, and that will be that. If my mother were alive, she would say, "Whatever happens, it's all for the best." I never believed it when she used to say it, and I don't believe it now. If Laurie leaves, it will not be for the best. It will be unacceptably awful, but I will accept it. Kicking and screaming, I will accept it.

I wake up in the morning resolved to focus on nothing but Kenny Schilling. My first stop is out to the jail to talk with him. He's less anxious and frightened than the last time I saw him, but more withdrawn and depressed. These are common reactions, and they must have something to do with the self-protective nature of the human mind.

I begin by telling him that I have decided to stay on his case, though he had always assumed that I would. I lay out my considerable fees for him, and he nods without any real reaction at all. Money is not an issue for him right now, though until a month ago he was a relatively low-paid player. The Giants are sticking with him and paying him according to his huge new contract. As far as my fees go, if I get him acquitted, it will be the best money he ever spent. If he's convicted, all the money in the world won't help him.

With the money issue out of the way, I start my questioning. "So tell me about the drugs," I say.

"There weren't any. I don't do drugs."

"They were found in your blood. The same drug was found in Troy Preston."

"They're lying. They're trying to put me away."

"Who's they?" I ask.

"The police."

"Why would the police want to put you away?"

"I don't know. But I didn't take no drugs."

His insistence on this point is surprising. Drug use in itself does not come close to a proof of murder. He could be protecting his public image, but his current incarceration on first-degree murder charges has blown that out of the water much more effectively anyway. It is extraordinarily unlikely that the police have conspired to frame him by faking the blood tests, though I will look into any possible motivations for their doing that.

The other possibility of course is that both the police and Kenny are being honest and that the drug was slipped to him. I need to consult an expert to find out if that is possible.

"Could someone have slipped you the drug without you knowing it?"

He grabs on to this like a life preserver. "Yeah, that must be it! Somebody put it in my drink or food or something. Maybe Troy did . . . he was there."

Once again the persistent "why" question rears its ugly head. "Why would he do that?"

He shakes his head, having discovered that this particular life preserver can't support his weight. "I don't know. But there's gotta be a reason."

I have Kenny rehash his relationship with Troy Preston, starting with their meeting at the high school all-star weekend. It turns out that they also spent a couple of days together at the NFL combine before they were drafted. The combine is a place where rookies come to demonstrate their physical skills to assembled NFL executives.

Kenny claims to have racked his brain trying to think of something relevant to Preston's murder, but he just can't come up with anything. "There's . . . there's just nothing."

I detect a hesitation, mainly because there was a hesitation. "What were you going to say?" I ask.

"Nothing. I've told you everything I know."

I've gotten pretty good at reading my clients, and for the first time I think Kenny's holding something back. Holding something back from one's defense attorney is akin to putting a gun to one's head and pulling the trigger, but my pressing Kenny for more information gets me nowhere.

Before I leave, I broach the subject of Adam Strickland becoming an employee of my office so that he can observe what's going on and perhaps someday write about it.

"But he can't write anything we don't want him to?" Kenny asks.

"He can't reveal any privileged information without our permission."

"What if he did?"

"You could sue him, and nothing he says could ever be used in court against you."

Kenny shrugs, having lost interest. He has no desire to focus on any subject that can't get him out of his cell. "Whatever you want, man. I don't care either way."

I tell him I'll decide one way or the other and then let him know. I head back to the office, where Laurie is waiting for me. I can tell by the look in her eyes that she has something to tell me, though my hunch is helped along considerably by her saying, "Wait till you hear this."

I decide to take a guess first. "Your old boyfriend changed his mind and offered you a job as a school crossing guard. And you said no, because they're giving you a bad corner and making you buy your own whistle."

"Andy," she says, "you're going to have to try harder to deal with this."

I already knew that, so I say, "What were you going to tell me?"

"Preston wasn't just using. He was dealing."

This is potentially huge. If Preston was dealing drugs, he was involved with big money and very dangerous people. The kind of people that kill other people. The kind of people that defense lawyers love to point to and say, "My client didn't do it; they did."

"Who told you?"

She smiles. "Police sources."

"Police sources" is Laurie-speak for Pete Stanton. Pete has long been a reliable source of information for both of us. He would never say anything damaging to the department, but nor does he have that knee-jerk police reaction not to have anything to do with anyone on the defense side of the justice system. There would be no downside at all to his supplying background information in this case, since it is under the jurisdiction of the state police.

"Did he give you specifics?" I ask.

She shakes her head. "Over dinner with you. Tonight. He invited me as well."

I nod with resignation. Since I've inherited my fortune, Pete's goal has been to make me poor again. He does this by selecting the most overpriced restaurants he can find and then stuffing himself to the point where he has to be lifted out of his chair with a crane, while I pick up the tab. "I hope he didn't choose the restaurant," I say.

"He did. It's a place in the city."

New York City. Pete hates New York City, always has, but he's apparently become disenchanted with the reasonable cost structure of New Jersey restaurants. "It would be cheaper to bribe the jury," I say.

• • • • •

PETE SAYS HE'LL meet us at the restaurant, so Laurie and I drive in alone. I'm not a big fan of driving in Manhattan; it calls for an aggressiveness that I simply do not have outside of a courtroom. I'm always afraid that Ratso Rizzo is going to pound on my car and yell, "I'm walkin' here! I'm walkin' here!"

The restaurant is on Eightieth Street near Madison, and as we get close, I start looking for a parking lot. I find one on the same block, with a sign proclaiming a flat rate of forty-three dollars for the night. They seem proud of this, as if it's so inexpensive it will be an enticement for people to park their cars here. I only wish Laurie and I had come in separate cars so we could take double advantage of this incredible deal.

"Maybe you should look for a space on the street," Laurie says.

I shake my head. "It's a nice thought, but the nearest space on a street is in Connecticut."

I park in the lot, and we walk half a block to the restaurant. It's French, with stone walls to give us the impression that we're having dinner in a cave. I approach the maître d' and tell him that I believe our reservation is in the name of Stanton.

He brightens immediately. "Ah, yes! They're waiting for you!"

Before I get a chance to fully weigh the significance of his using the word "they're" rather than "he's," Laurie and I are led to a private cave off the main dining room. We enter and see one table, set for fifteen people. The problem is, there are enough people in the room to fill it.

Pete jumps up, almost knocking over a lit candle in the process. "Our host is here!"

This draws a cheer, and I am soon surrounded by members of Pete's family. I know only two of them: his wife, Donna, and his brother, Larry. I've been out with Pete and Donna a few times, and I got Larry off on a drug charge four years ago. He's since turned his life around and does volunteer work as a drug counselor in downtown Paterson.

Laurie and I are soon introduced to a bunch of Uncle Eddies and Aunt Denises and Cousin Mildreds, all of whom think it's just wonderful that I've thrown this party for my good friend Pete.

"This is so nice of you," Donna says to me. "And his birthday isn't for six weeks."

Laurie jumps in, fearful of what I might say. "Andy wanted it to be a surprise."

I nod, staring daggers across the room at Pete. "And it was. It definitely was."

Pete is oblivious to my daggers; he's too busy holding bottles of expensive wine and asking, "Who wants white, and who wants red?" He looks at the labels and says, "I got the Lafeet something and the Pooly whatever..." This is from a guy who's never bought a bottle of wine without a twist-off cap.

I finally make it over to the guest of honor. "You're a cop," I say, "so you'd be a good person to answer this question. Who could I hire to kill you? After this dinner, I can't afford to pay very much, but I don't need a quality hit man. For instance, I don't care how much pain he causes."

"Don't tell me you're pissed off," he says.

"This was supposed to be a dinner where you gave us information about drug traffickers. Not a four-thousand-dollar family circle meeting."

He nods. "It turns out that Larry knows something about this, so I wanted him here. But he was having dinner with Aunt Carla, who was staying at Cousin Juliet's, and it sort of snowballed from there. You know how these things are."

With almost no family of my own, and no desire to impoverish my friends, I don't know how these things are, but I drop it. "So when can we talk?"

"You can drive Larry and me back. We'll talk then."

The rest of the evening is surprisingly pleasant, at least until the check comes. Pete's family is both close-knit and funny, and it feels good to be included in it. I'm not totally forgiving Pete for this fiasco, though, and I lash out by refusing to sing "Happy Birthday" when they bring out the three-tier cake I'm paying for.

It's not until we're on the George Washington Bridge driving home that Pete addresses the issue at hand. "Paul Moreno," he says.

"Who's Paul Moreno?" I ask. The question must be a stupid one, because it draws sighs and moans from Pete, Larry, and Laurie.

"He's a guy who makes Dominic Petrone look like

Mother Teresa," Pete says. Dominic Petrone is the head of the mob in North Jersey, which means Paul Moreno must be a rather difficult fellow to deal with.

"I just spent twenty-eight hundred bucks on your birthday. Can you be a little more specific?"

Pete, Laurie, and Larry then alternate being very specific, and the picture they paint of Paul Moreno is not a pretty one. About five years ago a group of young Mexican immigrants started a drug pipeline from their former country to their current home in North Jersey. It was mostly street stuff and relatively small money for this industry.

What distinguished this gang was the violence they were quite willing to use in running their business. Led by a young hood named Cesar Quintana, they became the area's primary source of cheap drugs and ruthless violence, and they were limited only by their inherent lack of intelligence. They were not businessmen, and business acumen is needed to sell all products, including illegal drugs.

Enter Pablo Moreno, born in Mexico to a family of very significant wealth, said to be dubiously earned. Moreno was educated in this country, graduated from the Wharton School of Business, after which Pablo Moreno became Paul Moreno. He returned to Mexico for a while and then settled in North Jersey two years ago to apply his business expertise in earnest.

It seems as if he conducted an analysis and determined that the best opportunity for success in this country was to become a part of the still-fledgling, unsophisticated operation Quintana was running. Moreno's style, reputation, and money overwhelmed him, and they soon became partners. They allegedly split the profits, but Quintana has allowed Moreno to call the shots, perhaps the first sign of intelligence he has ever shown.

In the eyes of law enforcement their operation now represents the worst of both worlds. Moreno provides the smarts and the capital, and Quintana supplies the muscle and willingness to use it. In the process they've branched out to higher-end drugs and higher-level clientele.

"Which is why they've become a major pain in the ass of Dominic Petrone," Pete says.

"And he hasn't taken them on?" I ask. Rumor has it that both end zones in Giants Stadium are built on a foundation of people who became pains in the ass of Dominic Petrone.

Pete shakes his head. "Not yet. Drugs have never been the main part of Petrone's operation, so he's let it go so far. There's no telling how long that will last. It's a war he'd win, but it would be ugly."

"So where does my client fit into this?"

Larry answers. "He probably doesn't, but Troy Preston does. Moreno loves football, and he took a liking to Preston. Preston in turn took a liking to Moreno and his lifestyle. The word is, they were really close."

"So Preston was dealing for him?" Laurie asks.

"Not in a serious way at first. More to his friends, certain other players . . . that kind of thing. People tell me it made him feel like a big shot. Then he started liking the fact that it was supplementing his income, so he branched out some. The bigger problem is, he started using what he was selling, which is not the best thing for a pro football career. And as his career went down, his need for money outside football went up."

My mind of course is focused on finding a killer other than Kenny Schilling. I start thinking out loud. "So Petrone could have killed Preston to send a message to Moreno. Or maybe Preston pissed Quintana off, and *he* killed him."

"Or maybe your client is guilty," Pete says, ever the cop.

"The victim's blood was in his car, and his body was in his house. Not exactly your classic whodunit."

"More like your classic frame-up," I say.

Pete laughs. "And exactly why would they pick Schilling to frame? It's not like they would have left evidence for the police to track them down. Petrone's been murdering people since he was four years old. You think we could have tied him to this?"

"You? No. The state cops? Maybe." I don't really believe what I'm saying; it's my pathetic attempt to get back at Pete for the birthday bash.

If Pete is wounded by my attack, he hides it well. He shakes his head. "Nope. Petrone didn't do Preston, and the job was too classy for Quintana. He would have sliced him up and dumped him in front of City Hall."

He's probably right, but at the very least this opens up a huge area for a defense attorney to explore and exploit. I'm already working out strategies in my mind; the money for this evening's fiasco may actually turn out to be well spent.

We pull up at Pete's car, and as he and Larry get out, Pete pats my arm. "Thanks, man. This is the nicest thing anybody's ever done for me, even if I was the one that did it. But you didn't get too pissed, and I appreciate it. You're a good friend."

"Happy birthday," I say. That'll teach him.

• • • • •

THERE ARE A FEW things I don't like
about my job. One is that it doesn't involve playing professional sports, though my placekicking brainstorm should
take care of that. Two is that it gives me the creeps to have
to call anyone "Your Honor." Three, and most important, I
don't like to mislead people.

But misleading people is something a good defense attorney does, and this case is about to become a textbook example. I do not believe that Troy Preston was murdered by
Dominic Petrone, Paul Moreno, Cesar Quintana, or anyone
else involved with illegal drugs. Those are not people who
would have gone to such lengths to frame Kenny Schilling.
They would have put a bullet in Preston's head and dumped
him in the river, or buried him where he'd never be found.
And, as Pete was quick to point out, they would not have
left a trail so they could be caught. And if they weren't in
legal danger, there would be no reason to frame somebody
else.

But these bad guys present perfect targets for me, people who I might get the jury to believe could have done it.

It helps me create reasonable doubt that my client is guilty, so I must pursue it vigorously, even though I don't believe it. I'm not lying, but it still makes me uncomfortable. I'll go forward with it, though, since our justice system makes no allowances for lawyer discomfort.

Adam Strickland is with Kevin and Edna when I arrive at the office. He takes notes as Edna regales him with more of her ideas for the crossword puzzle film, and I hear Kevin ask if Adam can use the actual name of Kevin's privately owned business in the Willie Miller movie. It's called the Law-dromat, and the gimmick is that Kevin gives free legal advice to his customers. Of course, he can only be there to do that when we are not busy on a case. The way the Schilling case is shaping up, there are going to be a whole lot of poorly ad-vised launderers running around North Jersey for a while.

Adam tells Kevin that he'll definitely put the Law-dromat in the script and refers to Kevin's idea as *My Beautiful Laundrette* meets *The Verdict*. Unfortunately, Adam forgets to mention that the script will ultimately travel through the pipe and into the sewer.

I haven't thought about Adam since I discussed him with Kenny, but I make a decision in the moment to let him hang out with us. Kenny didn't mind, and I made a commitment to the studio, so I might as well. I have Edna type up a stan-dard agreement, and within minutes Adam is an employee of my firm, bound by the same confidentiality guarantees as the rest of us.

I explain to Kevin what we've learned about Troy Pres-ton's relationship to Paul Moreno and the drugs he distrib-utes. I find myself feeling self-conscious with Adam listening in, especially since he is staring at me so intently as I speak that it feels like he's literally inhaling my words.

Because of Adam's presence, I don't mention to Kevin

my feeling that, while we now have some people to point the finger at, I don't really believe they are guilty. This is not a good start to this relationship; I'm going to have to either trust Adam or renege on our agreement and remove him from our team.

Kevin and I kick things around for about a half hour, until Laurie shows up with Marcus Clark. I had told her to bring in Marcus once I learned that we were going to be dealing with people as dangerous as Cesar Quintana and Paul Moreno. It makes me feel secure to have Marcus in our camp, in the same fashion that Don Corleone felt secure having Luca Brazi on his side. Having only seen Luca in the movie, and never meeting him in person, my view is that Marcus is far scarier. To me, Marcus makes Luca look like Mary Lou Retton.

Adam looks stunned when Laurie and Marcus enter, and it's easy to understand why. There could not be two human beings on this planet who look more different, yet each has achieved a type of physical near perfection. Laurie is white, tall, blond, and breathtakingly beautiful, with a face that combines intelligence, compassion, and more than a modicum of toughness. Marcus is African-American, short, bald, and carved from burnished steel, with a perpetual scowl so fearsome that my initial instinct is invariably to back away from him, even though he's on my side.

What Marcus and Laurie have in common is that they are both talented investigators, though their styles are as different as their looks. Laurie is smart and relentless, pushing and probing, until she learns what she has to learn. People provide Marcus with information in the hope that he will continue to let them live. And sometimes he does.

I introduce them to Adam, mentioning that Adam is a writer.

"Books?" asks Marcus, a man of few words.

"Movies," says Adam. He says it nervously, because when people talk to Marcus, the goal is not to say the wrong thing. "I write screenplays, and—"

"*Rambo*?" interrupts Marcus.

"Uh, no. I didn't write *Rambo*," says Adam, glancing quickly at me in the hope I'll jump in and help, which I won't. "But I liked it. It was a wonderful film. They . . . they were wonderful films . . . all the *Rambo*s."

Marcus just shakes his head and sits down, no longer interested in Adam or his portfolio. He also doesn't say a word as I go over everything I know about Paul Moreno and Cesar Quintana. I'm speaking strictly for Marcus's benefit, since Laurie already knows all of this, having been my date for Pete's birthday extravaganza.

When I'm finished, it's time to give out the assignments. I say to Marcus, "I'd like you to find out everything you can about Quintana and whatever connections he has to Troy Preston or Kenny Schilling."

Marcus just stares at me, not saying a word. Also not a nod or a blink or a shrug or any other human response. It's disorienting, but it's pure Marcus.

I continue. "Be careful, these guys are very dangerous."

Again I get the Marcus stare, but no other reaction.

"I'm glad we had this chat," I say. "I always find these exchanges of ideas very helpful."

Apparently also satisfied with the discussion, Marcus gets up and leaves.

"Jesus Christ," says Adam. "*Godzilla* meets *Shaft*. Are we sure he's on our side?"

"Let's put it this way," I say. "If we find out he's sleeping with the fishes, we're in big trouble."

With that, I leave to begin what may be an impossible

project. I'm going to attempt to reverse the tide of public opinion that has been building against Kenny, the overwhelming feeling that he must be guilty.

While Kenny has always been relatively popular, this belief in his guilt amounts to mass wishful thinking, by both the public and the press. The media see this as a monster story, sure to sell newspapers and lift Nielsen ratings for months. The public views it as entertainment, much more fascinating and exciting than whether Britney and Justin will get back together. They are looking forward to following the soap opera that will lead up to and include the trial.

All of this anticipated fun for everyone would be wiped away if something came out to vindicate Kenny and lead to the charges being dropped. So while no one would ever admit it, the wishful thinking is that he is guilty, so the show can go on.

I've decided to let our developing defense point of view leak out into the public discourse, but I can't do so openly. I have to do it in a sneaky, underhanded manner, which our system fortunately encourages. My only dilemma was in deciding which member of the press to make my partner, since the number of willing candidates would literally number in the thousands.

I briefly considered whether to go national, to slip my story to *Time, Newsweek,* or one of the cable outlets. The advantage would be immediate widespread coverage, but in this situation it's just not necessary. Any story, no matter its origin, will be picked up in the hurricane that has become this case and spread everywhere. I could plant this in the afternoon with a stringer for the *Okefenokee Swamp Gazette,* and it would be the lead on CNN before nightfall.

Once I made the decision to do this locally, the choice of whom to go to was a difficult one. Vince Sanders, editor of one of the local papers, has helped me a number of times in the past. He's also a good friend, which is the main reason I can't go to him. I can't have my fingerprints on this. Everybody will assume I'm behind it anyway, but if Vince breaks the story, they'll know it for an actual fact. Vince is going to kill me for not going to him, but I'll make it up to him later on.

I narrowed my choice down to two or three prospects and finally settled on Karen Spivey, a real pro who has covered the courthouse beat for as long as I can remember. She's a no-frills, old-fashioned reporter who grabs a story in her teeth and pulls on it until all the facts come out. She's also done me a bunch of favors in the past, and it's nice to be able to repay one.

I called Karen yesterday and told her that I had a scoop for her but that it was off the record—"background," as it's known in reporter jargon. We agreed to meet at the duck pond in Ridgewood, an out-of-the-way place where we'd be unlikely to be seen. Her office is in Clifton, but she was quite willing to travel the half hour or so to get to Ridgewood. The truth is, she was so excited to hear from me that she would have agreed to meet me in Beirut.

I stop on the way and pick up Tara, since the duck pond ranks with her favorite places on earth. We don't even bring along her favorite tennis ball, since throwing it causes a commotion that makes the ducks swim away from us. Tara likes them close-up, where she can observe them.

We arrive before Karen, and Tara immediately goes into staring mode, watching every move the ducks make. They watch her just as carefully; it's as if they're all here because they're writing a dissertation on the habits of the other species. The ducks don't seem at all threatened by Tara, though they shy away whenever other dogs show up.

Karen arrives, and as she gets out of her car and looks toward me, I point at a deserted picnic area. I call Tara to come along with me as I go to meet her, though Tara would much rather stay and watch the ducks. I don't like to take her away from them, but I care for Tara as I would a child, and you don't leave children alone at the duck pond or anywhere else.

Karen, in her business suit, looks completely out of place in these surroundings. Her reputation is that she works twenty-four hours a day, and it's unlikely her job brings her to very many duck ponds.

"Thanks for coming, Karen," I say, pretending that she's done me a favor.

She taps her foot on the ground. "What is all this green stuff?"

"Grass. And the brown material under that is dirt."

She shakes her head, as if in wonderment. "Damn. I heard about this stuff. But I didn't realize there was any around here."

"Next time I'll show you flowers."

"You do that. Are we going to make small talk all day?" Her trip to nature is over; she's back to business.

"Unless you confirm that we're off the record."

She nods. "We're off."

"You can say you got this from sources close to the defense," I allow, "but my name doesn't get mentioned."

"Agreed."

I proceed to tell her what I know about the drug connection Troy Preston had with Cesar Quintana. I don't mention Paul Moreno, and I don't mention the rivalry with Dominic Petrone, preferring to hold all of that until a later date. There is always the possibility that Karen, being a good reporter, will uncover it on her own, and that would be fine with me.

"Was Preston involved in their drug business?" she asks.

I nod. "That is our information, though we're not ready to prove it. He certainly had drugs in his system."

"As did your client."

"Preston took them voluntarily," I say.

She seems surprised. "And Schilling didn't?"

"Schilling didn't."

"So how did the body get in Schilling's house and the blood in his car?" she asks.

"We'll take that up next semester."

Karen looks skeptical, as she should be. "You think Quintana framed him? Why would they do that?"

I smile knowingly, even though I don't have the slightest idea what I'm talking about. "Come on," I say, "I'll show you how cute Tara is with the ducks."

Much to my amazement, Karen has no desire to see how cute Tara is with the ducks. She declines, then rushes off across the green stuff to her car so she can prepare her story.

• • • • •

THE PHONE WAKES me at six A.M., and

Laurie answers it.

"Hello," she says, then listens for a moment and hands the phone to me. "It's Vince. He wants to talk to the 'shit-head source close to the defense.'"

I take the phone. I've dreaded this conversation and was hoping to put it off until later than six in the morning. "Hello, Vince, old buddy," I say. "How are you?"

"You son of a bitch."

Vince has obviously read Karen Spivey's story already. "I'm sorry, Vince. If I gave the story to you, everyone would have known I planted it."

"Who do you think they suspect now? The queen of fucking England?"

I actually feel bad about this, but I'll get over it. "You'll get the next one. I promise."

"I'd better. And just to show there are no hard feelings, you can have *my* next one. It's about your client, and you're not going to like it."

"What is it?"

Click.

Vince hanging up on me is not a news event, but what he said leaves me a little unsettled. He's a terrific newsman with a first-rate staff of reporters and very capable of having come up with something on Kenny. If he said I'm not going to like it, it's safe to assume that I won't.

It's also safe to assume that calling him back won't help me drag the secret out of him, so I roll over and go back to sleep for another hour. When I wake up, I go out to the front yard and get the paper, an act that Tara has never accepted as dignified for golden retrievers to perform.

Karen has nailed the story well; it will certainly have the desired effect of shaking up the public perception of the case. Quintana is not likely to be thrilled with it; Karen has done some additional reporting that makes his connection to Preston seem even tighter.

I sit for a while and ponder what my next steps should be when Laurie comes in and reminds me that I have a breakfast with Sam Willis at eight.

Sam is my accountant, a position that increased significantly in importance when I came into my fortune. He is also my friend and my competitor in something we call song-talking. The goal is to work song lyrics smoothly into our conversation, and I am probably giving myself too much credit by referring to Sam as my competitor. He is a master at it and has long since outdistanced me.

I let Sam choose the restaurant for breakfast, and he picked a place called Cynthia's Home Cookin', which the signs say is noted for "Cynthia's World Famous Pancakes." I've only been to Europe twice, but no one has come up to me and said "Ah, an American. That's where Cynthia makes her famous pancakes." But Sam is a regular here and always chooses the place, and they do have great pancakes.

Since it's not fair to leave Adam in the office listening to
Edna all the time, and since he's supposed to be observing
me, I invited him to the breakfast with Sam. He's waiting for
me in the parking lot when I arrive, as always writing something in his notepad.

"Good morning," I say. "No trouble finding the place?"

He smiles. "Are you kidding? It's world-famous."

I point to the notepad. "You're taking notes about it?"

He nods. "It's a great setting for a scene."

We go inside the restaurant, which is basically a dump,
albeit a crowded dump. There is not an empty table in the
place. Sam sits in a booth near the window waiting for us.
He waves, then calls out to the waitress. "They're here,
Lucy."

"Coffee comin' up, Sam" is her response, then she comes
over to the table and pours coffee for all of us even before
we arrive. Decaf is not an option at Cynthia's.

I introduce Adam to Sam as we sit down. I notice my
chair is covered with crumbs and sweep them off before sitting. "Nice clean place you brought us to."

Sam shrugs and fires his opening salvo. "Sometimes you
wanna go where everybody knows your name."

Adam brightens up. "Hey, that's a song. *Cheers,* right?" I
had forgotten to warn Adam about the song-talking.

Sam says to me, "This guy's sharp as a tack."

"He's a big-time screenwriter," I say. "So be careful, or
he'll have Peewee Herman play you in the movie."

I start to tell Sam what I want, which is to have him use
his incredible computer expertise to hack into the life of the
deceased Troy Preston. Put Sam in front of a computer and
he can find out anything about anybody, and right now I'm
interested in financial dealings that can connect Preston to
drug money. I provide Sam with the personal information

about Preston that was in the police reports, as well as the information the Giants were able to provide.

Sam gives the material a quick look, then casts a wary glance at Adam, who is still taking notes. The kind of research Sam does is not always strictly legal, and his unspoken question to me asks if Adam can be trusted. I nod that it's okay, so Sam promises to get right on it.

The waitress, Lucy, comes over and spends a few minutes joking with Sam, who tells Adam that Lucy can "light the world up with her smile. She can take a nothing day and suddenly make it all seem worthwhile." Adam recognizes it as being from *The Mary Tyler Moore Show,* which surprises me, since he's not old enough to have seen it, other than in reruns.

Sam asks Adam a bunch of questions about the movie business, including one about how Adam got into it in the first place. He grew up in a poor rural area in Kansas, and his first and fondest memories are rooted in his love for movies. Five years ago he was living in St. Louis working at an ad agency and spending his free hours writing something called a spec script. That's a script that no one commissions in advance and therefore can be sold as a finished product to the highest bidder. His sold for "mid-five figures," as Adam puts it, and though it never came close to making it out of the sewer pipe, it resulted in his getting more work.

"But I had to move to LA so I could sit in meetings, look creative, and pretend to know what I'm talking about."

I see an opportunity, so I say to Sam, "They said that Californee is the place he oughta be, so he loaded up the truck and he moved to Beverlee—Hills, that is."

Sam nods in grudging respect to my *Hillbillies* reference. "Makes sense . . . swimming pool . . . movie stars."

I tell Adam that I will meet him back at the office, that there is something I need to talk to Sam about privately. Adam leaves, and Sam makes the logical assumption that I want to discuss my personal finances, which is not at all what I want to discuss.

"There's somebody else I want you to check out." I say it hesitantly because I'm more than a little ashamed of what I'm doing. "His name is Sandy Walsh. He lives in Findlay, Wisconsin."

Sam writes down the name. "You want to tell me why?"

As long as I'm doing something this slimy, I might as well at least come clean as to why. "He's Laurie's old boyfriend . . . he's offered her a job back in Findlay. She's thinking of moving there."

He shakes his head in sympathy; he likes Laurie and knows how devastated I would be if she left. "You think she will?"

"I don't know," I say honestly.

He shakes his head again. "Just walking out on you and going back to her hometown . . . damn, there must be fifty ways to leave your lover."

I'm going through this torture, and he's actually song-talking Simon and Garfunkel. The mind boggles. "This might not be the best time for song-talking," I say.

"Sorry, sometimes I can't help it. What do you want me to find out about this guy?"

"That he's a slimeball. Maybe a crook, a terrorist . . . whatever you can come up with. Something that will make Laurie decide to stay here."

"I assume you don't want her to know about this?"

I nod. "That's a safe assumption. It's not my proudest moment."

"Jeez, Andy . . . I thought you guys were gonna get married."

"We talked about it. Maybe we should have; things were going well enough. I certainly didn't expect anything like this."

"Ain't it always like that?" he asks.

"What?"

"I mean, the relationship goes on, you think you're making progress . . . I don't know . . . sometimes it just seems the nearer your destination, the more you're slip-sliding away." He smiles slightly, hoping I won't take offense at his inability to stop song-talking.

I don't. "Just for that you can pay the check," I say.

He nods. "Who do you want me to look into first, Preston or this Walsh guy?"

"Preston," I say with some reluctance.

"I'll get on them both right away," he says, understanding. "You can count on it."

I stand up to leave. "You're like a bridge over troubled water," I say.

He smiles. "I will ease your mind."

• • • • •

I MAKE IT A POINT to meet frequently with my clients during the pretrial period. It's not vital to their defense; the truth is that as time goes on, they have less and less to contribute. This is usually because they've already told me everything they know, though I'm not sure that's the case with Kenny Schilling. But with Kenny, as with all my clients, my visiting is vital to their sanity, and they are generally desperate to see me and learn whatever is going on in their case.

My visit to the jail this morning finds Kenny in surprisingly good spirits. A guard has slipped him the morning newspaper, and he's read Karen's story raising the possibility that Preston was the victim of a drug killing. It's the first positive news Kenny's heard in a very long time, and though it's totally speculative and publicly denied by Dylan, he chooses to be euphoric over it.

"So you think this Quintana guy could have done it?" he asks.

"Somebody did," I say, deflecting the question. "Preston didn't go in that closet and shoot himself, did he?"

"He sure as shit didn't," he says, laughing and punching me in the arm, which seems to be his way of being jovial. Since he's a two-hundred-thirty-pound professional football player with a punch that can dent iron, I'm going to have to give him any future good news over the phone.

Kenny's been getting visits from some of his teammates on the Giants, and that has made him more upbeat as well. I'm always torn in situations like this over how much to level with the client. His situation is fairly grim at the moment, but it would do no good to bring him down emotionally. There will be plenty of time for that later.

My next stop is back at my office, to receive a chemistry lecture from a professor at Fairleigh Dickinson University, located off Route 4 in Teaneck. The professor, Marianna Davila, will serve as my expert witness on the subject should I need one at trial. I've used her before and have always enjoyed the interaction. She's a very pleasant, attractive young woman who has developed an incongruous reputation as one of the leading authorities on street drugs in North Jersey.

I find with experts in any field that it is counterproductive for me to ask other than general questions early on in our discussions. I don't want to lead them where I want to go; there'll be plenty of time for that when I get them on the stand. I want the raw facts first, and then I can figure out how I want to manipulate them.

I have Kevin and Adam sit in on the meeting, and I start by telling Marianna that we are meeting on a matter relating to the Kenny Schilling case. She tries not to show it, but I see her perk up. I know from past conversations that she wouldn't know a football from an aardvark, but no one is immune from the barrage of media coverage this case has gotten. And it's only beginning.

"Tell us about Rohypnol," I say.

"Its nonproprietary name is flunitrazepam" is how she starts, and my eyelids begin drooping. "There is no medically accepted use for it in the United States, and it's produced almost exclusively outside the country. It's most prevalent in the U.S. in the South and Southwest, but lately, it's gotten up here in much bigger quantities. Most of it comes out of Mexico."

"How long does it take to have an effect?" I ask.

"Usually, thirty minutes to an hour, but it peaks in maybe two hours. Blackouts are possible for eight to twenty-four hours after taking it, which is why its main use is as a date-rape drug." Anticipating my next question, she says, "It lasts in the bloodstream for up to seventy-two hours."

"What kind of a high does it give?" Kevin asks.

She shakes her head. "It doesn't. It's more of a low. Think Valium, only way stronger. Very relaxing . . . gives a feeling of peace, serenity, when users know what they're doing."

We continue to question Marianna, whose knowledge of the subject seems complete. She'll make a fine witness if we need her, especially since she says that Rohypnol could absolutely be slipped into a drink.

Marianna leaves, and Adam does as well. I doubt it's a coincidence; Adam seemed to be so taken with her that he didn't even take notes while she talked.

I have to wait for Laurie to come by with the report on where she and Marcus stand in their investigation. I've structured it so that Laurie is in charge of the overall investigative efforts, and Marcus reports through her. Basically, I've set it up this way because I'm afraid of Marcus and Laurie isn't.

Laurie's not due for about an hour, so I play a game of sock basketball. It's a game where I take a pair of rolled-up socks and shoot it at the ledge above the door, which serves as the basket. I set up mock games, and it serves as a stress-reducer and confidence-builder, mainly because I always win.

I'm the Knicks this time, and we beat the Lakers 108–14, the highlight being my thirty-one blocked shots of Shaquille O'Neal. After the twentieth block he gets in my face, but I stare him down. When it comes to nonexistent three-hundred-pound, seven-foot basketball players, I make intimidating eye contact.

Destroying Shaq makes me work up a sweat, compounded by the fact that Edna doesn't believe in air conditioners and instead keeps the windows open so that we can have fresh air. It's a concept I've never understood. Where do air conditioners get their air in the first place? Don't they just cool off the same air we always breathe? Or is there some mysterious tubing that leads from some stale air factory direct to our air conditioners? Edna seems to think the air that comes from the dirty city streets through our windows is straight from the Rockies, although I don't remember seeing too many Coors commercials shot against the backdrop of Market Street in Paterson.

I wash up in the bathroom down the hall and then go back to the office to wait for Laurie and do some paperwork. It turns out that the paperwork part is going to be difficult because sitting at my desk is a large, very ugly man.

"This place is a shithole," Ugly says.

My first instinct is to run for it, figuring that no normal person, even a nonlarge, nonugly one, would enter my office and sit like that at my desk if he was up to any good. But it seems like a particularly cowardly and ridiculous thing to do; this is my office, and I should at least be able to find out what he is doing here before I bail out.

"Sorry it's not up to your standards," I say, "and by the way, who the hell are you?"

Ugly shakes his head. "That doesn't matter. What matters is who sent me and what he wants."

"Fine. Who sent you?"

"My boss. He doesn't like you talking about him."

"Cesar Quintana?" I ask.

"Didn't I just say he doesn't like you talking about him?"

"So that's why you're here, to ask me to be quiet?"

Ugly laughs and stands up, walking slowly around the desk. I start to gauge the distance between myself and the open door. "Right. I'm asking you to be quiet. And if you don't get quiet, he'll come see you himself, cut your tongue out, and strangle you with it."

He moves slowly as he talks, sort of toward me but at an angle. He's not stalking, just ambling. I move as well, and before I know it, I have been outmaneuvered to the point where I don't think I can make it to the door before he gets to me. This is not good, and for a moment I consider whether to move toward the double windows overlooking the street. Since Edna left them open, I could call out into the fresh air for help.

I can't think of anything to say, and my guess is, it wouldn't matter anyway. Ugly has been given an agenda, whatever that might be, and he wouldn't likely be entrusted by his boss to make decisions or changes in the moment based on circumstances.

For some reason I notice that he has a bit of a gut and is not in the best of shape. I contemplate whether this gives me any advantage at all and quickly realize that it does not. We're not going to run the marathon, nor am I going to bob and weave for ten rounds. He might huff and puff a little,

but it's nothing that will stop him from kicking the shit out
of me, if that is his mission.

I'm so intent on his motions that for a moment I don't realize that he is still talking. ". . . has something that my boss
wants. So you get it from him, and maybe we can let you
live."

"What?" I ask. "What are you talking about?"

"I'm talking about your client. You get it from him, give
it to me, and we'll be fine."

This is a little bewildering. "Get what?"

"Ask your client. He'll know. And tell him if he doesn't
come up with it, we can get to him in prison."

"Why don't you tell me what it is?" I ask, and I can immediately tell that I'm starting to piss him off. He's won the
strategic maneuvering game, and I can't make it to the door.
He starts to move toward me, more threatening now, and I
back up toward the window, finally leaning against the wall
next to it.

One moment I see him coming toward me, and the next
moment my view is blocked by Marcus Clark, standing between us and facing Ugly. I assume he came in through the
door and walked across the room, but he managed to do it
without either of us noticing him. I know this because I see
a flash of surprise on Ugly's face, but no real concern. He's
not afraid of Marcus, which makes him an idiot. But he does
seem to realize that Marcus will be somewhat more difficult
to contend with than I am.

"Step aside, friend," Ugly says.

Marcus, ever the gregarious conversationalist, just stands
there and doesn't say a word.

"I'm not going to tell you again," Ugly says, and then
without waiting for a response, pulls his fist back to take a

swing at Marcus. It is safe to say that Ugly is not a Rhodes scholar.

Marcus's movement is so quick as to be imperceptible, but the thud of his fist hitting Ugly's stomach echoes through the office. It is followed by a gasp and then gagging, as Ugly doubles over in stunned agony. As he leans over, Marcus picks him up over his shoulder, so that the very large Ugly is completely off the ground.

"Put him down, Marcus." The voice is Laurie's, and I look up to see that she has just joined the party. "Come on, Marcus, put him down."

Marcus looks over at her, nods, then walks a few feet and drops Ugly out the open double windows. I hear a thud as he lands and some screams from people one floor below on the street.

"I think she meant to put him down in the office," I say, but Marcus seems unconcerned with his mistake.

Laurie and I go to the window and look down. Ugly had crashed through one of the awnings above the fruit stand, crushing it. He then landed in a display of cantaloupes, which I hope were ripe enough to have cushioned his fall.

As startled bystanders come over, Ugly staggers to his feet, still apparently more hurt from the effects of Marcus's punch than his fall. He makes it to a nearby parked car, opens the door, and falls into the passenger seat. The driver, who was waiting for him, pulls out.

"I'll be right back," I say. "I've got to go buy some cantaloupes."

I go downstairs to pay Sofia Hernandez, the owner of the fruit stand, enough money to take care of the damage and aggravation. She's amazingly calm about it, as if thugs falling from the sky are an unfortunate but expected part of doing business.

I'm ready to go back upstairs when Pete Stanton pulls up, along with two other cars with patrolmen. Pete comes over to me, a grin on his face. "When I heard on the radio that the guy came flying out of your office window, I had to take the call."

"Thanks for caring," I say, and suggest that he come upstairs. "Marcus is up there."

Pete nods in understanding. "Ah, the human launching pad."

Pete comes up, and Laurie and I watch with barely concealed amusement as he tries to question Marcus. If a transcript could be done of this interview, and there were a thousand words spoken, Pete would be shown to have spoken nine hundred and seventy of them. Marcus simply has little to say, whether he is talking to Pete, the SS, or anyone else.

Finally, Pete turns to me as a witness to the events. I ask Marcus if I can speak for him, and he both nods and grunts, which represents a ringing endorsement of me as his spokesman.

I describe Ugly, though it is a basic, not very helpful description. I have no comprehension of how some people can remember faces as well as they do. More amazing is how they can describe them. It's not even just a question of memory; if you gave me a picture of someone to refer to, I still couldn't describe him or her well enough for a police artist to draw.

When I am finished, Pete says, "He sounds like any one of a hundred people who work for Quintana."

"Except this one can fly," I point out.

"Right. Now, exactly how did that come about?"

"It's pretty simple," I say. "He was hassling me, Marcus asked that he stop, he attacked Marcus, Marcus picked him up, Laurie asked Marcus to put him down, and Marcus put him down."

"Outside the window," Pete says.

Laurie says, "My mistake was in not telling Marcus which side of the window to put him down on."

"The guy was having trouble breathing," I say, "and Marcus has heard Edna mention that the air is fresher out there. He was doing him a favor."

"After this, Quintana's going to send people after you in bunches," Pete says, injecting some depressing reality. "Is Marcus always going to be there?"

I look at Marcus, who shrugs. It's not the most reassuring shrug I've ever seen. Marcus can stop a lot of people, but eventually, one is going to get through. To me. And if one of them gets through to me, it's game, set, and match.

Pete leaves, and Laurie, Marcus, and I talk about how we should proceed in light of this new, very disturbing development. Laurie is concerned for my personal safety, and while I pretend to be stoic about it, I certainly share that concern. Our hope is that Ugly's visit, while embarrassing to Quintana, might be thought to have served its purpose. I've been warned, and although our collective reaction to the warning was to toss Ugly out the window, Quintana can at least be sure the warning was delivered.

Almost as disturbing was Ugly's claim that Kenny had something belonging to Quintana, and his demand to get it back. If true, Kenny certainly hasn't shared the news with me. If not true, Quintana is just going to get more upset when he doesn't recover whatever it is he's missing.

We agree that Marcus will keep an eye on me for now, though from a distance. He's very good at it, and it makes me feel safer, at least for the time being. But the trick is not to throw all of Quintana's people out the window. The trick is to get Quintana to stop sending those people in the first place.

There is only one person who can do that.

• • • • •

PAUL MORENO'S personal assistant is so cute and perky she could be a cheerleader. She greets me at his office at PTM Investments with, "Hello, Mr. Carpenter, and welcome to PTM. My name is Cassie. It's so nice to meet you." If I gave her some pom-poms, I think she'd jump in the air and yell, "Give me a P! Give me a T!" I can't tell if she's completely sincere, but so far I like Moreno's staff a hell of a lot better than Quintana's.

There's a lot I don't know about PTM Investments. For instance, I don't know what the "T" stands for, and I don't know what they invest in. But I can find out that stuff some other time; right now my goal is to convince Paul Moreno to prevent me from being killed.

In the next five minutes Cassie announces my presence to Moreno, fields two calls, brings me some delicious hot coffee, and gets me in to see Moreno. All of this she accomplishes with a smile. She is the anti-Edna.

Moreno's office is done in chrome and steel, ultramodern to the point that it looks like it was furnished in the last couple of hours. His desk has only a phone on it; paper and writing instruments are nowhere to be seen.

Moreno's window looks out at Van Houten Street in downtown Paterson, and it seems incongruous considering the obvious expensiveness of the office furnishings. The street is not a slum, but nor is it the kind of view that's going to make Ritz Carlton buy up the adjacent land.

When I enter, Moreno is standing behind his round bar, making a couple of drinks. He gives me a warm smile. "Mr. Carpenter, welcome." For a ruthless drug dealer's office, things are pretty friendly.

"Thanks for seeing me on such short notice," I say.

He comes around the bar, holding two drinks. The liquid in them is pink, almost red. "Try one of these," he says.

"It's a little early in the day for me."

"Not for this. It's made from fruit trees at my home. They're crossbred, unlike anything you've ever had."

I take one and sip it. It hits me with a jolt; it's one of the best and most distinctive tastes I've ever experienced. "This is unbelievable," I say, and guzzle down the rest of the glass. He laughs and heads back to the bar to pour another.

"So what can I do for you?" he asks.

We're about to get to the unpleasant part of the visit; I briefly wonder if I should wait until he gives me another glass full of that great juice. I decide to go ahead. "Tell Cesar Quintana not to try and kill me."

I guess I haven't offended him too badly, because he hands me the drink before responding. "Who is Cesar Quintana, and why would he want to kill you?" he asks.

He's either playing a game with me or worried that I'm wearing a wire. Either way, I have to go along with it. "He's a drug dealer whose name came up in connection with the Kenny Schilling case. He sent an emissary to my office to

warn me not to mention him again." I decide to leave out
the part about Schilling having something that he wants;
Moreno is probably very aware of it, but just in case, it gives
me something to hold back.

"Why are you telling this to me?"

"Because he is either your partner or your employee,
and I'm told that you can control him."

"If that were true, and I'm certainly not saying that it is,
why would I want to control him? How would that be to my
advantage?"

"To keep your own name out of the press. Bad publicity, no matter how unfair, is bad for investments. Think
Martha Stewart." I hold up my glass. "Although you make a
better drink."

Moreno walks over to his desk, picks up his phone, and
says something I can't quite hear. Within five seconds the
door opens and two very large men in suits come in. I
would have preferred perky Cassie.

Before I can react, they have ahold of me and push me
up against the wall. One of them keeps me pinned, unable
to move, while the other frisks me, no doubt checking for a
wire. Finding none, they leave as quickly as they came. If
there was a secondary goal to leave me feeling intimidated
and vulnerable, Moreno has achieved that as well. Physically, I'm okay, except my heart is pounding so hard I don't
think I'll be able to hear over it.

"Mr. Carpenter, do you have any idea how much you will
shorten your life span by threatening me?"

I try to compose myself, to not look as frightened as I
am. "I didn't intend it as a threat," I say. "I see it as a nego-
tiation . . . a deal."

"With all the publicity surrounding this football player's

case, killing you now could bring unwanted attention to my business, but it would be a manageable inconvenience."

My mind flashes to my future headstone: "Here lies Andy Carpenter. He was a manageable inconvenience." I decide not to mention my headstone image to Moreno, for fear that he'll make it come true. "Think how inconvenient it would be for me," I say.

He smiles. "That's not really my concern. Cesar Quintana is not someone who can easily be controlled. Especially after the embarrassment in your office yesterday."

I return the smile, which is difficult, since my lips are shaking along with everything else. "Maybe you can reason with him. As one businessman to another."

He shakes his head, as if I just don't get it, but I decide to push it. "Look, after all this, the police would know where to look if anything happened to me. They'd come straight for Quintana and for you. Probably you could handle it, but maybe not. I'm just suggesting it's not worth it to find out."

He thinks for a moment, as if deciding what to do. My hunch is that no matter what decision he is about to announce, he had made it before I even walked into his office. "I would strongly suggest you hold up your end of the bargain," he says.

"So we have a deal?" I decide to be explicit. "You call off Quintana, and I keep your name out of it."

He nods. "We have a deal."

I look toward the bar hopefully. "Let's drink to it."

He shakes his head. "I don't think so. Goodbye, Mr. Carpenter."

My next stop is the courthouse, where there is a hearing before the judge recently assigned to the case, Henry Harrison. Judge Harrison is a sixty-two-year-old with an impressive résumé. He was a full marine colonel, a Vietnam hero with a Silver Star. He retired from the service at the age of forty-five, went to Seton Hall Law School, spent five years as a prosecutor, and eventually became a superior-court judge. Our backgrounds are quite similar, except for the fact that he's spent his entire life serving society, whereas I've spent my entire life living in it.

While assignment of judges is said to be random, my guess is that Judge Harrison was specifically chosen. His background is well known, and he has a large reservoir of respect from the public, which will help when his rulings are inevitably scrutinized. He is also firm and decisive on the bench, well equipped to deal with whatever bullshit Dylan and I try to throw at him. Lastly, he is nearing retirement age and not likely to be swayed by public pressure.

I'm a few minutes from the courthouse when my cell phone rings and Vince Sanders's voice cheerfully greets me with, "Where are you now, you traitor shithead?"

"How long are you going to hold a grudge, Vince?"

"Are you kidding? I still hate Jimmy Collins, a kid who pissed me off in kindergarten."

"Where is he now?" I ask, pretending I'm interested.

"He's a priest. Runs a soup kitchen and shelter on the Lower East Side of Manhattan. Dedicates his life to helping the sick and the poor . . . the son of a bitch."

I can't help laughing, though I know that will only encourage him. "What can I do for you, Vince?"

"Get your ass over here. We've got a deal to make."

"What kind of deal?" I ask.

"I give you some bad news about your client before it breaks, and you promise me future scoops."

Uh-oh. "What kind of bad news?"

"Not over a cell phone, bozo. Anybody could be listening in."

I explain to Vince that I'm on my way to court, and we
agree to meet at Charlie's tonight. I've got a bad feeling
about this one.

Dylan is already in court when I arrive, but he glances
quickly and then looks away as I enter. We are not going to
be friendly adversaries during this trial, which is fine with
me. I like to antagonize and annoy the opposing attorney in
hopes of goading him or her into a mistake or misjudgment.
It's part of my style, and its effectiveness varies according to
the opponent. Dylan has shown himself susceptible to this
strategy in the past, so I'm not about to blow that potential
advantage by getting chummy with him.

I work my way through the press and packed gallery to
join Kevin, seated at the defense table. Seconds later Kenny
Schilling is brought in. I usually like to talk to my clients before each appearance so as to let them know what to expect. I arrived too late to do so today, which is no tragedy,
since this will be little more than a formality. Kenny's role
will be merely to sit and watch.

Judge Harrison comes in and immediately gets the hearing started. He's basically an impatient man, and he usually
presides as if he's got a train to catch. Once Dylan and I are
introduced as the respective counsel, Harrison says, "Talk to
me, gentlemen."

Dylan surprises me by requesting a gag order on all interested parties. It is clear that he considers Karen Spivey's
story, and the furor that followed, to be a negative for the
prosecution. He wants the focus kept on Kenny as the only
possible killer.

"Your Honor, the defense has been advancing wild theories in the press, which can only serve to pollute the jury pool," Dylan says.

I'm torn here. Basically, I'd be fine with a gag order, since I've already put out Quintana's name, and I have nothing to add to that. I'm questioning myself, though, trying to make sure that I am not subconsciously in favor of it so that I can more easily keep my deal with Moreno. Keeping that deal has the additional benefit of keeping me alive.

I stand. "Your Honor, the prosecution has been publicly proclaiming that my client is guilty since the moment of the arrest. The press coverage has been overwhelmingly in the prosecution's favor. We would be in favor of the gag order as well; it's too bad it couldn't have been in place earlier."

Dylan half whirls in surprise, not knowing what to make of this. I believe he had been hoping I would be opposed to the gag order and that Judge Harrison would be reluctant to impose it. This would have allowed Dylan to play the aggrieved party while still playing to the press every chance he got.

Harrison lets him off the hook. "Despite the apparent agreement on this issue by both parties, I am not prepared to issue the order at this point. But I do expect both the prosecution and defense"—he looks at the gallery—"as well as the media, to behave responsibly, or I will revisit the issue."

Harrison announces his intention to set a trial date, and Dylan suggests the first week in November. That would be quick for a trial of this magnitude, which is why Dylan is again surprised when I propose the first week in September. Dylan is right to be surprised: It is straight out of Defense 101 to delay as much as possible. Unfortunately, Kenny did not take that course, and he's insisted on his right to a speedy trial.

Harrison is also surprised. He's six foot five, and from his position up on the bench it looks like he's peering down from Mount Olympus. "Are you sure about this, Mr. Carpenter? That's just six weeks from today."

I decide to try to turn this negative into a slight positive. "Yes, Your Honor. Mr. Schilling wants to miss as little of the season as possible." The football season starts around the same time as the trial will start, and I want any Giants fans on the jury to be keenly aware of their power to put Kenny back on the field.

Harrison handles a few minor "housekeeping" chores, then rejects my plea to set bail. I told Kenny that it was a formality, that there was no chance bail would be granted, yet I can still feel his disappointment when Harrison refuses.

I arrange to speak to Kenny in an anteroom for a few moments after the hearing. I tell him about the visit from Ugly and his comments that Kenny has something that belongs to Quintana.

"Man, Preston must have been in with some heavy guys," Kenny observes with some pleasure. Kenny's no dummy; he believes that the more dangerous Preston's associates were, the more chance that the jury will believe they killed him.

"Do you have anything of his?"

He shakes his head. "No, man. I don't have any idea what they're talking about."

I've given up trying to read the truthfulness of Kenny's statements. I'm unable to do so, and it doesn't do me any good anyway, so I just take them at face value.

I head back to the office to do some paperwork before going to Charlie's to hear whatever disaster Vince has in store for me. Alone at the office is Adam, typing away on his laptop. I feel a flash of guilt that I forgot to invite him to the hearing today and that I generally have not been that accessible.

"How's it going?" I ask.

"Great," he says with characteristic enthusiasm. "I'm working on an outline. I read through most of the transcript of the Miller trial today."

"What did you think?"

"You're damn good. I couldn't write you that good if I started from scratch. Lucky I don't have to."

"I could show you some other transcripts which wouldn't impress you quite so much."

"I doubt it," he says. I like this guy more and more every day.

I decide to invite him to Charlie's with Vince. He deserves some exposure to the inner workings of the case, and he's sworn to secrecy, so it doesn't seem as if it can hurt. He jumps at the opportunity. It's hard to imagine an opportunity he wouldn't jump at.

I check through my messages before we leave, just in case someone else has called to confess to the Preston murder. No such luck, and within a half hour Adam and I are in the car heading to Charlie's.

On the way Adam says, "I need to create an arc for you."

"An ark? Like a boat?"

He shakes his head. "No, a character arc. That's all movie executives care about. The character has to change, develop during the script. Have an arc."

"I pretty much haven't changed since I was eleven years old," I say. "Wait a minute . . . I just started eating mushrooms a few months ago. And I've got a couple of hairs growing on my left ear . . . that's new . . ."

He laughs. "I don't think that'll do it."

"So how can I help?"

"What about if you had a disease?" he asks.

"I don't think I want to help that bad."

"No," he says, "what about if I create a disease for you to have while you're handling the Miller trial? Life-threatening, but you don't let it stop you. You're fighting for your life and Willie's at the same time, staring your own mortality and his right in the face."

"How does that help you?" I ask.

"It's a catalyst for your change . . . your arc. Gives you a new perspective . . . that kind of thing. *Terms of Endearment* meets *Anatomy of a Murder.*"

"I don't like it," I say, "but as long as the pipe is going to take the whole project into the sewer, I don't care either way."

He takes this as a yes. "You got any preference? I mean, for the disease."

I think about it for a moment; it isn't every day one gets to pick the ailment he will heroically fight. "Just something that doesn't hurt and can't be sexually transmitted."

He nods. "That makes sense."

• • • • •

VINCE IS WAITING for us at our regular table when we get to Charlie's. He's watching a Mets-Yankees interleague game on the large-screen TV, and the first thing I do is look at the score, which will be a sure predictor of his mood. Vince is a die-hard Mets fan, but the Yankees are ahead 5–1. It could get ugly.

At least for the moment Vince has nothing obnoxious to say, because he has a hamburger stuffed into his mouth. All of us, Laurie, Pete, Vince, myself . . . we all have different reasons why Charlie's is our favorite restaurant. Vince's reason is that when he orders a hamburger, they don't assume he wants it with cheese. Other restaurants start with the cheeseburger, and that's what you get unless you specifically direct them to remove the cheese. Vince says that the historic status quo in America is just a hamburger, no cheese, and he resents that the cheese-ites, as he calls them, have taken over. Vince needs some significant therapy.

I introduce Adam to Vince and explain Adam's presence. Vince, no doubt anticipating his portrayal in the movie, flashes the charming side of his personality, which in his case means eliminating most grunting and spitting. Once we get the pleasantries and ordering of our food and beer out of the way, I try to get to the heart of the matter. Laurie is waiting for me at home, and that is a far more appealing prospect than this boys-night-out.

"So tell me about Schilling," I say.

As if on cue, Adam takes out his notepad and pen, causing Vince to give me a wary glance. "It's okay," I say, "he's sworn to secrecy."

Vince nods, though he doesn't seem convinced. "You screwed me by giving away that story on Quintana."

"We've been through that," I say. "I apologized. I begged for your forgiveness."

He sneers. "That was all bullshit."

I have the advantage of knowing that Vince can never stay mad at me. I defended his son, Daniel, last year on another headline-making case. Daniel was accused of being a serial killer of women, when in fact the actual killer was contacting him and providing information that would eventually frame him. I won an acquittal, though Daniel was subsequently murdered by the real killer. In the process I learned some secrets about Daniel that would hurt Vince terribly if ever publicly revealed. All in all, the episode won me "friend points" with Vince that can never be erased.

Vince finally gets around to what he has to tell me. "I've got something on your boy. In return I want to be your media contact until this is over. You got a story to plant, I'm your gardener."

"What if what you have isn't good? What if I know it already?"

"Then the deal is off," he says, which both surprises and worries me, since he's confident his bad news is significant.

"Fine," I say as the waitress arrives with our beer.

"Six years ago Schilling was involved in another shooting death."

Adam reacts, almost coughing up his beer. "Tell me about it," I say to Vince, though I dread hearing it.

"He went out hunting with some buddies, in a town called Hemmings, about two hours outside of Milwaukee. One of the group got shot."

"By who?" I ask.

"They couldn't pin it on anybody . . . finally classified it as an accident. But there are people that believed Schilling was involved. He had argued with the dead guy an hour before it happened."

If this piece of news is as Vince describes it, I instinctively know three things. One, this is not good. Two, it will come out whether Vince breaks the story or not. And three, when it comes out, it will create a media firestorm, further messing with prospective jurors' minds. "Can you give me the particulars? Names, places . . ."

Vince takes out a piece of paper from his coat pocket and hands it to me. "You've got three days to find out what you can before the shit hits the fan."

It's very important to me that I get on this before the entire world is after the same information I am. "Three days? Come on, Vince, you can do better than that."

He shakes his head. "Nope. I go with it on Monday. Somebody could be beating me to it right now."

I inhale my hamburger and beer and head home, leaving Adam behind to hang out with Vince. It'll be a clash of the titans, Adam's irresistible upbeat enthusiasm versus Vince's immovable grouchiness. Adam may be in over his head. My guess is that within an hour Vince'll have him writing *The Vince Sanders Story*.

Laurie is waiting for me when I get home, and I'm anxious to talk to her about the information Vince has given me. Laurie, it turns out, is anxious to have sex. I weigh my options, debating with myself whether to talk or have sex, while I'm ripping my clothes off. Then, since I'm not comfortable with naked talking, I decide to go with the sex.

After we're finished, I decide to go with sleep rather than talk, but Laurie again has other ideas. "You said you wanted to talk to me about something," she says.

I nod and tell her about the shooting in Wisconsin.

"You want me to go out there to check it out?" she asks.

I'm jolted awake by the realization that Hemmings must be reasonably close to Findlay, her hometown and possible future place of employment. "No," I say, "I need you working here. I'm the one with the least to do right now, so I should go."

Laurie doesn't argue with me, acknowledging that she really is busy and adding that Wisconsin will likely be a temporary safe haven from the danger of Quintana, just in case Moreno hasn't successfully called him off.

She doesn't try to dissuade me, nor does she mention the proximity to Findlay. It pops into my head that maybe I should go to Findlay and check out the place, maybe personally catch this Sandy Walsh loser doing something slimy. I doubt I'll have time, but the thought is pleasant and intriguing enough to let me sleep with a smile on my face.

The next morning I get into the office before Edna, which is not exactly a news event. I decide to go online and make my own travel arrangements to Wisconsin, to leave late this afternoon.

I am a complete computer incompetent, and every time I try to do something some ad pops up in my face. It takes me forty-five minutes, but I finally get through it. Just before I'm finished, I have an amazing stroke of luck. A message comes on the screen, telling me that if the bar at the top is flashing, I'm a winner. And it's flashing! I haven't been on-line in weeks, and here I am the chosen one. It's simultaneously thrilling and humbling, so much so that I forget to click the bar to see what I've won.

Adam comes in with a request to go with me, and I say yes, mainly because I can't think of a valid reason to say no. The studio will pay for his ticket, and he calls their travel department and within thirty seconds is booked and ready to go. Of course, he missed out on the flashing bar and the incredible win.

I've scheduled a ten o'clock meeting with Kevin and Laurie to assess where we are in our trial preparation. Kevin has been meeting with various members of the Giants, ironic because Kevin knows so little about football, and sports in general, that I could tell him Kenny played shortstop and he'd believe me.

Kenny's teammates are thoroughly supportive, uniformly claiming to be positive that Kenny could not possibly be guilty of such a crime. Not realizing that I had already talked to Bobby Pollard, the paralyzed trainer who is one of Kenny's best friends, Kevin has done so as well, and he is especially taken with Bobby's expressions of loyalty. He is also, as I was, impressed by the fact that Kenny has seen to it that his friend has stayed employed.

Laurie and Marcus have made considerable progress buttressing our contention that Preston was involved with drugs, as both seller and user. Their information is supplemented by things Sam Willis has found out about Preston's finances. It helps, especially since we have little else to hang our hat on. The evidence against Kenny, while circumstantial, is very compelling, and we have almost nothing to refute it.

On the plus side we haven't uncovered anything striking or unusual about the relationship between Kenny and Preston. Certainly, there is no obvious motive, at least none that we can see. This is not to say Kenny is innocent; the murder could have been the result of a sudden argument or a rash act clouded by the fog of drugs.

Our meeting ends early, since I have to get to the airport. I'm late and only have time to kiss one of them goodbye, so I choose Laurie over Kevin. It's a tough call, but I'm paid big bucks to make this kind of decision.

Kevin leaves, and I say to Laurie, "Making any progress on your decision?" I say it nervously because I'm nervous about hearing the answer.

She shakes her head. "Not really. I'm trying not to obsess about it. I just think, when I know, I'll know." That's pretty tough to argue with, so I don't.

On the way out I walk by Sam Willis's office, and he yells out for me to stop in. He tells me that he's been checking into Sandy Walsh, and I instinctively look up to make sure that Laurie hasn't come in and overheard this. It's another sign that I'm aware that what I'm doing is nothing to be proud of.

"He's got real money," says Sam. "Not as much as you, but loaded."

"From where?"

"Hard to tell. Maybe investments, maybe family money . . . but it's not from his business."

"What is his business?" I ask.

"Rental car agency. One location in town, one just out-side of town. Solid, but not big enough to be responsible for his wealth."

"Thanks, Sam," I say, and prepare to leave.

He stops me. "Andy, there's one other thing."

"What's that?"

"The guy's married."

"Laurie said he wasn't," I say.

He shrugs. "Maybe that's what he told her. Got married three years ago February. Wife's name is Susan."

I nod and leave, considering what this news means. It's a mixed bag. On the one hand, it could result in some pain for Laurie, but on the other hand, it could be used by me to get her to stay.

I wish all my bags were this mixed.

• • • • •

THE TEMPERATURE in Milwaukee when
we land is eighty-seven, not quite what I picture when I
think of this town. It's in stark conflict with my mental
image of Vince Lombardi prowling the sidelines, smoke
coming from his mouth into the frigid air as the Packers
march across the frozen tundra in nearby Green Bay.

The airport is modern and efficiently run, and within a
very few minutes we're in a rental car driving the two
hours to Hemmings. I drive and Adam takes out his
notepad, no doubt making sure he can keep track of how
many rest stops we pass.

An hour from Hemmings we pass a sign telling us that
we are three miles from the exit for Findlay. I haven't yet
decided whether to check out Laurie's hometown, but the
highway god is obviously throwing it in my face. Am I man
enough to resist temptation? I never have been before, so
I doubt it.

"Isn't that where Laurie is from?" Adam asks.

"She told you that?" is my quick response.

Adam reacts to my reaction. "Sure. I didn't know it was a secret."

This is the last thing I want to talk about, so I switch the conversation toward Adam's life. "You like LA?" I ask.

He shrugs. "I love it, but just for now. It's especially great with my lifestyle; being a writer absolutely beats working. But if I hit it big, I'm out of there."

"Why?"

"Because when they need you, and you don't need them, you can work from anywhere. You hardly ever have to go to meetings and schmooze; all you have to do is write."

"So where would you live?"

He points at the green fields we are passing. "Near my parents in Kansas. I want to have enough money to buy a house for them and one for me. After all these years they deserve a nice house."

"You wouldn't miss a big city?" I ask.

"Maybe a little, but I could always go there on vacations. I want to be somewhere I can raise a big family and not have to worry about drive-by shootings."

"Do you have a girlfriend?" I ask.

"No," he says, then laughs. "Why, do I need one of them first?"

We drive on for a while longer, at which point Adam apparently decides it's my turn. "Are you and Laurie engaged or anything?"

"No," I say. "I'm a swinging single."

He laughs. "Yeah, right."

The terrain gets more and more desolate as we reach Hemmings, which can't really be called a small town, or a town at all. It's really just three or four streets of houses in various states of disrepair, surrounding a cardboard box factory.

The houses have deteriorated over the years, yet most have well-kept small lawns and gardens separating them from the street. It is as if the residents do not have the bucks necessary to renovate their homes, but their gardens make the statement that they would if they could.

One of the better-kept homes belongs to Brenda and Calvin Lane, and they are standing on the porch waiting for us as we arrive. I had spoken to Calvin yesterday, alerting him to our coming to see them, and confirming that they would talk to us. He appeared anxious to do so, and their waiting for us on the porch would seem to confirm that.

Within two minutes we are inside on the couch, being barraged by homemade breads, jams, and pastries. Brenda could make a fortune running a bakery on the Upper East Side of Manhattan, but my hunch is that doing so is not on her radar screen.

Calvin thanks us profusely for coming, as if it had been his idea and we were doing them a favor. "When I saw what happened on television, I knew I had to talk to somebody about it." He seems unconcerned when I tell him I'm representing Kenny; he just wants to tell his story to anyone who will listen.

"I told him it was silly," says Brenda, "but he wouldn't listen." She laughs. "He never does."

"I think getting things out in the open is always a good thing," I say. "What is it that's bothering you?"

"It'll be five and a half years this November that we lost our Matt," Calvin says, and for the first time I notice that some of the pictures on the wall are of a strapping young man. A few of them are in football uniform.

Now that the conversation has turned to their son, their movements are as if choreographed. Calvin moves his chair closer to me, and Brenda brings out a photo album to show Adam. Clearly, they think I'm the guy to talk to about this matter, and in this case they're right.

I can hear Brenda start to identify the pictures that Adam is looking at; as if she has to entertain him while Calvin is telling me his story. They start in kindergarten and peewee football, so apparently, it's going to take Calvin a while.

"He was a great kid . . . a great kid," says Calvin. "Not a week goes by we don't look at those pictures."

"What happened to him?" I ask, trying to move this along, but feeling a little bad about doing so. Talking about their boy is clearly one of their favorite pastimes.

Calvin goes on to tell me the story of a fateful November weekend, just after Matt's freshman season as a University of Wisconsin football player had come to an end. Matt had a fine year; he was a top player his entire young life, and the coach at Wisconsin was predicting huge things for him.

A bunch of guys whom Matt knew, mostly football players, had come up to do some camping. They weren't all from Wisconsin—some were from big cities—but Matt was going to educate them in the ways of the wild. They'd do some camping, fishing, maybe a little hunting, and in the process drink far more than their share of beer.

It was a trip from which Matt never returned. He took a few of the guys hunting and was the victim of what was ruled a tragic accident. The police version is that a hunter must have shot at motion in the woods, thinking it was a deer when in fact it was Matt. This despite the fact that the hunter apparently fled and was never identified, and the additional fact that Matt was wearing the bright orange jacket designed to prevent just such accidents.

Kenny Schilling was there that day, having previously established a friendship with Matt through football. The police questioned each of the young men thoroughly, and Calvin did as well, trying to understand why this young life had been snuffed out.

Calvin says that Kenny had aroused his suspicions at the time, but Brenda's slight accompanying groan indicates that she doesn't share that feeling. Kenny had been tentative in describing his whereabouts and had not returned to the camp after the shooting until well after the others.

"And I heard him arguing with Matt about an hour before they left," Calvin says.

This time Brenda's groan from across the room is louder. "They were probably arguing about football," she says. "They always argued about football. Big deal."

Calvin gives me a slight smile and wink, in the process telling me that I should discount everything Brenda is saying. But I actually think she's probably right, as the police did as well. According to Calvin, the police did not appear suspicious of any of the group, and the case never went anywhere.

I'm greatly relieved to hear what Calvin has to say; it's not nearly the blockbuster that Vince led me to believe. When this breaks, if it does at all, my assessment is that it will be a twenty-four-hour story, ultimately going nowhere and doing no damage.

My plan had been to visit with the local police in the morning and get whatever information I could from them. That no longer seems necessary and in fact could be counterproductive, calling more attention to a story that in no way incriminates Kenny. I'll ask Pete Stanton to call them, cop-to-cop, and find out what he can.

Now of course we have more time on our hands before our return flight tomorrow evening. I can't go fishing because I didn't bring any bait. I can't go hunting because I left my twelve-gauge at home. I can't farm the land because I don't own any land and I never applied for a plow license.

I guess I'll just have to go to Findlay and check out Sandy Walsh.

• • • • •

WE FIND A HOTEL just outside of Find-lay, no expensive minibar or robes in the bathroom, but clean sheets and a television that gets forty-eight channels, including both ESPN and ESPN2.

Adam and I are tired, but we go out to grab a quick bite to eat. I'm forced to grudgingly admit that Laurie's home-town is not totally without culture when we find a Taco Bell that's open late. When Adam tells me he can charge it back to the studio, I order an extra grilled stuffed burrito to take back to the hotel.

When I'm traveling, I usually call Laurie before I go to sleep, but I avoid the temptation this time. I don't want to lie to her about where I am, and I certainly don't want to tell the truth, so conversation at this point could be a little diffi-cult.

In the morning we have the buffet breakfast in the hotel. I try the fruit, which appears to have ripened about midway through the first term of the Clinton administration. The bis-cuits are the consistency of something Mario Lemieux would shoot from just inside the red line. But the coffee is good, and I'm able to use the time to tell Adam where we're going.

It's the "why" I'm not quite so forthcoming about. I tell him I want to surreptitiously check out this guy Sandy Walsh, but I imply that it has to do with a case. Adam can hang out in town while I do it, and he's not to say anything to anyone about it when we get back. I think he knows I'm full of shit, but he's nice enough to just shrug and go along.

Findlay is a small town but considerably bigger than I expected and much nicer than Hemmings. It has a four-block shopping area of treelined streets, where cars park headfirst at an angle. All in all, a nice town . . . a nice place to have grown up . . . I'm afraid a nice place to go back to.

I was hoping for a lot worse. I was hoping there would be a sign when we pulled in saying "Welcome to Findlay, Pedophilia Capital of the World." Or "Welcome to Findlay, World's Leading Fungus Producer."

I'm feeling uncomfortable with this whole thing. Laurie's actions remind me of *The Wizard of Oz,* like she's going to click her heels and say, "There's no place like home, there's no place like home." Which is bullshit, or Dorothy wouldn't have run away from the dump in the first place.

I ask Adam, "If Dorothy ran away from home because the dog catcher was going to ice Toto, how come she clicks her heels and goes back? And what happens to Toto when she gets there? Can we assume he gets a needle in the arm?"

He has no idea what brought this on, but it's about movies, so he's into it. "You know something, you're probably right. They should do a sequel, *The Wizard of Oz 2: Toto's Revenge.*"

"You should write it."

"Maybe I will," he says, but I can't tell if he's serious.

Once I leave Adam in the shopping area, I call one of

the rental car offices that Sam told me Walsh owned. The office I reach is the one about five miles out of town. They tell me that Walsh is not there, but at the office in the center of Findlay. It turns out to be a few stores down from where I left Adam. I don't even have to get back in the car; I just walk down the street and go in.

My plan is to ask for him and then hit him with a diversion I've created about my company and its need to rent a large amount of cars in a small time frame. By presenting such a lucrative opportunity, I figure I can engage him in conversation, then see where it goes from there.

I enter the small office and approach the counter, an ingratiating smile on my face. "Hi," I say to the young woman, "I'm looking for a Sandy Walsh."

As I am saying this, I can see into the office behind her, where a man is sitting at a desk. He gets up and walks toward me, a little better-looking and in better shape than I would prefer. I was hoping for someone a little more on the grotesque side, with some open, oozing sores on his face.

"Who shall I say is here?" the clerk asks.

I'm about to tell her a made-up name when the man from the office approaches, extends his hand, and says, "Andy Carpenter?"

This is baffling. How could he know who I am? Unless it's from all those stupid legal cable shows I do. "Have we met?" I ask.

He smiles. "No. Laurie told me you'd be dropping by."

So I've gone through this whole clandestine operation when Laurie knew all along that I'd go snooping around Findlay. Laurie is smarter than I am; the counter I'm leaning on is smarter than I am. "Well," I say, trying not to appear pathetic, "I was staying in town, and I figured any old friend of Laurie's is a friend of mine."

"Let's go get a cup of coffee," he says, and we go off to do just that.

Within fifteen minutes of our sitting at a table in the local diner, probably twenty people come over and say hello to Sandy. He has a pleasant word and a smile for each of them; it's apparent that this is a nice guy. It's going to be hard to reconcile that with the fact that I hate him, but I think I can pull it off. Besides, I still have an ace up my sleeve, the knowledge from Sam that Sandy is married, though Laurie thinks he isn't.

We're chitchatting away about a variety of subjects when I smoothly bring up the subject. "Are you married?" I ask.

He shakes his head. "Not anymore. My wife passed away about two years ago. We were only married a year."

"I'm sorry," I say, but I should add, "that I'm such an idiot." Sam obviously saw a computer record of the marriage but never thought to check for a death certificate.

He nods. "Thanks. It happened all of a sudden . . . brain aneurysm. Makes you think, doesn't it?"

"Sure does."

Just when I'm positive I couldn't feel stupider, a woman comes over and gives Sandy a kiss on the cheek. "You must be Laurie's friend Andy," she says, holding out her hand. "She told us all about you when she was here."

Sandy introduces the woman as Jenny, his fiancée. I smile through the pain; I can almost hear Laurie laughing at me from back in Paterson. It flashes through my mind that maybe I shouldn't go back home at all, that maybe I can avoid humiliation by living the rest of my life in Europe or Asia or Pluto.

But for now I just say my goodbyes, pick up Adam, and head for Milwaukee. I can decide where I'm going when I get to the airport.

I opt for going home, and on the plane I have some time to reflect on what I've seen in Findlay. I'm sure it has its warts and problems like any other town, but it seems to be a nice place to live, in the classic "Americana" sense. I understand how Laurie must feel about it and how it must have felt to be ripped away from it.

If those feelings are anything like mine for Paterson, I'm going to be sleeping alone pretty soon. Paterson is a part of me and always will be. I even like its idiosyncrasies, such as the fact that all its famous citizens are number two in what they did. Louis Sabin, a Paterson scientist, invented the oral polio vaccine. It would have been a bigger deal had not Jonas Salk come first. Larry Doby of Paterson was the second black baseball player, three months after Jackie Robinson. Even Lou Costello, perhaps the most famous person from Paterson, drew second billing behind Bud Abbott.

Laurie is at the airport to pick me up when our plane lands. My big-picture plan is to apologize and ask her forgiveness for my surreptitious meddling; it's the nuances of the apology plan that I haven't figured out yet. For instance, I haven't decided whether to include pleading, moaning, whimpering, sniveling, and drooling in the process. I'll have to see how things go and take it from there, but I'm certainly not planning to let things like dignity and self-respect get in the way.

Adam says his goodbyes, and Laurie and I go to her car. Much to my surprise, she starts to bring me up-to-date on the investigation.

"We've got good news and bad news," she says. "Which would you like first?"

"The bad news."

"I found a witness who heard Kenny and Preston arguing the night of the murder," she says.

"Has Dylan gotten to him yet?"

She nods. "He has now. The guy was afraid to come forward. Didn't want to become Kato Kaelin when the shit hit the fan." She's referring to a key witness in the O. J. Simpson case, who became the butt of months' worth of late night jokes on television.

"The good news better be really good," I say.

"I think it is. The witness heard the argument when Kenny was dropping Preston off at his house. He saw Preston get out of the car and Kenny's car pull away."

She's right; this is very good news. For Kenny to have committed the murder later that night, he would have had to come back. If he was going to do that, why leave in the first place? It doesn't exonerate him by any means, but it makes it more reasonable to argue that someone else entered the picture that night.

"Did he say what they were arguing about?" I ask.

She shakes her head. "Not really . . . he just heard bits and pieces. And he didn't actually see Kenny, but he ID'd the car. I wrote a full report; there's a copy on your desk, and I have one with me."

This is such intriguing information that for a moment I forget the Findlay disaster. I'm prepared to bring it up when Laurie starts talking about this great walk and run she went on with Tara today. Is it possible she's letting me off the hook?

We get home without any mention of the dreaded F-word, which is how I've come to think of Findlay. Tara meets me at the door, tail wagging furiously and head burrowed into me to receive my petting. Her excitement at seeing me is something I never take for granted; it's a gift to be loved this much.

I take Tara for a walk and go back to the house. Laurie

is in the bedroom, looking much as she did when I left, except for the fact that she's not wearing any clothes. It's a comfortable look, so I try it myself. I like it, so we try it together. It works really well.

After our lovemaking my mouth decides to once again blurt something out without first having discussed it with my brain. "I was in Findlay," I say. "I met Sandy Walsh."

She nods, though she seems slightly groggy and ready for sleep. "I know. He called me. He liked you a lot."

"And I liked him. But I went there behind your back to check up on him . . . and on you. I was looking for ammunition to use to keep you here."

"Mmmm. I know. Can we talk about this in the morning?"

I'm anxious and nervous about this subject, and it's barely keeping her awake? "Laurie, I'm sorry I did it. It was devious and petty, and you deserve better."

"It's okay, Andy. I'm not angry with you. I appreciate what you did."

"Excuse me? Earth to Laurie, Earth to Laurie, come in please, come in please. Why aren't you pissed at me?"

She gets up on one elbow, apparently having given up for now on the possibility of imminent sleep. "Andy, you did what you did because you love me, because you don't want to lose me. You also might be concerned that I could make a decision I'd regret. So what if you didn't tell me about it in advance? What you did wasn't terrible, nobody got hurt. All in all, it makes me feel good that you did it."

"Oh," I say. "Good night."

"Good night."

A few minutes later my mouth opens up again. "Laurie, I'm not sure I can stand it if you leave."

She's asleep. She can't hear me.

• • • • •

TODAY'S A ROUGH day for Kenny Schilling.

Not that there's an easy day for him in County Jail, awaiting a trial that will determine if he'll ever have another day of freedom. But today is the day of the Giants' first exhibition game, and it's a further, agonizing reminder to Kenny that he lives in a seven-by-ten-foot world, with no road trips.

My arrival today is a welcome diversion for Kenny from the boring hours with nothing to do but lie around and worry, but he no longer has that look of hopeful expectation when he sees me. It's gotten through to him that there are not going to be any miracle finishes here, no Hail Mary passes. If we're going to prevail, it will be at trial, and the road is straight uphill.

I ask Kenny about the death of Matt Lane, and his initial reaction seems to be surprise rather than concern. He tells pretty much the same story that Calvin told, though of course he claims to have had nothing to do with the shooting. In fact, he says, no one has ever even hinted at the suggestion.

"They're not saying I had anything to do with Matt getting shot, are they?" he asks, the worry growing.

I shake my head. "The prosecution doesn't even know about it yet, but they will. Unless there's something you're not telling me, it won't be a problem."

"I'm not holding back anything."

"Good. Then tell me about your argument with Troy Preston when you dropped him at his house."

This time the flash of concern is immediate and transparent. He tries to cover it, but as an actor he's a very good football player. "I don't remember no argument," he says.

I decide to take the tough, direct approach, not my specialty. "Yes, you do."

"Come on, man, we were just talking. It was probably about a girl . . . okay? No big deal."

"Who was she?" I ask.

He shakes his head. "I don't know . . . I'm not even sure it was about a girl. We'd argue all the time . . . it could have been about football. I'm tellin' you, it didn't mean nothing."

I can't shake him, and he's probably telling the truth, so I let it drop for now. If Dylan wants to, he can use his resources to run it down, then provide it for me in discovery.

As I'm leaving the jail, I run into Bobby Pollard, his wife, Teri, and their son, Jason. Bobby's been coming to see Kenny on a regular basis, and since the prison has not exactly been designed with the handicapped in mind, Teri comes to help him navigate the place in his wheelchair.

"I was going to call you, but I figured I shouldn't," says Bobby.

"What about?"

"I don't know . . . just to see how things were going. To see if I could help in any way. And I heard you went up to Wisconsin to see Matt's father."

His knowledge of this surprises me. "How did you hear that?"

"Old Calvin keeps in touch with some of the guys. You know, he tells one person, they tell another . . ."

Teri smiles and winks at me. "It's the old football players' network. They spread the news faster than CNN."

"Did you know Matt?" I ask.

Bobby nods. "I sure did. And I was there that day. I was with his parents when they got the news. It was the worst day of my life." He points to his useless legs. "Worse than the day this happened."

I ask Bobby a bunch of questions about the day Matt was killed but get basically the same story. It must have been a hunting accident . . . nobody has any idea who did it . . . Kenny could never have done such a thing. I have no reason to believe otherwise, but it's starting to nag at me a little.

I also ask Bobby if he'd be willing to testify on Kenny's behalf, mostly as a character witness, and he once again vows he'll do whatever he can to help.

Before I leave, Teri motions me to the side and talks softly, so that Jason can't hear. "Jason wanted to see his 'Uncle Kenny.' Do you think there's anything wrong with his being here?"

I shrug. "I wouldn't think so, if you answer his questions honestly about what's going on. But I'm not the best guy to ask about how to treat a seven-year-old. I can barely take care of myself."

She laughs, and they go inside. I head back to the office for a meeting with Kevin, Laurie, and Adam. The trial date is starting to bear down on us, and we are way behind. Of course, I always feel we are way behind, and this time is no worse than most. What we're really lacking is evidence to present in our client's favor, which is generally a good thing to have.

We discuss whether to hire a jury consultant, and even though Kevin is in favor of it, I decide not to. I find that I always spend a lot of time with them and then just go ahead and follow my own instincts anyway.

Another decision to be made is whether to challenge the blood evidence. The Simpson trial and verdict have had an unfortunate effect, besides the fact that a double murderer was set free. It's also made police far more diligent and careful in their handling of evidence, especially blood evidence. Kevin has gone over the collection done in this case, and there are no grounds on which to convince a jury that the lab reports are not legitimate.

On the investigative front we've made gradual progress, but with few favorable results. All that is really left to do now is continue to follow up and talk to friends of Kenny's and Preston's, especially those people who knew them both. The pro football community is a large and close one, and that list is very long. The Giants, because of all the research they did on Kenny before the draft, have provided much of it, and it goes back to his early high school days. Pro football teams don't like to make mistakes with first-round draft picks.

Kevin reports that he has attempted to reach at least seventy-five people so far and has been successful in talking to perhaps fifty. Almost all are cooperative. Five are in prison, three have left the country, and another three have died, including Matt Lane.

The one positive development is that Cesar Quintana has not yet killed me. Moreno has kept his end of the bargain, and even Laurie agrees that Marcus can be assigned other tasks than surreptitious bodyguard for me. Once the trial begins and we start to throw Quintana's name around some more, that may change. I still don't know what he thinks Kenny has of his, but he seems to have backed off for now.

Adam has proven to be surprisingly helpful and insightful in these conversations, and I suggest that Kevin let him take over some of the burden in checking out the list of friends. After all, we're paying Adam a dollar; we might as well get our money's worth.

Laurie has put off her decision until after the trial, when we both can have more time to think clearly. I view this as a positive sign: She loves this work and loves working with me, and it's a priority for her. I also view this as a negative sign: She's planning to leave and doesn't want to crush me during such a crucial trial.

Stable I'm not.

• • • • •

ARRIVING AT THE courthouse for jury selection day, it doesn't feel only like a football player is on trial. It feels like a football game is about to take place. Every parking lot within a mile is overflowing, and there's actually a tailgating environment, with some people even bringing picnic lunches. There's also a tangible excitement in the air, which I can only liken to a play-off game at Giants Stadium.

I'm good at jury selection; it's one of my strengths. I'm not sure why, except it is a commonsense process, and that's how I treat it. But as soon as we get started, it's quite clear that this is unlike any other jury selection I've ever been a part of.

Ordinarily, potential jurors come in armed to the teeth with excuses not to serve. Few people have the time or the inclination to tie themselves down to a lengthy trial, in the process putting their own lives on hold. They all seem to have reasons why their business or their sick relative or their very future cannot survive the ordeal.

Not this time. Jury service in the trial of *New Jersey v. Kenneth Schilling* is seen as a plum assignment, guaranteeing a shot on *Regis and Kelly,* if not a lucrative book deal. This is the first trial-of-the-century trial, and everybody wants a piece of it.

Everybody but me. I'm always a pessimist at the start of a trial, but this time it's justified. We have done little to counter the physical evidence and could never do anything to counter the image that America has of Kenny holed up in his house with a gun, fending off the police. Things can change within a trial—there is an inevitable ebb and flow—but from my vantage point right now it looks like there will be a lot more ebbing than flowing.

The media have been speculating on whether I am going to play "the race card" and that if I'm going to do so, it will most likely be evident in jury selection. I'm not above playing any cards that are dealt to me, but I honestly have no idea what the race card is. Kenny Schilling and his alleged victim are both African-Americans, so if there is an advantage to be gained, I'm not a good enough card player to pick up on it.

Kevin and I meet briefly with Kenny in an anteroom before the court session begins, and I can tell that he is pumped. The endless waiting is over, and he thinks we can go on the offensive. I have to spend some time educating him on what constitutes jury selection and how boring it can be.

The courtroom is a place where the truth is revered, so it's a bad sign that at least ninety percent of the prospective jurors here today are full of shit. Almost without exception they claim to have an open mind, to have no preconceived notions about the case. In fact, most of them claim to have had little exposure to it, which means they have been spending the last three months in a coma.

Judge Harrison seems even more cynical about the process than I am. He exercises his right to question the jurors along with the lawyers, and at times he is openly incredulous at their claims of purity of thought and knowledge.

I infuriate Dylan by asking many of the prospective jurors if anyone they know or any members of their family have had any drug problems, or drug-related encounters with the police. The press in the gallery buzzes at the mere mention, knowing that I'm going to be using Quintana as a possible other suspect. Dylan wants drugs to enter this case only in that Preston and Kenny were both under the influence when Preston was killed.

The juror wannabes fall into two categories: those who sit on the stand and stare at Kenny and those who deliberately avoid staring, stealing quick glances whenever they think they can do so without being noticed. Kenny was a popular player before, but he has now achieved true stardom through this case. Somehow these jurors, though professing to be open-minded and barely aware of the facts of the case, seem to understand that.

Dylan seems less annoyed by the dishonesty running rampant in the courtroom than I am, but we both use up most of our challenges. We finally empanel a jury that I can live with, though am not thrilled by. There are eight males, of which three are African-American and one Hispanic. The four females are three whites and one African-American. The chosen group seems to be reasonably intelligent and likely to at least listen to our case, should we happen to find one along the way.

Judge Harrison asks Dylan and me if we want to sequester the jury. We both say that we do not, which is pretty much what we have to say. Neither of us wants to be responsible for imprisoning these people in a motel for weeks; they might take it out on us when it's time to reach a verdict. Harrison agrees, and the jury will not be sequestered, though he lectures them sternly on the need to avoid all media coverage of the case. Yeah, right.

During a trial I make it a practice to have our team meet every night to prepare for the next day's witnesses, as well as go over everything, so as not to let anything slip between the cracks. Tonight will be the first of these regular meetings, with the main purpose being to prepare for opening statements.

The regular team for the duration of the trial will consist of Laurie, Kevin, Adam, and myself. Marcus will come when he has something specific to contribute, but these are basically strategy sessions, and strategy is not Marcus's strong point.

We kick around the limited options open to us in our opening statement, until it gets too depressing. I like to speak more or less off the cuff so as to sound natural and more sincere. The difficulty I sometimes have is when I have a lot of points to make, and want to make sure I don't forget anything. That is not the case here; I have disturbingly few points to make.

The meeting ends, and Kevin is about to leave when Pete Stanton shows up. Pete lives more than a half hour out of town, and I wouldn't expect him to be working this late unless something significant had happened. I also wouldn't expect him to drop by without calling; he knows as well as anyone the intensity with which we work during a trial.

Pete greets everyone, but I can tell by the look on his face that something is wrong. He asks, "What's the word for when you make a contract with someone and then they die, so the deal can no longer be enforced?"

Kevin answers, "The contract is voided."

Pete nods and speaks to me. "Then you just got voided. Paul Moreno took a bullet in the head coming out of the Claremont tonight. Pronounced dead at the scene."

We throw questions at Pete and learn that in recent weeks the situation has grown increasingly tense between Moreno and Quintana on the one side and Dominic Petrone on the other. More and more Petrone has felt his operations being challenged by the Mexican drug ring, and it had apparently become financially intolerable, as well as personally and professionally embarrassing.

Local and federal authorities alike were expecting a war to break out, though the expectation was that it would not be full-scale, but rather a couple of messages sent in the form of killings. No one believed that Petrone would start it by taking out Moreno.

Pete considers it a brilliant stroke by Petrone. Moreno was the absolute brains of his operation, and though Quintana will no doubt respond with violence, Pete doesn't consider him smart enough to prevail in a war.

Laurie disagrees. In Moreno she believes that Petrone had an adversary smart enough to make a deal when one was called for, a deal that could leave both sides alive and in profit. No deal is possible with Quintana, she feels, and on that Pete agrees.

What hasn't yet been mentioned is the effect this will have on me. My deal with Moreno to get Quintana to keep away from me is no longer operative. "Anybody want to take a stab at where that leaves my general life expectancy?" I ask.

"I certainly wouldn't make any long-term plans," Pete says.

Laurie tries some optimism. "I think Quintana will have his sights set on Petrone and his people. And that should certainly be enough to keep his hands full."

"But I represent an easier target. He could take me out for practice."

"I've got a black-and-white outside with two patrolmen," Pete says. "They'll keep an eye out tonight, but I think that tomorrow you should get Marcus back watching your ass."

I look out the window, and sure enough, Pete has called for a patrol car to protect me. It's a sign that he's worried for my safety, or maybe he's worried that he'll have to find new financing for next year's birthday bash.

The timing of this is particularly terrible. Quintana was pissed off that I brought his name into the Kenny Schilling furor, and my entire strategy in the trial that starts tomorrow is to bring Quintana's name into the Kenny Schilling furor. Since rational is not one of the many adjectives I've heard used to describe Quintana, it could provoke a deadly reaction. Or if he *is* rational, he could well decide it's a hell of a lot easier to show how macho he is by taking on me rather than Dominic Petrone.

"Maybe I'm just being selfish," I say, "not thinking about my client."

"How's that?" asks Kevin.

"Look at the irony here. We're trying to convince the jury that Quintana is a killer. If he kills me, or even tries to, it makes our case." It's a poor attempt at lightening the mood, yet it actually contains a grain of truth.

"I'd better call Marcus," Laurie says, and I don't try to stop her.

The meeting finally breaks up, and though this is Tuesday, not one of the nights that Laurie and I stay together, she says that she'd like to. I can't tell whether she wants to be with me or wants to watch out for me in Marcus's absence. I don't dwell on it for more than a few seconds. Laurie wants to sleep with me, and whatever the reason, passion or protection, it's more than fine with me.

• • • • •

DYLAN HAS A surprise waiting for me when Judge Harrison asks if the lawyers have anything to bring up before he calls the jury in. He introduces a motion asking that the defense be prohibited from bringing irrelevant matters, like the drug underworld, into the case.

"If there is evidence that these people killed Troy Preston," says Dylan, "then by all means it should come in. However, mere evidence that they simply knew Troy Preston has no place in this trial."

Harrison turns to me. "Mr. Carpenter?"

"Your Honor, the motion is without merit, and would be so even if it weren't totally untimely. The prosecution has known for weeks of our intention in this area, yet they chose to wait until opening statements to contest it."

Dylan responds, "Your Honor, we would submit that the murder last night of Mr. Paul Moreno, which was widely reported this morning, makes this motion more pressing. The potential exists that it can turn this trial into a media circus, without having any real relevance."

"How about if you rely on me not to turn this trial into a circus?" Harrison responds dryly.

Dylan immediately goes into damage control mode. "I'm sorry, Your Honor, but I was referring to the atmosphere outside of court. I worry about the influence on the jurors."

Harrison turns to me. "Your Honor," I say, "the prosecution position is ludicrous on its face. As I understand it, they have asked the court that we not be allowed to present evidence showing that the victim associated with murderers. They choose to make that request the very morning after those same people are involved in another murder. Speaking for myself, the mind boggles."

Harrison rules promptly, as is his style. He refuses to prohibit our pointing toward Preston's associates in our defense, though he will not let us go too far afield. Dylan is annoyed; he believed he had a chance to undercut our defense before we even began. Now he has to collect his thoughts and give his opening statement.

He begins by thanking the jurors for their service, praising their sacrifice and sense of duty. He doesn't mention their future TV appearances and book deals, just as I won't when it's my turn. It's the unfortunate duty of us lawyers to kiss twelve asses and six alternate asses during every trial.

"There is a lot of attention being paid to this case," Dylan says. "You have only to try and park near the courthouse to know that." He smiles, and the jurors smile with him.

"But at its heart it's a very simple case. A man was murdered, and very conclusive evidence, evidence that you will hear in detail, pointed toward this man, Kenny Schilling, as the murderer. The police went to talk to him about it, and he pulled out a gun and prevented them from entering his house. And why did he do this? Because the victim's body was in his bedroom, stuffed in his closet."

Dylan shakes his head, as if amazed by what he is saying. "No, this is not a complicated case, and it is certainly not a whodunit. Troy Preston, a young man, an athlete in the prime of life, was shot through the back of the head. And this man"—he points to Kenny—"Kenny Schilling, supposedly his friend, he's the one who 'dunit.'

"Mr. Carpenter will not be able to refute the facts of the case, no matter how hard he tries. He will realize this—he does already—and he'll try to create diversions. He'll tell you that the victim, who is not here to defend himself, associated with bad people, people capable of committing murder. Some of it will be true, and some not, but I'll tell you this: None of it will matter. Even if Troy Preston hung out on a street corner every night with Osama bin Laden and Saddam Hussein, it still would not matter. Because those people, bad as they are, did not commit this particular murder, and that's all you're being asked to care about. And soon it will be very clear to you that Kenny Schilling committed this murder, and that's the reason he's the man on trial."

Dylan goes on to detail some of the evidence in his arsenal, knowing full well he can back it all up with witnesses and lab reports. By the time he's finished, he's done a very good job, and it doesn't take a mind reader to know that the jury was hanging on his every word. The entire world believes Kenny Schilling is guilty, and as members of this world, that's the predisposition the jurors brought here with them. Dylan's words only served to reinforce their belief, so they considered him totally credible.

Kenny looks depressed, and I lean over and whisper a reminder that he is supposed to look interested and thoughtful, but not to betray any emotional reaction at all. It's easier said than done; the words he's just heard from Dylan would be enough to depress anyone.

I stand up to give our opening statement with a modest goal. Right now the jury is thinking that the prosecution has all the cards, and though that may be true, I've at least got to show that this is not a mismatch, that we are a force to be reckoned with.

"I'm a curious guy" is how I begin. "When something happens, I like to know why. I want things to make sense, and I feel comfortable when they do.

"When the thing that happens is a crime, then the 'why' is called motive. It's something the police look for in trying to figure out who is the guilty party. If there is a reason or a motive for a person to have done it, then that person becomes a suspect."

I point toward Dylan. "Mr. Campbell didn't mention motive; he didn't point to a single reason why Kenny Schilling might have killed Troy Preston. Now, legally, he doesn't have to prove what the motive was, but wouldn't it be nice to have an idea? If someone is on trial for his very life, wouldn't it be nice to understand why he might have done something? And wouldn't it be nice to know if someone else really did have a motive and a history of murder?"

I walk over to Kenny and put my arm on his shoulder. "Kenny Schilling has never committed a crime, never been charged with a crime, never been arrested. Never. Not once. He has been a model citizen his entire life, achieved a high degree of success in a very competitive field, and as you will hear, has been a good friend to an astonishing number of people, including the victim. Yet Mr. Campbell would have you believe that he suddenly decided to shoot his friend and leave a trail of evidence that a five-year-old could follow."

I shake my head. "It doesn't make sense. We need to have an idea why.

"Well, let's try this on for size. Troy Preston had other friends, friends with a record not quite as spotless as Kenny's. In fact, they were more than friends; they were business associates. And that business was a dangerous one: the importation and sale of illegal drugs. And it turns out that Troy's other friends kill people.

"Yet you will hear that almost no investigative effort was made to determine whether one of the people they killed was Troy. Kenny was an easy suspect, because he was set up to be one by the real killers. The police accepted everything they saw at face value, and here we are, still wondering why.

"Now, Kenny did a stupid thing, and if he was charged with committing a stupid act, he would have already pleaded guilty. He took out a gun, for which he has a legal permit, and fired a shot in the air. Then he prevented the police from entering his house for almost three hours, before voluntarily giving himself up.

"Yes, it was stupid, but there was a *why* behind it, a *motive* for what he did. He had just found his friend's body, a bullet through his chest, in the back of his house. Suddenly, men were at the door trying to get in, men who within moments had guns drawn. How could he know that these men were really police? He had no idea why his friend was shot, and was afraid that the same thing was about to happen to him. He panicked, of that there is no question, but it's easy to understand why.

"Kenny Schilling is not a man capable of murder. You will come to know him, and you'll understand that. You'll also hear about other people, people very capable of murder, and you'll understand that as well.

"All I hope, all Kenny Schilling hopes, is that you keep asking why and keep insisting that things make sense. I know that you will."

I get a slight nod from Kevin, telling me that it went reasonably well. I agree with that, but I also know that "reasonably well" is not going to cut it. Not in this case.

It's late in the day, so Harrison tells Dylan that he can call his first witness tomorrow. It'll give me something to look forward to.

• • • • •

A TRIAL IS AN incredibly tense, hectic process, yet for me there's something calming and comforting about it. It's the only time in my life when I have a rigid schedule, a self-discipline in my actions, and it's a refreshing change.

Tonight is a perfect example. We have our team meeting at my house, after which Kevin leaves and Laurie and I settle down to dinner. We have take-out pizza, though hers is of the vegetarian variety and in my humble opinion not worthy of the name "pizza." Luciano Pizza or Jeremiah Pizza or whoever the hell invented it would cringe at the sight of the healthy mess that comes out of Laurie's pizza box.

Laurie turns out the overhead lights and instead lights candles she had put on the table. It makes it a little tough to see the pizza, but she seems to like it that way. We talk about the case, about what's going on in the world, about how great Tara is, or anything else that comes to mind. Everything except the Findlay situation.

After dinner my ritual is to go into the den, turn on CNN or a baseball game as background noise, and read and reread our files on the Schilling case. In order to react in a courtroom the way I want to react, I need to know every detail of our case, every scrap of information we have.

Each night, I go over the next day's witnesses, as well as an area of our investigation that I select more or less randomly. Tonight I'm going over Kevin's and Adam's reports on their work in locating and talking to Kenny's friends and acquaintances, especially those he shared with Preston.

At ten-thirty Laurie and I go up to bed, where I continue to go through the papers. She makes a phone call, which is disconcerting, since she speaks to Lisa, a high school girl-friend from Findlay. Laurie is making real connections, or re-connections, back there, and the knowledge of it makes it a little hard for me to concentrate.

I'm trying extra hard to focus, since I have the uneasy feeling that there is something in these particular reports that is significant and that I'm missing. I'm about to discuss it with Laurie, now off the phone, when Tara starts to bark. Moments later the doorbell rings.

"Let me get it," Laurie says, which means she's at least a little worried that it could relate to Quintana.

I'd love to say, "Go ahead," but I'm too macho for that, so I throw on a pair of pants and go downstairs. I get to the door just as the bell rings again, and I ask, "Who is it?"

"Marcus" is the answer from the other side of the door.

I turn on the porch light, move aside the curtain, and sure enough, there is Marcus. I open the door. "What's wrong?" I ask.

"Rope," says Marcus.

"Rope?"

"Rope."

"What about rope?" This conversation is not progressing that well.

"He wants to know if you have any rope," says Laurie from the top of the steps.

"No, I don't have rope," I say to Laurie. "Who am I, Roy Rogers?"

I turn back to Marcus. "I don't have any rope. Why do you need some?"

Marcus just shakes his head and closes the door. I turn to Laurie once he's gone.

"What is he doing? Should I get him some rope?"

"From where?" she asks.

"How the hell should I know? Maybe there's a rope store open late around here."

Marcus seems to be gone, so I go back upstairs and once again get into bed with Laurie. My sense is, I haven't heard the last of this rope situation, and this is confirmed about five minutes later when the doorbell rings again.

Once again I trudge down the stairs. "Who is it?"

"Marcus."

I open the door and immediately see a sight that will forever be etched in my memory. Two men, one of whom I recognize as Ugly, the guy Quintana sent to threaten me, are tied up with my garden hose. They are head-to-toe and back-to-back, but stretched out full length against each other. They look like a two-sided human bowling pin, and Marcus walks into the house carrying them over his shoulder. He comes into the room and drops them on the floor, and the thud could be heard in Hackensack. Tara sniffs around them, having absolutely no idea what is happening. Join the club.

"Laurie!" I call out. "You might want to get down here!"

She comes downstairs, surveys the bizarre scene, and takes over. "Marcus, what's going on?"

He tells her in a series of barely decipherable grunts that they were outside, trying to break in, and he caught them.

His plan now is to question them. Marcus questioning people is not a pretty sight.

"I think we should call the police," I say.

Marcus looks at me, then calls Laurie off to the side. They
whisper out of earshot of me, Ugly, and his friend. The intruders are rolling back and forth in a futile effort to untie
themselves and/or get up. It would be funny if it were happening in someone else's house.

"Come on, Andy. Let's go upstairs," says Laurie.

"Why? What's going on?"

"Marcus is going to question our guests."

I start to argue, but Laurie silences me with a look, and a
head motion directing me upstairs. I have confidence in her
in situations like this, and none in myself, so I follow duti-
fully behind.

As we near the top of the steps, Marcus calls up to her.
"Knives?"

"In the kitchen. Second drawer on the right," she says.

When we get in the bedroom, Laurie closes the door.
With Marcus, Ugly, and his buddy now out of range, I become a little more assertive. "What the hell is going on?"

"Marcus said we can call the police in fifteen minutes.
He'll know what he needs to know by then."

"What is he going to do?"

She shrugs. "Be Marcus. But he said he won't kill them,
and he won't do anything on the carpet."

I nod. "Well, that's comforting."

"Andy, those guys were trying to break into this house.
They might well have killed you, or even us."

She's got a point. "Fifteen minutes?" I ask.

She nods. "Fifteen minutes."

Except for the agonizing times I've felt waiting as verdicts
were about to be delivered, these are the longest fifteen min-

utes I've ever spent in my life. I strain to hear any noises coming from downstairs, but it seems, as they used to say in Westerns, to be "quiet out there, too quiet."

At the moment the fifteen minutes are up, I pick up the phone and call 911, reporting that two men have broken into my house. I then call Pete Stanton at home, and he agrees to come over. I think he gets some kind of perverse kick out of Marcus and doesn't want to miss out on what is going to be an entertaining evening.

Laurie and I go downstairs. I don't know about her, but I'm cringing at what I think I am about to see. The trio is not in the living room or den, and we find them in the kitchen. Ugly and his pal are sitting with Marcus at the kitchen table, drinking diet sodas. They look unhappy but are no longer tied together with the hose and look none the worse for wear. Marcus looks impassive, which is not exactly a stunning piece of news.

Five police cars pull up less than two minutes later. The process takes only a short time; I explain that these two guys tried to break in and that my bodyguard caught them and held them here so that they could be turned over to law enforcement.

Pete Stanton arrives just as the cops and their captives are leaving, and I let him listen with Laurie and me to the mysteries of the agonizing fifteen minutes, as told by Marcus Clark.

It takes almost an hour and a half for us to understand his cryptic grunts, but basically, the pair admitted to him that they were sent by Quintana and this time were told to "kick the shit out of the lawyer." They also revealed that it was money that Quintana believes Kenny took from Preston that night, a total of four hundred thousand dollars. The night Preston died was drug receipt payment night, but Preston was killed before he could make that payment. My two visitors were supposed to find out with certainty whether I know where that money is.

Pete points out the obvious. "Quintana's going to keep coming at you."

"Why can't you arrest him once these guys tell you what they told Marcus?"

Pete shakes his head like I just don't get it. "They won't talk to us. We're not allowed to be as persuasive as Marcus. They go down for breaking and entering, then maybe serve a little time, maybe not. There's no way they rat out Quintana."

"Which means Quintana remains a big problem," I say.

"I could kill him," says Marcus.

Pete jumps up as if somebody shoved a hot poker up his ass. "I'm outta here," he says, and walks out the door. He's a friend, but he's also a cop. He has no love for Quintana, but he's not going to sit and listen while somebody plots his murder.

Once Pete leaves, Laurie says, "Don't kill him, Marcus. That's not going to solve anything."

I'm torn here. I'm not usually one to countenance murder—after all, I'm an officer of the court—but in this case I'd be tempted to make an exception. To say the least, if I heard that Quintana died, it wouldn't prompt me to sadly shake my head and say, "Boy, that really puts things into perspective, doesn't it?"

"You need to protect Andy full-time," Laurie continues.

I turn to Marcus and nod. "I want you on that wall. I need you on that wall." Either he recognizes the line from *A Few Good Men* or he doesn't; with Marcus it's hard to tell. He grunts a couple of times and leaves.

"That is one scary guy," I say after I'm sure that he can't hear me.

"Just be glad he's *your* scary guy," Laurie points out.

It's now two-thirty in the morning, so Laurie and I get back into bed. I take some time to think about the case. I find I'm starting to believe my own PR now, considering it more and more possible that Preston actually was the victim of a drug killing. The money was certainly substantial enough that people from that underworld might kill for it, and I'm certain, too, that members of Quintana's gang would have been aware of it.

I've been thinking all along that it wasn't a drug hit because Quintana, Moreno, or even Petrone wouldn't have bothered to frame Kenny. They've got the people and the experience to have murdered anonymously, without real fear of it being traced back to them. Therefore, there would be no reason to frame anyone.

But what if it was one of Quintana's men who did the killing so as to get the money? He might well have framed Kenny, not to throw the police off his trail, but rather to make sure Quintana did not catch on. Quintana's justice would be far more swift and deadly than the police.

There is also the chance that Kenny found out about the money and went for it, but this seems far less likely. Sam has checked and found no evidence that Kenny had anything but a rosy financial picture, and he's been paying his substantial legal bills on time.

I always want to believe that a client is innocent, but there's believing and *really believing*. For the first time, I'm starting to *really believe,* and it's a nice feeling. It doesn't quite make up for my knowledge that a murderous maniac in command of an entire gang of other murderous maniacs is trying to kill me, but it's a nice feeling.

• • • • •

DYLAN'S FIRST witness is Patrolman Jared
Clayton, the officer that found Kenny's abandoned car. I
would have expected Dylan to build his case more method-
ically, to perhaps put on team officials of the Jets to talk
about Preston not showing up that day and how uncharacteristic that was. As I reflect on it, I realize that Dylan's strategy is a good one: He doesn't want to give me a chance to
cross-examine based on Preston's character. As far as Dylan
is concerned, this is a physical evidence case, and he's going
to focus on that as much as possible.

Patrolman Clayton testifies that the car was abandoned
maybe ten feet into the woods off the road but that he was
able to see it.

"What made you approach?" Dylan asks.

"Well, I thought maybe somebody was in it, in some kind
of distress or something. It wasn't really a normal way to
leave a car. Then, when I got close, I saw the license plate."

"It was an unusual plate?"

Clayton nods. "It said 'GIANTS25.'"

"Why was that particularly interesting?"

Clayton looks sheepish, a look he can pull off, since he can't be more than twenty-three years old. "There had been a report that a football player was missing and . . . well, I'm not really a football fan, so I didn't realize he played for the Jets." Most of the female jurors smile their understanding.

"What did you do when you reached the car?" asks Dylan.

"I looked inside and determined there was no one in the car. Then I opened the door and saw what looked to me like bloodstains on the passenger seat and passenger side dashboard. Then I immediately closed the door, called in for a detective team and forensics, and secured the area."

Dylan introduces evidence proving that the car in question is Kenny's. Having done that, he could let the witness off the stand, but Clayton is an appealing witness, so he keeps him up there for another ten minutes before turning him over to me. Clayton hasn't done us much damage—that will come later from the lab results—but my strategy is to make points with every prosecution witness, no matter what they testify to. It reduces the chances of a "steamroller effect," in which the jury starts to view the prosecution as an unstoppable force.

"Patrolman Clayton," I begin, "were you on a special assignment on that day? Or just on your regular patrol?"

"Regular patrol," he says.

"So you weren't looking for this specific car? This make and model?"

"No."

"So it was the way it was left in the woods, the way it was abandoned, that attracted you to it?"

"Right," he says. "It was unusual for a car to be partway into the woods like that."

"Almost as if it were meant to attract attention in the way it was positioned?"

Dylan objects that Clayton could not possibly know the intent of the person who left the car there. Harrison sustains, but I'm starting to make my point.

"Would you say there was a significant amount of blood," I ask, "or just some small specks?"

"I would say a decent amount, certainly not just specks."

I nod. "And you testified you saw it immediately and that as soon as you saw it, you were positive what it was?"

"Yes."

"Were there wipe marks? As if somebody had tried to clean it up?"

"I didn't see any," he says.

"Patrolman, let me ask you a hypothetical question. If that were your car, and you had murdered someone, would you have done a better job hiding it? Would you have cleaned up the blood?"

Dylan objects, but Harrison lets Clayton answer. "I guess I would have, sir. But I wouldn't murder anyone."

I accept that and move on. I get Clayton to describe where the car was on the highway, then ask, "And where was the taxi stand?"

"Taxi stand?"

"Right. Because if the defendant left his car there, he couldn't walk home, could he?"

"Well . . ."

"Are you aware of any theory of an accomplice, someone who drove Mr. Schilling home after he *carefully hid* the car?"

Dylan objects that this is out of the witness's area, and I don't push it. Clayton responds to another question by saying that there is a rest area with a telephone a half mile away. I don't ask if there is any record of that phone calling a taxi company, because Dylan would object again. I know from the discovery that two such calls were made during the days when the car might have been left, but they were both by women, so Kenny is in the clear on that.

I let Clayton off the stand, satisfied that I've done as much damage as I could, but I'm all too aware that Dylan's big guns are still loaded and ready to fire.

Next up for Dylan is Dr. Janet Sheridan, the lab director who did the DNA tests on the blood in Kenny's car. I know from the reports that the results are conclusive, that it is without question Preston's blood.

Dylan takes three hours to get Janet to say this in as many ways as she knows how. Her conclusion is that the chance of its not being Preston's blood is one in two point five quadrillion, or something like that.

My cross-examination is quick and to the point. "Dr. Sheridan, how did Mr. Preston's blood get in the car?"

"I'm afraid I have no idea. That's not within the scope of my work."

I nod. "Sorry. Who was driving the car when it was left where it was found?"

Dylan objects, but Harrison lets her say she doesn't know this either.

"So if I were to say that someone other than Mr. Schilling took his car, murdered Mr. Preston, and then left the car with the blood in it, is there anything in your test results that would prove me wrong?"

"Not in these results, no."

"Thank you."

Kevin and I go back to the office. Adam is there working, and I realize that he wasn't in court today, though he had said he would be. Maybe the studio is pressing him for what he calls a first draft, but that's the furthest thing from my mind at the moment.

Adam stops what he's doing to listen to Kevin and me

dissect the day in court. Kevin is a very good barometer of the trends in a trial, and he thinks we did okay, but not great. He's quick to say that there was no way we could have done great, but it's not necessary because I wasn't insulted. He's absolutely right: Dylan had the upper hand.

After about a half hour of this, Adam rather tentatively asks a question. "Let me ask you guys something. Forgetting people you've met while practicing criminal law . . . I'm talking about in your personal lives . . . how many people your age . . . friends . . . do you know that have died in the last ten years?"

"One" is my answer, thinking of Susan Goodman, a girl I went to high school with who was hit by a car about two years ago.

"Two," says Kevin. "Why?"

"I've checked out maybe a hundred and twenty people identified as friends or acquaintances of Kenny's. Eight—all males—have died in the last seven years. None were over twenty-five years old."

• • • • •

I DON'T BELIEVE in coincidences. Never have, never will. It's not that I don't think they can happen, and it's certainly not that I think everything that happens is by a grand design. I've just found that it's always best to assume apparently related events have a logical reason for being, and there is nothing logical about coincidence.

Eight friends of Kenny's dying before the age of twenty-five: I don't know what the actuarial tables would say, but the odds against that must be off the charts. And these are young people, mostly athletes, in the prime of their lives. This is very scary stuff.

We have got to get into this in detail right away. Adam does not yet know the particulars of the deaths, nor does he have any indication there was foul play. Who knows, there could have been a leukemia cluster, in which case it will turn out to be a false alarm for our case. He also does not know the specifics of the connections between Kenny and the deceased, or the connections, if any, between the unfortunate young men themselves.

If these deaths are suspicious, related, or in any way tied

to Kenny, we're in deep trouble, and our Quintana theory is most likely out the window. But we're a long way from determining any of that, and my hope and expectation is that when we find out what we need to know, the problem will go away.

In any event, we have a lot to learn, and we damn well better learn it before Dylan does. Kevin and I are not going to be of much help, and Laurie's busy on a million other things, so I decide to let Adam do much of the legwork, since he seems good at it and that legwork can be done on a computer and telephone.

Adam is eager to dig into it, and I'm confident he can get it done. The truth is, he showed a really good instinct in picking up on this situation in the first place; someone else could easily have missed it or not thought it represented a problem.

"Let Sam Willis help you on this," I say. "He can find out things on a computer in ten minutes that could take you ten weeks to track down."

"Great," says Adam.

"And from now on you're really going on the payroll, with an investigator's pay. You're not just hanging around anymore."

"Don't worry about it," he says. "The top actors and directors are going to be fighting over this one. Besides, this is really cool. I'm glad I can help, and I'm enjoying myself."

That makes one of us.

I go home, take Tara for a walk, and then call Laurie. Tonight's not one of our sleepover nights, but I want to talk to her about Adam's discovery. I would do so even if she were not involved in the case, even if she were a pharmacist, ballet dancer, or software designer. When something important happens, good, bad, or confusing, it's comforting to talk to her. And I've got nobody to back her up in this area, no real bench strength, so if she bails out, I'll be talking to myself. That would be another hell of a loss.

Laurie's reaction to the news mirrors my own, viewing this as a potentially ominous development and unwilling to chalk it up to coincidence. "Do you need to share this with the judge and Dylan?" she asks.

It's a question I haven't thought about, which doesn't say much about my abilities as an attorney. I think about it now and decide that I don't have to share the information now, and perhaps never. Even if we were to determine that Kenny was involved, even if he's a serial killer, we would not legally have to divulge the information. We would actually be prohibited from revealing it, the only exception being if we were aware of another murder that was going to be committed.

I get into bed and think about the situation some more. I don't want to discuss this with Kenny yet; I want to have more information first so I can better judge his response. On some level I can see the possibility that he had an argument with Preston and killed him, but I simply cannot see him as responsible for multiple deaths. Of course, I've been wrong before.

The window drapes are open, and my mind flashes to Michael Corleone in the bedroom of his Vegas compound, realizing just in time that the drapes being open means he should hit the ground before the bullets come flying.

I get up and close the drapes, cowardly doing it from the side of the window so as not to expose myself should Bruno Tattaglia want to take a shot at me. As I do, I get a look out into the darkness, and I can only hope and assume that Marcus is there.

They never mentioned anything about this crap in law school.

I wake up at six in the morning and call Vince Sanders. I've made a deal with him to make him my initial media contact, and I'm honoring that now. I had come to the conclusion that he sent me on what was basically a wild-goose chase to Wisconsin to check out Matt Lane's hunting accident, but now I'm not so sure.

Vince grunts angrily at my waking him up, so I tell him that he can go back to sleep and I'll give the story to someone else. That tends to increase his alertness, so I suggest he meet me at a coffee shop on the corner of Broadway and Thirty-second Street in an hour.

I take Tara for a walk that ends up at the coffee shop, and we sit at our regular outdoor table. I get her a bagel and a dish of water, and she's already polished it off by the time Vince arrives, ten minutes late.

"This better be good," he says.

"It is," I say, launching quickly into what I wanted to tell him, since I'm in danger of being late for court. "My house was broken into by two of Quintana's thugs. They were going to kick the shit out of me."

"But they didn't?" he asks.

"Marcus."

He nods. Enough said.

"Quintana is trying to keep his name out of the trial, but he's also after four hundred thousand that Preston was supposed to give him the night he was killed. He assumes Kenny has it and somehow further assumes that I can get it."

"Four hundred thousand?" Vince repeats, obviously impressed. "These guys who tried to break in . . . why would they tell you this?"

"Marcus."

He nods. Enough said.

"But they won't tell it to the police . . . so I'm telling it to you. You can break the story tomorrow morning, and then I go national with it."

"I'm happy to do it," he says, "but won't that just piss Quintana off even more?"

"Maybe, but he's coming after me to keep me quiet. Once I go completely public, he's got nothing to be gained anymore by shutting me up. Besides, if he's got any smarts at all, once I do this he'd know that he'd be the first one the cops would go after if anything happened to me. I'm going to shine as much light on him as possible."

"And it helps your client in the process," he says.

"Yes. It does."

Vince thinks about this awhile and then seems to smile in satisfaction at what I've just told him. "Works for me," he says. "I'll even buy the bagels."

"Good. I was just going to order Tara another one."

I get to court with only ten minutes to spare, and I'm barely settled in when Dylan calls Teri Pollard, Bobby's wife, to the stand. It's a smart move. He wants someone to testify that Kenny left with Preston to take him home, but he doesn't want to call one of the football players who were there that night. They are celebrities, and Dylan doesn't want that celebrity factor to play in Kenny's favor.

Teri is clearly not happy to be doing Dylan's dirty work, but she's obligated to tell the truth. That truth includes describing to the jury the details of the night at the Crows Nest and the fact that Kenny and Preston left on the early side.

"Did anyone else go with them?" Dylan asks.

"No," Teri says, but then throws in, "unless they met someone outside."

Dylan won't let her get away with that. "But you did not

see them meet anyone? And you're not aware of any expectation they had of meeting anyone?"

"No" is her grudging response.

I attempt to get Teri to provide support for Kenny's general character and goodness, but Dylan objects, since I'm only allowed to cross-examine on areas he covered in direct. That's okay; Dylan's objecting makes it look like he's hiding something.

"Was that night the first time you had been with Kenny and Preston at the same time?" I ask.

"No. Bobby . . . my husband . . . and I have been out with them together maybe five or six times." She points toward Bobby, sitting in the gallery aisle in his wheelchair. "But we spend time with Kenny very frequently."

"Ever see them argue?" I ask.

"No."

"Ever see them threaten each other?"

"No."

"You never thought Mr. Preston might be in any danger by going with Mr. Schilling?"

"No, of course not." Then staring right at Dylan, she says, "Kenny's one of the nicest people I've ever met."

Way to go, girl.

Next up in Dylan's parade is the county medical examiner, Dr. Ronald Kotsay. Dr. Kotsay was brought in about six months ago to replace a man who held the position for thirty-eight years, and he's had a rough go of it. Dr. Kotsay made the mistake of quickly trying to modernize procedures, which did not go over very well with the staff or DA's office. Simply put, everybody was just used to his predecessor, and Dr. Kotsay's "sweep out the old" approach faced a lot of resistance. Things have calmed down since, and most people have come to realize what an outstanding medical examiner he is.

"Dr. Kotsay, you were called to the defendant's house in Upper Saddle River, were you not?" Dylan asks.

"I was."

"And you examined Mr. Preston's body at the scene?"

Kotsay confirms that and goes on to say that he found the body in the closet where I had seen it.

"Were there any other wounds on the body, other than the fatal bullet wound?" Dylan asks.

"Yes, there were some cuts and abrasions on the wrists. I believe they were the result of a restraint of some sorts, probably metal."

"Handcuffs?"

"It's possible, but likely something with a rougher edge. It's impossible to be sure."

Dylan goes over the autopsy, which reports the less-than-shocking news that the corpse with a bullet hole in its chest died of a bullet hole in the chest. "Did you run toxicological tests on Mr. Preston?"

Dr. Kotsay confirms that he did and that Preston's blood tested positive for Rohypnol. Under questioning he goes on to explain the properties of the drug.

There is little I can do with Dr. Kotsay, since everything he has said is one hundred percent accurate. "Dr. Kotsay, would the amount of Rohypnol in Mr. Preston's system have rendered him unconscious?"

"No, I certainly would not think so."

"Is it an amount one might take recreationally?"

"Yes."

"What effect would the drug have?"

"Depending on the person's tolerance of course, it most likely would make him mellow, serene, perhaps tired."

"So it is what is commonly known as a downer?" I ask.

"Yes."

This is an important point for me to have gotten in, since Dylan will be bringing out the fact that the same drug was in Kenny's system. A mellow, serene, tired person is not the type one would expect to commit a murder.

"Did you have occasion to examine Mr. Preston's prior medical records, including those from the NFL drug testing program?"

He confirms that he did and also that those records left no doubt that Preston had been using drugs for quite some time.

"Was he also selling these drugs?" I ask.

Before Dylan has a chance to object, Dr. Kotsay says, "I have no idea."

"Dr. Kotsay, if you know, what percentage of adults over twenty-one in America are frequent users of hard drugs? And I would exclude marijuana from this category."

"I could get you the accurate information, but I believe it is between four and eight percent."

"And what percentage of adult murder victims that you do autopsies on are frequent users of hard drugs?" I ask.

He thinks for a moment. "Again, I don't have the figures in front of me, but I would say in excess of twenty-five percent."

"How would you explain that?"

Dylan objects, but Harrison lets him answer. "Well, I would say that their use and especially their purchase of the drugs brings them into contact with dangerous people. Criminals. Their need for money also can cause them to commit crimes."

"So you would say the drug business is a dangerous

one?" I ask, fairly secure that the jury will remember I said in opening statements that Preston was selling drugs.

"Yes, I would certainly say that."

I smile, hoping the jurors will think I've accomplished more than I have. "Thank you, Doctor, I couldn't agree more."

• • • • •

LAURIE LAUGHS after we make love. Not every time, but tonight she does. I have to admit that the first couple of times it bothered me a little. I mean, I'm not the most confident guy in the world; I wouldn't take one of those "How sexually secure are you?" tests in *Cosmo* unless I could cheat.

But I soon came to understand that her laughter is from the sheer enjoyment of it. Most people I know, myself included, laugh when something is funny, and Laurie does as well. But she also laughs when she is experiencing something that she thinks is wonderful, and at those times it's an uninhibited, unrestrained laugh that sounds as good as it must feel.

I have other, different physical reactions after sex, but they are competing. I get simultaneously sleepy and hungry, and the only way to satisfy both would be to set up an intravenous system in the bedroom. One of the problems with this is I don't think M&M's and Oreos come in liquid form, so I'll just have to wait for medical science to figure it out.

For tonight, hunger wins out, and I trudge down to the

kitchen for a snack. Since I am psychologically incapable of being alone in a room without the television on, I turn on the little one on the kitchen counter.

CNN comes on, with a "Breaking News" banner across the screen. This no longer has the significance that it used to; in a desire to attract viewers surfing through channels, news stations have latched on to these kinds of banners as a way of getting the surfers to stop. So breaking news can be anything from the start of a war to an unusually large rainfall near Topeka.

This one gets my attention immediately, since I recognize a street in Paterson. The street is filled with police, and the helicopter shot clearly shows a body lying in the center of it all, covered by a sheet. I turn up the sound and hear the announcer say that the victim is a reputed mobster, allegedly a member of the Petrone family in North Jersey.

This is no doubt part of a developing war between Quintana and Petrone, and the first shot fired in revenge for the killing of Paul Moreno.

I turn off the television and go upstairs without eating anything. I also find that once I get into bed, I can no longer sleep. Since I can't do the two things I usually do after sex, I try to copy Laurie and laugh. I can't do that either.

If Quintana has his way, I could be the next one lying on the street with a sheet over me.

Murders take the fun out of everything.

I fall asleep at about two o'clock, and the alarm wakes me at six. I groan and tell a sleeping Tara to get the newspaper. She groans slightly and stretches, dog talk for "Get it yourself, asshole."

The two stories on the front page of Vince's paper are the Quintana break-in at my house and the murder of one of Petrone's lieutenants. My story is the more prominent, and when I turn on the television news, the same is true there. Such is the media power of the Schilling trial that a failed break-in is considered more newsworthy than a successful murder.

The phone starts ringing, and Laurie helps out by dealing with the onslaught of media requests for interviews. I take a few of the calls, easily enough to keep the story going full blast.

Before I get to court, I call Adam and ask for an update. He's learned the cause of death in each of the cases: There are five heart attacks, an ocean drowning, a hit-and-run, and Matt Lane's hunting accident. None was considered murder by the police who investigated each death, and the only one that attracted criminal attention was the hit-and-run. The driver is still at large.

I can hear the ·disappointment in Adam's voice; he doesn't think he's accomplished much, but he's not understanding the significance of it. Five heart attacks in men this age seems an impossibility and therefore ominous. Adam wants his discoveries to solve the case. I don't share his goal; if these deaths turn out to be related, it will likely be a disaster for Kenny.

I suggest to Adam that he give Sam Willis another assignment. By accessing Kenny's records, especially his credit cards, I want to know where Kenny was when each of these people died. It's a sign that I don't trust my client, but I don't want to just take his word for things. I want the absolute facts. Besides, assuming he wasn't involved in these deaths, he would have no way of remembering where he was at specific times over the years.

Before Dylan calls his first witness, Harrison calls us into his chambers. He has seen the news reports and wants to know if I am concerned for my safety. If so, he will order the marshals to provide special protection for me in and around the courthouse.

I think Marcus has things fairly well under control, and I certainly don't think the courthouse area is where Quintana will come after me, but I don't tell this to Harrison. "Thank you, Your Honor, I would appreciate whatever protection you can arrange."

I want the media, and maybe even the jury, to see that the court thinks I am in danger. This will tell them very clearly that there are killers involved in this case other than my client.

Dylan is smart enough to pick up on this. "Your Honor, I certainly want to ensure Mr. Carpenter's safety . . ."

I turn to Judge Harrison and interrupt, pointing to Dylan. "Is he a heck of a guy or what?"

Dylan stares a dagger at me and finishes his sentence. ". . . but I am concerned that this can be played to the defense's advantage." He goes on to explain how, accurately summarizing my reasons for wanting the protection in the first place.

Harrison takes this under consideration, then decides to order the extra protection, with a directive that it be as unobtrusive as possible. He also orders me not to mention it outside of these chambers. Unless the media are extra aware, my advantage has effectively been negated. Point to Dylan.

I'm sure it's the first of many points that Dylan will make today. He calls State Police Detective Hector Alvarez, who led the group of four detectives who first arrived at Kenny Schilling's house that day. He was in command until Captain Dessens was called to take charge of the explosive confrontation.

Alvarez describes a very nervous Kenny refusing to let the officers in. When they became more insistent and threatened to enter forcibly, Kenny brandished a handgun and fired a shot to fend them off. They then took out their own weapons, retreated, and called for backup support. As told, the jury could not help but think that Kenny's actions demonstrated a clear consciousness of guilt.

Kenny has been steadfast in claiming that the officers took out their weapons first, but in cross-examination I am unable to get Alvarez to agree with that. The closest I can come is to get him to admit that his men were surrounding the house and he could not see a number of them. He claims that they would not draw their weapons without being so ordered, but they were not in his line of sight at the time.

"Detective, were any of your men shot or wounded?"

"No."

"But a shot was fired by Mr. Schilling?"

"Yes," he says emphatically.

"So he missed?"

"Fortunately."

"Did you retrieve the bullet?"

He shakes his head. "No. We couldn't find it."

"Might he have fired into the air?" I ask.

"It's possible."

"As if he was trying to scare you away but not hurt you?"

Dylan objects that Alvarez couldn't know Kenny's motivation for firing, and Harrison sustains. I move on.

"Detective, is it possible that Mr. Schilling didn't believe that you were police officers?"

"I verbally identified us as such and held up my badge to the peephole in the door."

"Are you sure he was looking through it? Can you tell

from the outside?" I know from examining it that it's impossible, so I'm hoping to trap him.

"I believe he was. I can't be sure," he says, avoiding the trap.

"Were any of your men in uniform?"

"No."

"So it's possible he thought you were lying? That you were not police, but rather intruders that might cause him physical harm?"

"That doesn't make sense," he says.

"What if he had just received a major emotional jolt, one that made him fearful, panicked, before you arrived? A jolt in which he, just for argument's sake, found his friend murdered in a closet with a bullet in his chest? Might that have caused him to worry about your men coming at him with guns?"

"I believe he knew we were the police, and that's why he didn't want to let us in." He shakes his head firmly. "Mr. Schilling's actions were not those of an innocent person."

"Lieutenant, does the name Luther Kent mean anything to you?"

Alvarez reacts, stiffening slightly. "Yes."

"Please tell the jury how you came to be aware of Mr. Kent."

In a softer voice he describes a night four years ago when he and his partner came upon Mr. Kent on a street. They approached him, since he resembled the sketch of a man wanted as a serial rapist in that neighborhood. Kent panicked and ran, and in the resulting chase he was shot and killed by Alvarez's partner.

"Was Mr. Kent later shown to be the rapist?" I ask.

Alvarez takes a deep breath; this is not easy for him. "No.

DNA tests cleared him. The actual rapist was arrested two days later."

Dylan sees where I'm going and objects as to relevance, but he should have objected earlier in the questioning. Now that it's gone this far, Harrison is not about to stop it, and he doesn't.

I continue. "Did Mr. Kent have a criminal record? Any indication he had ever done anything which should have made him afraid of the police?"

"No."

"But different people react differently to stressful situations, isn't that right?"

"Of course, but that has nothing to do with this case."

"Because since then you've become a master at predicting and judging reactions? You've taken a mind-reading course at the Police Academy?"

Dylan objects, and this time Harrison sustains, but I've made my point, and I let Alvarez off the stand.

It's been another day of making small points that do not affect the big picture. I have absolutely no ability to prove that Kenny did not commit this murder; my only hope still rests with trying to convince the jury that it could well have been a drug killing by Quintana's people. I can only introduce this during the defense case, so I have to be patient and bide my time.

I head back to the office to pick up some papers to read over after tonight's meeting, and before I leave, I stop in at Sam Willis's office. He's been working hard with Adam, and I haven't had a chance to thank him.

"Happy to do it," Sam says. "He's a natural on a computer. He can dig things up that I can't."

That's obviously an overstatement, but Sam doesn't

throw praise around indiscriminately. Adam must be picking up Sam's tricks really well.

"You've both been a really big help."

"He's doing most of it," Sam says. "I'm telling you, he should give up this California movie bullshit and come work here. Him and me and two computers, we could rule the world."

I smile at the image. "You told him that?" I ask.

"Sure did. I said, say goodbye to Hollywood."

Uh-oh. That sounds like a song, but I can't place it, and once again I didn't prepare any material to engage in song-talking competition.

"Okay," I say, ready to bail out before I become inundated in lyrics.

Sam goes on. "Then I figured I shouldn't have said it, that it's none of my business. So I said, 'Hey, Adam, don't mind me. California's okay, but I'm in a New York state of mind.'"

Got it. Billy Joel.

"I should go, Sam. Laurie's waiting for me."

He's not quite ready for me to leave. "How are things going with her?" Sam asks.

"Nothing new. Still deciding."

Sam shakes his head in sympathy for my situation. "I think you need to be aggressive. Don't just stand around and wait for her to make the move. Talk to her."

"And say what?"

"Well, I can't put myself in your shoes, but I'll tell you what I said when I was in a similar situation. After I graduated college, this girl and I moved in together. We were thinking of getting married, but she kept threatening to leave. Finally, I told her, 'Hey, babe, I don't care what you say anymore, this is my life. Go ahead with your own life and leave me alone.'"

He's going to keep song-talking until I come up with a response, but none comes to mind at the moment.

"I mean it; you gotta take a stand," he continues. "And don't worry; I know Laurie. She's not gonna move to that hick town. She's an uptown girl; she's been living in her uptown world."

Ah, hah! An idea. "That's not what I'm going to tell her," I say.

"What are you gonna say?" he asks

"I'll be honest; I'll tell her the truth. I'll say, 'I just want someone that I can talk to. I love you just the way you are.'"

He nods his understanding. "Good for you, man. But that honesty, it's such a lonely word."

• • • • •

WEEKENDS ARE VERY difficult during a trial. Each day in court is intense and pressure-filled, and when the weekend comes around, the need to withdraw and relax is palpable. But there is no withdrawing, and no relaxing, because there is too much to do, and in the back of my mind I know that the opposition is always working.

I meet Walter Simmons, the Giants' legal VP, for breakfast. I had told him I'd keep him informed of progress, within the confines of lawyer-client privilege. He's been helpful in getting his players to meet with various members of our team, so I feel I owe him this time.

The Giants won their first game last week, but did it by passing for three hundred fifty yards and returning two interceptions for touchdowns. The running game gained an anemic sixty-one yards. After I update him on the status of the trial, he says, "Sounds like we should trade for a running back."

"We've got a decent chance," I lie.

"Yeah. And we're going to win the Super Bowl."

I shake my head. "Not without a better kicker. But before too long I may have somebody for you."

He doesn't pick up on it, and I decide against telling him my plans. Since it takes very little physical prowess, he could decide to try it as well. One thing I don't need is more competition.

Adam calls me on my cell phone to tell me that he's in the office and that he hopes it's okay with me. "The computer here is much faster than using my laptop at the hotel," he says.

"No problem," I say. "When do you want to update me on progress?"

"Pretty soon. There's a couple more things I need to check out first."

I head home for an afternoon of reading and rereading of case material. First I take Tara for a walk and a short tennis ball toss in the park; I've been feeling guilty at how little time I've spent with her. That guilt is increased when I once again see how much she enjoys it. Afterward, we stop off for a bagel and some water, and by the time we get home, I've thoroughly enjoyed the brief respite away from the case.

I plunge into the material and barely notice the college football game I have on in the background. Laurie comes in at about four carrying grocery bags. She says, "Hi, honey," and comes over to give me a kiss. It's domestic bliss straight out of *Ozzie and Harriet,* and for all my cynicism it feels really good.

"Have you seen David and Ricky?" I ask.

She's never seen *Ozzie and Harriet,* since she doesn't watch old reruns as religiously as I do, so she has no idea about whom I'm talking. Once I explain it to her, she doesn't seem interested in it. This isn't working; I need a woman who can be my intellectual equal.

She starts unloading the groceries. "I thought we'd barbecue some seafood tonight."

"Fish?" I ask, my disappointment showing through.
"What is there, a hamburger strike going on?"

With all the work I have, the idea of stopping to cook
fish is not pleasing. Of course, I have no idea how long it
will take because I don't know how long one is supposed
to cook fish. I know some should be cooked through, some
rare, and some just seared, but I don't have a clue which is
which. "I don't have a lot of time," I say.

"I'm going to cook it," she says.

Uh-oh. Another sign of independence. "Are we forgetting who the boy is in this relationship? I am the barbecuer,
you are the barbecuee."

"You're a man's man," she says, and then goes off into
the kitchen to marinate the fish in whatever the hell you
marinate fish in. They spend their whole life in liquid, and
then they have to soak in liquid before you cook them? The
ocean didn't get them wet enough? Hopefully, these particular fish have to marinate for two weeks, but I doubt it.

They're soaking for about ten minutes when the phone
rings. Laurie gets it, and from the kitchen I hear her say, "Hi,
Vince . . . What?" She listens some more and then says,
"Vince, he's here with me. He's right here." There is a tension in her voice that chills me to the bone.

She comes rushing into the room and goes right to the
television, changing the football game to CNN. I stand up—
I'm not sure why—and start walking toward the television,
as if I'll find out what the hell is going on if I'm closer.

I see myself on television; it's footage from a panel show
I did some months before. My lips are moving, but the
sound is muted so that the announcer can talk over me. I
don't hear what he is saying because my eyes are riveted to

the blaring message across the bottom of the screen: "Schilling lawyer murdered."

My mind can't process what is going on. Why would they think I was murdered? Can it be Kevin? Is he the person they're calling a Schilling lawyer? Then why are they showing me?

"Andy . . ." It's Laurie's voice attempting to cut through the confused mess that is my mind. "They're saying that you were shot and killed in your office this afternoon."

And then it hits me, with a searing pain that feels like it explodes my insides. "Let's go," I say, and run toward my car. Laurie is with me every step of the way, and within five minutes we are approaching my office.

We have to park two blocks away because the place is such a mob scene. Laurie knows one of the officers protecting the perimeter, and he lets us through the barricades. Pete Stanton is standing next to a patrol car, in front of the fruit stand below my office.

"Pete . . ." is all I can manage.

"It's the writer, Andy. Adam. He took two shots in the face and one in the chest. Died instantly."

I can't adequately describe the pain I feel, but I know I've felt it before. Sam Willis had a young assistant named Barry Leiter who was murdered because he was helping me investigate a case. Like then, I find my legs giving out from under me, and I have to lean against the car for support.

"Why?" I say, but I know why. Adam was blown apart by bullets that were meant for me.

"We just arrested Quintana, Andy. I don't know if we can make it stick, but he ordered it done. No question about it."

"I want to see him," I say, and push off from the car. It's only then that I realize that Laurie has her arm around me, and she keeps that arm around me all the way up the stairs. She is supporting me, and she is sobbing.

There are officers and forensics people everywhere, finishing up their work. They seem to part as we approach, mainly because Pete is with us telling them to. Suddenly, there just inside the office door, we see a body covered by a sheet. I am getting goddamn sick of seeing people I care about covered by sheets.

I'm not sure how long we're at the office, probably a couple of hours. Pete has a lot of questions he has to ask me, but he doesn't make me go down to the station to answer them. Sam Willis shows up, having heard the news on television, and he lets us use his office. It's the first time I've ever seen Sam cry.

There is little I can tell Pete that he doesn't already know. He's aware of the incident where Marcus threw Ugly out the window, and he was there the night Marcus stopped Ugly and his friend from breaking into my house and roughing me up.

Pete tells me that Ugly and his friend are still in custody and have been since that night. "That probably cost Adam his life," I say. "Whoever Quintana sent didn't know me by sight . . . they thought Adam was me."

Pete shakes his head. "Maybe, maybe not. They probably came in shooting and didn't even wait to look. Maybe Adam never knew what was coming."

For the record, and for Pete's tape recorder, I take him through the reason Adam came here in the first place. I also describe Adam's gradual evolution into being helpful on the Schilling case, but I refuse to provide details, citing attorney-client privilege.

Pete tries to probe, to find out as much as he can, explaining that the murder has to be investigated fully. Though he strongly believes that it was a case of mistaken identity and that I was the target, the investigation cannot prejudge that. It has to start with the assumption that Adam was the target and look for reasons why. I understand that, and I'm fine with Pete doing an inventory of the office where Adam was working and taking whatever he needs.

"Just remember that his notes about the Schilling case are privileged, so I'd appreciate it if only you'd look at them first to see if they're relevant. And I'll need them back as soon as you can."

Pete's fine with that and tells me that I can go. As we reach the street, Willie Miller screeches to a halt in his car and jumps out. He sees me, and his eyes just about bug out of his head. "Man, they said you . . ."

Without another word he hugs me. I can count the number of male hugs I've liked on very few fingers, and I don't like this one, but I appreciate it. After a few moments I break it off. "Adam was killed, Willie. They shot him thinking it was me."

Willie looks at me disbelieving, then his face briefly contorts in a kind of rage I'm not sure I've ever seen before. Without a word, in a lightning-quick move he puts his hand through the front window of his car, smashing it to bits. I know Willie holds a black belt in karate, but it's still an amazing sight to behold.

I put my hand on his shoulder. "Come on, we'll drive you home."

Laurie drives, and after we drop Willie off, we go home. She makes us drinks, and we sit down in the den. I just can't seem to clear my head, to accept as fact what has happened. I don't want to be a part of this; I don't want people to die because of what I do for a living. I don't want to be around this anymore.

"You want to talk, Andy?" Laurie asks.

"All I do is talk."

"It's not your fault," Laurie says. "You couldn't know this was going to happen."

"What do I need this for? I'm a lawyer. Did I cut the class in law school when they said that people were going to die just because they knew me?"

"Andy—"

I interrupt. "I want to do what other lawyers do. I want to sue doctors for malpractice because they forgot to remove the sponge after my client's appendectomy. I want to represent huge corporations when they merge with other huge corporations. I want to make cheating husbands pay through the nose in alimony. I want to do everything but what I'm doing."

"No," she says, "you're doing exactly what you should be doing. And you do it better than anyone I know. As one of your former clients, I can say with certainty that you're needed right where you are."

I shake my head, not giving an inch. "No, you've got the right idea," I say. "Findlay is a better place to live than this. I think you should go. I should go with you."

She shakes her head. "You can't run away, Andy. I won't do that, and I won't let you do it either. If I go, if we go, we'll be going *toward* something, not running away."

I know she's right, but I refuse to say so, because then I might have to stop feeling sorry for myself. An old Joe Louis expression pops into my head, as if he were talking about me. "He can run, but he can't hide."

Right now all I want to do is hide.

• • • • •

I TAKE IT UPON myself to call Adam's parents in Kansas and notify them of the death of their son. It is one of the more difficult conversations I've ever had in my life, but I can only imagine how much worse it is for them. They want his body flown home for the funeral service, and I promise I will help them make the arrangements. It's a murder case, so by law an autopsy must take place first, but I don't see any need to mention that right now.

They seem not to want to end the phone call, as if I am their final connection to their son and they want to keep that connection going as long as possible. They show incredible generosity by telling me that they had been receiving phone calls from Adam, telling them how much he enjoyed working with me and how excited he was to be meeting important sportswriters. He'd been meeting football players, not sportswriters, but I certainly don't bother to correct them. Memories are all they have, and I don't want to blur them in any fashion.

I tell them Adam was hoping to buy them a house, that

he talked about them lovingly and often. They thank me and finally say goodbye, to retreat into their agony.

In the morning I have Kevin, Sam, Marcus, and Edna join Laurie and me at the house for a rare Sunday meeting. Willie comes over as well, since he wants to be involved in whatever way he can in protecting me and nailing Adam's killer. I'm happy to have him; the trial is not going to stop while we mourn for Adam, and I have to make sure that as a group we are ready to deal with what happened and move on.

We spend the first hour or so talking about Adam and how we felt about him. He had made a very deep impression on each of us with his enthusiasm for life, an enthusiasm that makes his death feel that much more tragic. Marcus even adds two words to the discourse: "Good guy." It's the Marcus equivalent of a normal person delivering an impassioned twenty-minute eulogy.

Kevin forces us to look at the impact that this horrible event will have on the Schilling case. I've been thinking about asking Judge Harrison for a two-day recess, to give me time to get my head together, as well as helping to catch up on the work Adam was doing.

Kevin thinks a recess is a bad idea, that the publicity from Adam's killing can only have the unintended and ironic effect of helping in Kenny's defense. Despite Judge Harrison's admonition to the jurors not to expose themselves to media coverage of this case, there is no realistic possibility that they haven't heard what has happened. The inescapable conclusion to be reached is that there are murderers, not sitting next to me at the defense table, who are involved in this case. We might be able to convince the jury that it is "reasonable" to assume that those same people murdered Troy Preston as well.

I think Kevin is probably right, though his point is probably moot, since it is unlikely Judge Harrison would actually grant the recess anyway. So I decide to push on, even though there is nothing I would rather do less.

I ask Sam to bring us up-to-date as best he can on Adam's work, but there isn't much he can offer. Adam had given him specific things to do, and their assignments really didn't overlap. We are not even aware of how Adam put together the list of people he was checking out. When Pete returns Adam's notes, it will make Sam's job easier.

Sam has been working hard, though, and his report on his own progress is very worrisome. He has managed to place Kenny within a three-hour drive of three of the deaths, not including Matt Lane's hunting accident. This is no small revelation: We are talking about four cities in very different parts of the country. To make matters worse, Sam hasn't ruled out Kenny's presence in the other death locations; he just hasn't finished the complicated process of checking.

I am both nearing and dreading the time when I will confront Kenny with what we have learned. His reaction, his explanation, will determine how I handle things and, more important, will most likely determine his entire future.

Laurie brings up the matter of my protection. Quintana is in jail, but Pete has told us off the record that there is little concrete evidence to tie him to Adam's death. He undoubtedly hired someone to do the killing, keeping his own hands clean. There is a real possibility that he will be released, and a just as strong possibility that he will come after me again.

Laurie makes the suggestion that Marcus's total focus be on protecting me and that he recruit some of his more energetic colleagues to help in that endeavor. Marcus grunts his agreement, but it is clear that he considers more aggressive action necessary. He's got a point: Had we let him go after Quintana when he suggested it the first time, Adam would be alive today.

Everybody leaves, and I start to go over my case notes, hoping to get myself emotionally geared up for the resumption of the trial tomorrow. It's not going to be easy, and within a half hour I find myself turning on the television and taking comfort in NFL football.

In the morning Judge Harrison once again calls Dylan and me into his chambers to discuss the events outside of court. He and Dylan express their condolences, and Dylan is somewhat regretful for his comments last time, when he intimated that my revelation of the threat was mostly an attempt to sway the jury.

Harrison unsolicitedly offers me a one-day recess, which I decline. Dylan asks that Harrison poll the jury, to see if they've actually been deligently avoiding press coverage. It's a surprising request and makes me realize just how worried Dylan is about what is taking place outside the courtroom. If the jury admitted to having seen the coverage, the only real remedy would be a mistrial, and I am stunned to realize that apparently Dylan would consider that.

Harrison declines to poll the jury; this is not a judge who is going to give up on this trial. He agrees to admonish the jury in even stronger terms than previously not to expose themselves to any press reports.

Dylan calls Stephen Clement to the stand. Clement is the neighbor of Preston's whom Laurie discovered and who has information that cuts for both the prosecution and the defense. Dylan is making the smart move of calling him, since his ability to question him first will allow him to frame the testimony, both positive and negative.

Clement, under Dylan's questioning, tells the situation in simple, direct terms. He was out walking his dog that night when a car pulled up and Preston got out. He never saw the driver, but he describes the car, with the GIANTS25 license plate. He also knows that the driver was a male, because he heard Preston and the driver arguing.

"Could you tell what they were arguing about?" Dylan asks.

Clement shakes his head. "I really couldn't hear them . . . I was across the street, and the car was running. It might have been about a woman; the driver might have said, 'You leave her alone.' But I could just as easily be wrong."

"But you were close enough to be sure that they were arguing?" Dylan asks.

"I'm quite certain of that."

Dylan asks what happened next, and Clement says that the car pulled away, at a higher-than-normal speed.

"Did the car return?" Dylan asks.

"Not while I was there. But I only walked the dog for another three or four minutes."

"So the car could have returned after that and you wouldn't know it?"

Clement nods. "That's correct."

Informationally, I have no reason to even question Clement, since everything he has to say has been said. I just need to spend a little time putting a more favorable spin on it for our side. Laurie has questioned him extensively, so I have some information at my disposal.

"Mr. Clement, when you were out walking, did you have a cell phone with you?"

"Yes. I always carry one."

"When you heard these men arguing, did you call the police, fearing violence was about to break out?"

"No."

"Did you try to intervene yourself? Try to prevent anyone from getting hurt?"

"No."

"Did you quickly leave the area so that you and your dog wouldn't be injured?"

"No."

"So it was not an argument that was unusually loud or volatile? Not one where you were worried that someone could be badly hurt? Because if it were that bad, I assume you would have taken one of the actions I just mentioned. Isn't that right?"

"I guess . . . I mean, they were just yelling. It wasn't that big a deal."

Having made the point, I ask him how fast the car was driving when it pulled away, since Clement had referred to the speed as being higher than normal.

"I would say about forty miles an hour," Clement says. "It's a residential neighborhood, so that's pretty fast."

I put up a map of the neighborhood and get Clement to explain that he walked home in the same direction that the car pulled away. That adds a few minutes to the time he would have had to see the car if it returned. It's a small point, but it works against the image of an outraged Kenny storming back after the argument and killing Preston.

Court ends for the day at noon, giving two jurors time to attend to personal business, probably doctor's appointments. I can certainly use the time, and I call Pete Stanton and ask for a quick favor. He knows he owes me big-time for the ridiculous birthday party, so he readily agrees.

One of the names on the list of mysterious deaths was a drowning in the ocean in Asbury Park, a Jersey beach resort about an hour south of Paterson. I know that Pete has a number of connections with the police department down there, and on my behalf he calls one of them to arrange for me to be able to talk to the officer most familiar with the young man's death.

I don't hit much traffic going down there, since it's a weekday and not during rush hour. Arriving in Asbury Park provides a bit of a jolt; I spent a good deal of my youthful weekends down here, and the city hasn't held up very well. The buildings have eroded considerably faster than my memories.

Sergeant Stan Collins is there to meet me when I arrive at the precinct house. He didn't speak to Pete directly, but he knows what I'm there to learn and suggests that we drive to the scene of the drowning.

Within ten minutes we're near the edge of Asbury Park, and the ocean seems rougher than it did when I drove in. Collins says that this is common and has something to do with the rock formation.

He points out where Darryl Anderson died on a September day six years ago. "There was a hurricane warning, or a watch," he says. "I can never remember which is which."

"I think the warning is worse," I say.

He nods. "Whatever. A bunch of local teenagers weren't too worried about it, and they decided it would be really cool to ride the waves in the middle of the storm."

"Anderson was one of the teenagers?" I ask.

"Nope. I think he was twenty or twenty-one. His brother was one of the kids out in the water. Anderson heard about it from his mother, who was upset and asked him to make sure the kid was okay."

Collins shakes his head at the memory and continues.

"The undertow was unbelievable, and Anderson started yelling at the kids to get out of the water. He was a big, scary guy, a football player, so they did. Except one kid, a fourteen-year-old, couldn't make it. The current was pulling him out."

"So Anderson went in after him?"

He nods. "Yeah. Got to him and grabbed him but couldn't make it back. Their bodies were never found."

"Is there any way," I ask, "any way at all, that he could have been murdered?"

His head shake is firm. "No way. There were twenty witnesses to what happened, including me, although I got here for the very end of it. Everybody who saw it said the same thing. It was preventable . . . those kids should never have been in the water . . . but there is absolutely no way it was murder."

It's a sad story, but one that has the secondary effect of cheering me up. Kenny obviously had nothing to do with this death, and if I can find that to be true of most of the others as well, then coincidence will actually have reared its improbable head.

When I get back home, an obviously distressed Laurie comes out to meet me at the car. I hadn't told her where I was going, and she was panicked at the possibility that Quintana had gotten to me and dumped my body in the Passaic River.

"I'm sorry I upset you," I lie, since I'm thrilled that she's upset. "I had to leave in a hurry."

"You had a cell phone, Andy. You could have called me."

She's right, I could have called her, and I'm not sure why I didn't. It's not like me. I didn't consciously think about it, but was my subconscious trying to worry her? Or am I subtly separating from her, so as to prepare myself and lessen the devastation when and if she leaves?

"I should have."

She lets it drop, and I update her on what I learned. She is relieved, as I am, but points out that it's not proof that Kenny wasn't involved with any of the other deaths. She suggests that it's time that I speak to Kenny about it, and I make plans to do so before court tomorrow.

Laurie and I had planned to go to Charlie's for dinner tonight, but she doesn't want to leave the house. She wants to make a quick dinner and get into bed. With that as the ultimate goal, there is no such thing as a dinner quick enough. But I inhale some kind of a sandwich, and Laurie and I are in bed by nine o'clock.

Our lovemaking tonight is more intense than usual, and Laurie is one hundred percent responsible for that. I think that she was really shaken and worried about me today, and this is how it is manifesting itself. Of course, the next time I successfully read a woman's mind will be the first, so I stop trying to figure it out and simply go with the flow.

It turns out to be one of the best flows I've ever gone with.

● ● ● ● ●

I WAKE UP WITH that awful feeling of remembrance about Adam. I know these feelings will be with
me for a long time, because I still have them about Sam's assistant, Barry Leiter, and he died almost two years ago. I'm
going to have to start allocating scheduled time for my various guilt issues so I don't get them confused.

I arrive at court an hour early for my scheduled meeting
with Kenny about the information Adam was developing. I
bring Kevin with me, not for him to participate, but to have
an independent opinion on Kenny's reaction to my questions.

Kenny seems surprised and a little concerned when he's
brought in for the meeting, since the unusual nature of it
makes him think that something has come up.

I get right to the point, reading him the names of the
eight young men who have died. When I'm finished, I ask,
"Do those names mean anything to you?"

Kenny thinks for a moment, then says, "Well, Matt Lane
is the guy who died in the hunting accident that we talked
about. And Tony George played for Penn State, a linebacker.

I don't know where he is. And I think Mike Rafferty played out West somewhere; I met him a long time ago. I think I heard something happened to him. Are these guys all football players?"

"They were," I say. "Now they're all dead."

If the look of surprise on Kenny's face is an act, it's a damn good one. "What do you mean, they're all dead? What happened to them?"

"Various things . . . you don't know anything about it?"

The awareness starts to dawn on Kenny that we might be tying this to him. He stands up. "Hey, wait a minute! Are you saying I killed them? Are you out of your fucking minds?"

He's yelling so loud that I'm afraid the guards outside the door will hear him and come rushing in. "No, Kenny, that's not what I'm saying. But you can be sure that's what the prosecution will be saying if they find out."

"Find out what? Except for Matt, I don't even know where these guys live. How could I have killed them?"

"Okay," I say. "You've told me what I need to know."

He is far from calmed down. "Jesus Christ," he says, "I thought you were on my side."

We talk for a brief while longer, then Kevin and I leave for some last-minute preparation for today's witnesses. Kenny still seems upset, but he'll just have to deal with it.

Once we're out of earshot of Kenny, I ask Kevin what he thinks. "He obviously got upset," Kevin says, "but that could be because he's innocent *or* guilty. I'd vote for innocent; he really seemed confused before you told him what you were talking about."

That's my feeling as well, but like Kevin, I'm well aware that I could be wrong.

As Judge Harrison is about to come into court, I go to

turn my cell phone off. It's something I do every day, to save myself the embarrassment of his confiscating it if it should ring during the court session. I see that there is a text message on the phone from Sam, asking me to call him and identifying it as "important." The cell phone probably didn't get reception in the anteroom where I met with Kenny.

I'm worried about what Sam might have discovered, but I have no time to call him now. I also have to switch my mental focus to Dylan's first witness, Captain Dessens. As the lead investigator and arresting officer, Dylan will use him to sum up his case.

In truth, Dessens has little to add to the facts of the case. The jury has already heard about the blood evidence, Kenny's actions the day of the arrest at his house, and the discovery of Preston's body in the closet. Those are the main facts, and all Dessens does is repeat and embellish them. It is almost as if Dessens is giving Dylan's closing argument for him.

Dylan is painstaking in his questioning, and he doesn't turn the witness over to me until almost noon. Harrison decides to take the lunch break before I cross Dessens, and as soon as I can get to where I can talk privately, I call Sam.

"What have you got, Sam?" I ask.

"Nothing good. I've got Schilling within seventy-five miles of six of the eight deaths at the time they happened. I've cleared him on one, and I'm still working on the eighth."

"Shit," I say, once again displaying my characteristic rhetorical flourish.

"Andy, these deaths took place all over the country. The odds against Kenny being in each of these places at those particular times are astronomical. Beyond coincidence. Way beyond."

"I know," I say, because I do know, and there's nothing to be gained by my first choice, which would be to remain in denial. I make arrangements to see Sam after court is over, and go to find Kevin. His reaction is the same as Sam's, and we agree to figure out tonight just how we are going to deal with this.

Dessens gets back on the stand, no doubt prepped by Dylan for a full-blown cross-examination covering everything. He's not going to get it; I've made whatever points I've had to make with previous witnesses. Instead, I'm going to use this cross to start presenting the defense's case.

"Captain Dessens, you testified that Mr. Schilling became the focus of your investigation early on. I believe you said that within twelve hours he was your prime suspect."

He nods. "That's correct."

"Who were your less-than-prime suspects?"

"I don't know what you mean."

"Let me try to be even clearer. Who were on your list of suspects; who were the people you crossed off that list when you decided Mr. Schilling was your man?"

"There were no specific names; it was early in the process, and we hadn't had a chance to go deep into our investigation."

"So Mr. Schilling was your *only* suspect as well as your *prime* one?"

"Yes."

"Generally, in a murder investigation, when the prime suspect doesn't jump out at you so fast, is it fair to say you have a large list of suspects and then you pare them down?"

"Generally, but every case is different."

"But you never prepared such a list for this case? You stopped looking after Mr. Schilling was arrested?"

He shakes his head. "We continued our thorough investigation, but we had our man."

"Did your 'thorough' investigation uncover the fact that the victim was dealing drugs?"

Dylan jumps out of his chair to object that this is not within the scope of his direct examination, but I argue that it is, since Dylan had Dessens talking about his investigation. Harrison agrees with me and allows Dessens to answer.

"We had indications of that, yes. Nothing that has been proven."

"In the same way that Mr. Schilling's guilt in this case hasn't been proven, since the jury has not yet returned a verdict?"

Dylan objects that this is argumentative, and Harrison sustains.

I push on. "Did you learn where Mr. Preston got the drugs he was selling?" I ask.

"Not with enough certainty that I can name anyone here today."

I nod. "Fair enough. I'll name some people, and you tell me if they were possible drug suppliers to Mr. Preston. Here goes . . . Albert Schweitzer? Pope John Paul? The queen of England?"

Dylan objects again, calling my questions "frivolous," which is not exactly a news event. Again Harrison sustains.

"Captain Dessens," I ask, "is it your experience that drug suppliers are dangerous people, who often employ other dangerous people?"

He agrees to that but little else. I let him off the stand having basically made my point: Troy Preston associated with people who seem a lot more credible in the role of killer than does Kenny Schilling.

As Dylan rests the prosecution's case, I believe I have a slight but real chance of convincing the jury that Kenny doesn't fit the bill as the killer of Troy Preston.

That's because they don't know what I know.

• • • • •

SAM LAYS OUT THE information he has
learned in a straightforward, serious way. He doesn't even
song-talk, such is his understanding of the implications of
this material. Sam is a numbers guy, and he understands
the laws of probability. These facts do not obey those
laws.

The question is what to do now. I do not see how we
can ever bring any of this before Judge Harrison. If we determine the best, that Kenny has no culpability, then that is
the end of it. If we determine the worst, that Kenny has
committed a series of bizarre murders, we are prohibited
from revealing it. Anything in between, if there can be anything in between, would likewise be privileged.

All this work we are doing is essentially to satisfy our
own curiosity, and our energies could be better spent in
helping defend our client against the charge he faces, not
what he might have done besides that. The only legally eth-
ical justification for our actions is to claim that we are
preparing for the remote possibility that Dylan will learn
what we are learning, and we will have to defend against his

use of that knowledge against Kenny. Having said that, I certainly won't be charging Kenny for any of the hours we spend on this end of the investigation.

I ask Laurie to devote herself full-time to learning about these mysterious deaths. I want her to investigate each one individually, much as I did Darryl Anderson's drowning in the ocean off Asbury Park. Maybe she can clear each case as definitely not a murder, but I doubt it.

Marcus is going to continue to guard me, since our concerns about Quintana are absolutely real. Quintana may not have killed Preston, but he's already sent people after me, and Adam's fate is testimony to his ruthlessness. This is a bad guy, whether our courtroom claims of his involvement in the Preston murder are true or not.

Lying in bed is when I do some of my best thinking. Tonight Laurie lies next to me, awake, so instead of just rattling around in my head, the words I am thinking come out through my mouth. "The thing that gnaws at me, in a good way, if there can be such a thing as good gnawing . . ."

Laurie gets frustrated with my lengthy preamble. "Spit it out, Andy."

"Okay. None of these other deaths were ruled murder by the police, not a single one. Assuming the worst, that Kenny killed all of them, why would he have done such a good job covering up his guilt those times, and then with Preston he just about holds up a neon sign saying 'I'm guilty'? That doesn't make any sense to me."

"So maybe someone else did them all, including Preston."

"That fails the same logic test," I say. "Whoever it was that did it, why would they make all of the others not look like murder and this one so obvious? To frame Kenny? They could have done that just by killing Preston. Why kill all the others?"

"Somehow the Preston killing is different," she says. "If it wasn't Kenny that did it, but instead somebody trying to frame him, the other killings weren't part of that plan. Don't forget, if Adam didn't happen to notice them, we'd think Preston was the only death in the case."

I'm just about to fall asleep when something makes me think of Bobby Pollard, the wheelchair-bound trainer who has known Kenny since high school. Pollard was in a terrible accident, one that cost him his ability to walk. It clearly could have cost him his life but did not. Should he be on our list as well? Was he supposed to be another victim?

It's eleven-thirty at night, but the Pollards told me I could call on them at any time, so I take that literally and dial their number. Teri answers, and I explain that I need to talk to her husband. My plan is to meet with them after court tomorrow, but such is their eagerness to help that they give me the option of coming over tonight. They apologetically say that they can't come to me because their son is asleep and it takes Bobby time to get dressed and become fully mobile.

I'm wound up too tight to sleep, so I figure I might as well go over there. I wake Laurie and tell her where I'm going so that she won't be worried again. She offers to go with me, but I tell her I'm fine on my own, and she seems quite happy to accept that and go back to sleep.

I leave the house, glancing around for Marcus on the way to my car. I don't see him, but I know he's there. I hope he's there.

Twenty minutes later the Pollards are serving me coffee and cinnamon cake in their dining room. "Bobby, I want to talk to you about your accident" is how I start.

His face reflects an understandable confusion. "My accident? I thought this was about Kenny."

"There's a great deal I can't tell you, including how the various pieces come together. I just ask that you answer my questions as best you can, and reserve any questions of your own until the time I can answer them."

Bobby looks over at Teri, and she nods her assent, which I think is the only reason he lets this continue. "What about my accident?"

"Tell me how it happened."

"I already did. I was driving in Spain, and I went off the road. The car rolled over, and I never walked again." His voice is angry, as if I shouldn't be making him go through this. He's right; I shouldn't.

"What caused you to go off the road?" I ask.

"Another car went out of its lane. I tried to avoid it, give it room, but I ran out of room myself."

"Who was driving the other car?"

He shakes his head. "I don't know. They didn't stop. I don't even know if they saw what happened to me."

"Do you think they did what they did intentionally?"

"I never have, no. Do you know something I don't?"

I ignore the question, trying to get through this. "Who was with you on the trip to Europe?"

He thinks and names four male friends, unfortunately including Kenny. Then, "Teri and I had just gotten married a few months before; it was sort of a last fling with the guys." He looks at her. "Not that kind of fling . . . you know what I mean."

She smiles her understanding, not particularly jealous of anything that might have happened almost a decade ago, before her husband was paralyzed. Then she turns to me. "I was pregnant, so we got married. We were only eighteen."

I ask Bobby, "Why weren't your friends with you when you went for the drive?"

He shrugs. "I don't remember. They probably went to the beach."

I'm learning more than I need to know, so I apologize for bothering them and leave without answering their questions. What I did was not fair to them, but it provided me with another piece of information. The list of tragically unlucky friends and acquaintances of Kenny Schilling's now includes Bobby Pollard.

Heading to court for the first day of the defense's case, I can't remember ever being a part of a situation like this. I'm defending my client against a murder charge while at the same time leading an investigation to determine whether or not he is a serial murderer. And whether I win or lose the trial, I can never reveal the results of that investigation.

I've decided to break our defense case into two parts. The first will deal with showing the jury who Kenny Schilling is and how unlikely it is that he would suddenly turn killer. The second phase will be devoted to presenting the jury with other alternatives, other possible killers, and to show them the dangerous world in which Troy Preston lived. Neither of the two parts is likely to carry the day; the overwhelming physical evidence, plus Kenny's behavior during the siege at his house, are still looking impregnable. We are in very deep trouble.

Just before the session begins, I call Sam Willis and ask him to add Bobby Pollard to the list of people he is investigating. I tell him not to bother checking whether Kenny had the geographic proximity to have caused the accident, since Bobby has already said that he did. Rather, I want Sam to check into the accident itself, to learn whether the Spanish police considered it a possible attempted murder.

I spend the day parading a group mostly consisting of professional football players in front of the starstruck jury. Each witness talks of his admiration for Kenny and the total absurdity that anyone could believe Kenny could take another life.

I would be bored to death if Dylan did not look so uncomfortable. He's afraid that the jury will buy into what these people are saying just because of who they are, and he spends little time cross-examining so that they'll leave more quickly. Dylan does get each to say that he has no actual knowledge as to the circumstances of Preston's death and cannot provide Kenny with any kind of alibi.

I call off our meeting tonight; I'm well prepared for tomorrow's witnesses, and I'm better off spending the time trying to extricate myself from my well-deserved depression. It's not one of our regular sleepover nights, but I ask Laurie to stay, and she does. I barbecue, and in deference to my fragile mental state, she doesn't even insist on fish.

We're just sitting down to eat when Pete Stanton, with characteristic perfect timing, shows up. We invite him to join us, since I always make extra, and he does. At least he didn't bring his extended family with him.

Once Pete is finished inhaling his food, he gets around to telling us why he came by. Quintana was released from custody this morning, and the police have heard from informants that he's going to come after me. Pete wants to make sure that I'm well protected, and Laurie tells him that Marcus and Willie are on the case.

"But you're sure it was Quintana that had Adam killed?" I ask.

Pete nods. "It was Quintana, unless you've got some other homicidal maniacs after you. With your mouth it wouldn't surprise me."

"So the investigation is closed?"

He shakes his head. "Unsolved murders are never closed. But this one ain't getting solved, if that's what you mean."

I know exactly what he means, and I don't want to spend the rest of my life fearing for my life. I'm forming the germ of an idea on how to deal with the situation, but I'm not ready to verbalize it yet, and certainly not to Pete.

"When can I get Adam's notes?"

"There weren't any."

"Come on, Pete, of course there were. He took notes on everything." Pete's shaking his head, so I ask, "Did you check his hotel room? And his car?"

"What kind of a moron do you think I am?" he asks. "I'm telling you, there were no notes, zero."

Laurie jumps in. "He had them, Pete. Legal pads . . . lots of them. I watched him take them."

Laurie and I look at each other, each knowing what the other is thinking. If whoever killed Adam took his notes, then it may not have been Quintana's people at all. They would have no use for them. And if it was somebody else, and they wanted those notes, then it's just possible that I wasn't the target after all.

The murderer may have killed exactly whom he intended to kill. Adam may have come upon something that caused his death, something that he never got a chance to tell me.

We tell our suspicions to Pete, who cautions us against

jumping to quick conclusions. Adam could have done something else with the notes. He could have shipped them back
to LA or left them in some storage place we don't know
about.

I don't buy it and I tell him so, which causes him concern that we are going to view Quintana as less of a danger.
"He's coming after you, Andy. We know that, whether he
killed Adam or not."

"Pete, do you know that Quintana is a murderer? I mean,
know it for a fact?"

"Of course."

I press him. "I don't mean know it like you 'knew' he
killed Adam. I mean absolutely know it beyond any doubt."

He nods. "I know it beyond any doubt. And I'm not talking about the people he's destroyed by selling his drugs. I'm
talking about murder. I would flick the switch on him
tonight if I could."

Pete thinks I'm asking the questions in order to confirm
that Quintana is a danger to me, but I'm not.

I have no intention of telling him why I'm asking.

• • • • •

I CALL A SEVEN A.M. meeting at my office with Kevin, Laurie, and Sam Willis. Laurie and I lay out our developing theory about Adam's murder, and Kevin's excitement is obvious. Not only does he agree with our reasoning, but he makes the point that if someone killed Adam because of what he learned about the deaths of the athletes, then Kenny is innocent. He's been in jail and is thus the one person with an ironclad alibi for Adam's murder.

I ask Sam if it's possible to go on my computer, the one Adam was using, and retrace where he had been on it.

"I can't do it in depth, but I know someone who can. I'll bring him in right away."

"What about the phone records?" I ask. "If he made calls those last couple of days, can you find out who he called?"

He nods. "That's easy. And once I'm in there, I can also lower your phone bill if you want."

We agree to meet right after court at my house to get an update on Sam and Laurie's progress. Kevin and I head for court; we've got a case to put on and a client to defend. A client who just might well be innocent.

Just before court starts, I go out to the side of the building where I won't be overheard. I call Vince Sanders on my cell phone and tell him I have a big favor to ask.

"What else is new?" he asks sarcastically.

"I want you to set up a meeting for me tomorrow night with Dominic Petrone." Vince knows Petrone fairly well, as he knows pretty much everyone in America, and he has served as an intermediary between myself and the mob boss before.

"You mind telling me why? 'Cause he's gonna want to know."

"Just tell him it's about Quintana. That's all I can tell you right now."

"I'll get back to you." A click indicates the call is over; Vince never says goodbye.

My first witness today is Donald Richards, a private investigator whose main client is the National Football League. Walter Simmons had put me in touch with him. I take Richards through the way he works for the NFL, leading him into a discussion of the great lengths they go to in protecting the integrity of their game.

"What kinds of things does the NFL worry about?" I ask.

"Gambling is number one. Drugs are a close second."

He describes the drug testing program, which is not as rigorous as it could be, but substantially more intrusive than those for the other major sports. The NFL, he explains, has comparatively good relations with the players' union, and therefore the players will submit to testing that the baseball players, for example, will not.

"Was Troy Preston one of the people you were hired to investigate?'

He nods. "Yes. On three separate occasions."

He goes on to explain that Preston had failed a drug test,

which is a red flag for the NFL. Richards was assigned to find out the extent of Preston's involvement with drugs, and based on his initial reports, follow-ups were deemed necessary.

"Why is that?" I ask.

"Because I learned that Mr. Preston was not just using . . . he was selling."

I ask Richards to provide the details of his investigation, and he doesn't hesitate to implicate the deceased Paul Moreno and the unfortunately very alive Cesar Quintana. It's a weird sensation that I feel while he is doing this, knowing that Quintana will freak out and redouble his efforts to kill me when he finds out that I have once again exposed his name to unwanted worldwide publicity.

Richards is on the stand all morning, and his performance is impressive. I make a note to mention him to Laurie, in case we want to add him to our team on future cases. It hits me that Laurie may well not be on that team, the first time I've thought about that possibility in a while. This has been a difficult and frustrating case, but if nothing else, it has served its purpose as a diversion from my personal concerns.

Judge Harrison cancels the afternoon session because of some other matters that he has to attend to, so Dylan's cross-examination of Richards will be put off to Monday. I call and ask Sam to come to the house at three to report on what he's learned, and I tell Kevin and Laurie to be there as well. Willie Miller joins us, along with his dog, Cash. Willie has been hanging around as part of my "security detail," and it does make me feel more secure, though I would never admit it.

Sam starts off with an apology that he hasn't made more progress, but he's only had a handful of hours to work on it. Sam has learned that Adam was apparently focusing on something involving the media; he was trying to locate a Web site for a magazine called *Inside Football,* which hasn't existed for a number of years. He also placed three phone calls to the *New York Times* in the thirty-six hours before he died.

"Any other significant calls?" I ask.

He shakes his head. "No, doesn't seem to be. Mostly to players Kenny knew . . . families of the deceased guys . . . that kind of thing."

"Any idea why he would be interested in a sports magazine and the *New York Times?*" Kevin asks me.

"No . . . but Adam's parents mentioned that he was excited about talking to famous sportswriters. I thought they meant football players, but I didn't question them about it. Maybe they were right."

I call Vince, whose connections would make him the ultimate authority in matters of this type. He's not in, and I leave a message for him to call me back ASAP. In the meantime Laurie brings us up-to-date on what she has learned.

None of the deaths were considered possible homicides by the various police entities that investigated, which we already knew. However, Laurie has checked into four of them so far, and when viewed through the prism that we now hold, they could look quite suspicious. As examples, she cites the hit-and-run and Matt Lane's hunting accident. The five heart attacks are bewildering, and I ask Laurie to check with a doctor, one we sometimes use as an expert witness, about whether there is a drug that can cause a heart attack and not show up in an autopsy.

Vince calls back within a few minutes and sounds annoyed. "I told you I'd call you back when I set up the meeting," he says.

"That's not why I'm calling," I say.

"Jesus, what the hell do you need now?"

"Vince, I'm going to ask you a question. I just want you to answer it and not assume it's important to the Schilling case. I don't want you to start tracking it down as a possible hot story."

"Then you must be trying to reach a different Vince," he says.

"You'll get whatever I have first. But this can't go public in any way now."

He thinks for a moment. "Okay."

"Did you ever hear of a magazine called *Inside Football?*" I ask.

"Sounds familiar, but I can't place it."

"It's a magazine that's folded. I need a list of the people that wrote for it in the last ten years and copies of any stories that included Kenny Schilling or Troy Preston." I have a hunch and decide to throw it in. "I also want to know if any of the writers are currently at the *New York Times.*"

"That's all?" he asks.

"That's all."

"Give me two hours," he says.

"You're a genius."

"No shit, Sherlock."

Vince then proceeds to use up five minutes of the two hours making me swear repeatedly that he will get whatever story comes out of his labor, as well as any story that doesn't. I'm happy to do so. Vince's contacts are amazing, and if I'm going to need to learn anything in the media world, he is a person who can absolutely make it happen.

Two hours gives me just enough time to take Tara for a short tennis ball session in the park, as long as I drive there. I haven't thrown a ball with Tara in a while, but one of her twelve million great qualities is that she doesn't hold a grudge. Willie and Cash join us, which is fine with me: Though Tara doesn't have many dog friends, she has always liked Cash.

Cash is the more competitive of the two dogs; it's very important to him that he retrieve each thrown ball. Tara is more out for the fun of the game, though I toss the ball in her direction often enough that she gets her share.

Willie lets me do the throwing, and I note that his eyes are constantly sweeping the park, probably looking for one of Quintana's people. I'm just about to suggest that we leave when I hear Willie say, "Andy, get the dogs and get in the car."

We are near the Little League fields, and I see Willie looking off in the direction of what we called Dead Man's Curve when we rode bikes down it as kids. It's about three hundred yards away, and I can see a dark sedan navigating the curve, which will eventually lead to where we are. It is a classically ominous-looking car.

I don't pause to ask questions, yelling for Tara and Cash to follow me. All three of us are in the backseat within seconds, and Willie follows along right behind us and gets in the driver's seat. He pulls out, quickly but without screeching the tires, and in moments we're driving in the security and anonymity of Route 4.

"Was that who I think it was?" I ask.

Willie looks at me in the rearview mirror and shrugs. "Don't know. But I didn't think we should wait around to find out."

"I can't run away every time I see a car," I say.

"What are you gonna do, stay and fight?" he asks. "They've got Uzis, you've got a tennis ball."

This is no way to live.

• • • • •

THE PHONE IS RINGING as I walk
into the house.

"You want me to fax you the articles?" is Vince's re-
placement for a normal person's "Hello."

"Fax them."

"I'll include the list of writers, but only one of them
works for the *Times*."

"What's his name?"

"George Karas."

George Karas has, over the last few years, become one
of the more well-known sportswriters in the business. He's
done this, as have others, by branching out past writing into
television, becoming one of the pundits that are called on to
give opinions about the games men play.

Karas would therefore certainly qualify as a "famous"
sportswriter, someone Adam might well have bragged to his
parents that he had spoken to. It gives me more hope that
we're on the right track.

"How do I get to him?" I ask.

"He's waiting for your call," Vince says, and gives me Karas's direct phone number.

"Vince, this is great. I owe you big-time," I say.

"You got that right. That reminds me, I set up the meeting with Petrone."

"For when?"

"Eight o'clock tomorrow night. They'll pick you up in front of your office."

"Thanks, Vince. I really appreciate all of this."

Click.

Since Vince is no longer on the phone, I hang up my end and call Karas at the number Vince gave me, which turns out to be his cell phone. We're only ten seconds into our conversation when I catch another break: He's on his way home to Fort Lee and offers to meet me for a cup of coffee.

We meet at a diner on Route 4 in Paramus, and Karas is waiting at a table when I arrive. I recognize him because I watch all those idiotic sports panel shows that he's on. I introduce myself, then say, "I really appreciate your meeting me like this."

"Vince told me he'd cut my balls off if I didn't talk to you," he says.

"He's a fun guy, isn't he?"

He nods. "A barrel of laughs. Does this meeting have something to do with the Schilling case? Vince wouldn't tell me."

His question is a little jarring on a personal note. I keep forgetting that the Schilling case, more than ever before, has at least made me nationally recognizable, if not a celebrity. The truth is that more people in this diner would know who I am than the "famous" sportswriter I'm having coffee with.

"It may. It depends on what you have to say. But I have to tell you that this is on background . . . off the record."

He's surprised by that. "Am I here as a journalist?"

"Partly," I say. "But I need assurance that you won't use it as a journalist, at least for the time being."

He thinks for a few moments, then reluctantly nods. "Okay. Shoot."

"A man that was working for me as an investigator was murdered last week. His name was Adam Strickland. Did he contact you around that time?"

Karas's face clouds slightly as he searches for a connection to the name. It's disappointing, but that disappointment fades when I see the light go on in his eyes. "Yes . . . I think that was the name. My God, that was the young man that was murdered in your office?"

"Yes. You spoke to him?"

Karas is quiet for a few moments, either trying to remember the conversation or trying to deal with this close brush with someone's sudden death. "He didn't tell me he was working for you . . . he just said he was a private investigator. I assumed he was working for some tabloid rag . . ."

"Can you tell me specifically what he asked you?"

"He was interested in the days when I did some freelance work for a magazine called *Inside Football*. I put together a high school all-American team, and we ran it as a large spread."

"Is that the team that Kenny Schilling and Troy Preston were on?"

He nods. "Yes. That's what he was asking me about."

"What specifically did you tell him?"

He shrugs. "Really not much. I told him that we picked players from all over the country. It's not an exact science;

these are high school kids, playing against all different levels of competition. We looked at their size, their stats, how hard the big-time colleges were recruiting them, that kind of thing."

I nod; as a sports degenerate I know something about this stuff. Great high school basketball players are far easier to spot than their football counterparts. Kids that stand out in football in high school often can't even cut it on the college level.

"Did he ask you for a list of players that were there?"

He nods. "Yeah, I wasn't going to go to the trouble of finding it, but he seemed like a decent guy . . ."

"He was a very decent guy," I say.

"I could tell. Anyway, I keep good files, so I faxed it to him."

I'm now close to positive that we're on to something. The list was faxed to Adam, it was important to Adam, but it was nowhere to be found in his possessions. The killer almost certainly took it, and I don't know any drug gang killers that like football quite that much.

Karas tells me about the weekend the players spent in New York, and I ask him if he can recall anything unusual about it, especially anything concerning Schilling or Preston, but he cannot.

"I wasn't a chaperone, you know? There were around twenty-five guys, and most of them had never been to New York, so they weren't too interested in me telling them stories."

He thinks some more, then adds, "We rented out the two upstairs private rooms in an Italian restaurant that Saturday night. I think it was on the Upper East Side. Divided it up, offense in one room, defense in the other. I must have been with the offense, because I remember Schilling being there."

He has nothing more to add, so he asks me a few questions about what this is about and how it relates to the trial.
I deflect them, but promise he'll be the second to know,
after Vince. Knowing Vince as he does, he understands.

I thank him for his help, and we both leave. He promises to fax me the list tonight, and I tell him the earlier the
better.

That list could answer a lot of questions—and raise new
ones. We're getting somewhere; I can feel it.

I go home and tell Laurie what I've learned, and I can
see the excitement in her face as she hears it. It's not the
look of a woman who wants to go to Findlay and plan a
schedule for the school crossing guards, but I don't say anything like that. I don't want to blow it.

Laurie and I spend the next hour and a half watching the
fax machine not ring. I take advantage of the time to think
about the trial, which is weirdly running on a parallel track.
When we learn more about the mysterious deaths, I'm going
to have to find a way to bring those two tracks together.
That's not going to be easy.

The fax machine finally rings, and it seems as if it takes
a little over a week for the paper to come crawling out. It
turns out there are two pages, and the first is a note from
Karas. He writes that he's just remembered that at the Saturday night party the offensive players asked him to leave the
room for a brief time. They said they were going to have a
"team meeting." He considered that a weird thing to request
and feared that they had brought some drugs that they were
going to use once he left. Not too long later they invited him
back in, and to his relief he saw no evidence of drug use.

The second faxed page is the list of high school players
who were brought to New York that weekend. Laurie and I

compare it to the names of the deceased young men, and we make a stunning discovery.

Seven of the eight who died were members of the offense, the same group that included Kenny Schilling and Troy Preston. The same group that asked George Karas to leave the room so that they could have a team meeting.

Kenny Schilling was close enough geographically to have killed each of those people, though they were spread out across the country. Kenny played professionally, and he traveled extensively, and those young men died at times when Kenny was nearby. Darryl Anderson, the Asbury Park drowning victim, is not on the list.

But there is another name on that list, and if Kenny was there, he was there as well. I've been viewing him as a victim, and there's still a good chance of that, but I've just adjusted my view.

I am talking about Bobby Pollard, high school all-American, Giants trainer, friend of Kenny's.

Possible victim, possible serial killer.

• • • • •

MY CLIENT IS INNOCENT. I am al-

most positive of that now. It would be nice if I had known it sooner, since I might have been able to develop an effective strategy to defend him. A secondary but significant benefit would be that Cesar Quintana would not be hell-bent on killing me.

There are a few questions that need to be resolved before I can include Bobby Pollard on my list of legitimate suspects. The primary one is his injury: I'm not sure he is really paralyzed. If I'm wrong about that, I'm wrong about his possible guilt, because there's no way he could have committed these murders without mobility.

The key factor that applies to both Bobby and Kenny, the one that leads me to suspect Bobby, is their availability. Most of these deaths occurred while the Giants were in a nearby town for a game. Players are pretty busy during those trips, and I'm not sure they would have the time to plan and execute these camouflaged killings. I assume that trainers also have serious constraints on their time, but I'll have to check that out. But if Kenny was in the town, Bobby was there as well.

I call Kevin and Sam, give them each some assignments, and ask them to come over tomorrow at noon. I'll be spending the morning at the jail, talking to Kenny.

I have a tough time sleeping tonight. There is so much to be done, and we have very little time and no real idea how to proceed. That's not a great combination.

I'm up early and leave for the jail by eight-thirty. Willie arrives just before I go, for the purpose of accompanying me. He seems to be relishing the role of bodyguard, and that's fine with me because my concern about Quintana is pretty much with me twenty-four hours a day.

We're at the jail by nine o'clock, and though I don't offer Willie the option of going inside with me, he makes it a point to decline just in case. Willie spent a lot of years in prison and is not about to enter one again, even if he's free to leave.

Kenny thinks I'm there to discuss the possibility of him testifying. It's something he has expressed a desire to do, but until now I've put off the discussion as premature. That hasn't changed.

"That's not what I want to talk about," I say. "Something important has come up."

If a person can look hopeful and cringe at the same time, Kenny pulls it off. He doesn't know whether this is going to be good or bad news, but he instinctively knows it will be important. "Talk to me," he says.

"I want you to think back to your senior year in high school, when that magazine made you an all-American and brought you to New York for the weekend."

He nods. "That's where I met Troy. I told you that."

"Can you think of anything unusual, memorable, that happened on that weekend?"

He thinks for a moment, then shakes his head and smiles. "Not unless you call drinking beer unusual."

"I'm thinking a little more unusual than that."

"Then I can't think of anything," he says.

"On that Saturday night you went to a restaurant with the rest of the players. There was a sportswriter there, and you and the other members of the offense asked him to leave the room so you could have a team meeting. Do you remember that?"

Again he thinks for a while, searching his memory. That weekend seems not to be something that he has thought about in a long time and maybe never was terribly significant in his life. I'm finding I believe his reactions, now that I believe in his innocence. It's a feeling of substantial relief.

"It definitely rings a bell. Let me think about it for a minute," he says.

"Take your time."

He does, and after a short while he smiles slightly and nods. "I remember . . . we had it all figured out. We knew some of us would make it big in the pros someday and that some wouldn't. Nobody thought they'd be the ones not to make it, but with injuries and stuff you never know."

"Right," I say, hoping to move him along.

"So we decided that the ones who did make it would get these huge bonuses, and we all agreed that they would take care of the guys who didn't. Like an insurance policy."

"So it was a pact?" I ask.

He grins. "Yeah. I told you we had a lot of beer."

"This pact . . . is that why you've taken care of Bobby Pollard all these years? Gotten him a job as your trainer?"

He shakes his head. "Of course not. I hadn't even remembered about that high school thing until you just asked. Bobby's a friend . . . and everything he dreamed about fell apart. So I helped him. But it wasn't charity, you know? He's a damn good trainer."

"Could anyone in that room have taken that pact seriously? Could Bobby?"

His head shake is firm. "No way . . . once the beer wore off . . . no way. Come on . . . we were kids. Why are you asking me this stuff?"

"Remember those guys I asked you about . . . the ones that had died? They were all there that night. They were all members of the offense on the *Inside Football* high school all-American team." I take out the list and show it to him, along with the list of the deceased.

"Goddamn," he says, and then he says it again, and again. "You're sure about this?"

I nod. "And I'm also sure that you were in the general area at the time of each death. You and Bobby Pollard." I'm not yet positive that what I'm saying about Pollard is true, but I have no doubt that the facts will come out that way.

"You think Bobby killed these people?" he asks.

"Somebody did, and he's as good a bet as any. And he may have killed a young man who was working for me as well, when that young man discovered the truth."

"It just doesn't seem possible. Why would he kill them? Because they didn't give him part of their bonuses? Some of these guys didn't even get drafted by the NFL."

It's a good point, and one of the things I'm going to have to figure out. "How good a player was Bobby?" I ask.

"He was okay . . . not as good as he thought. He wasn't real quick, but in high school he was bigger than the guys he was playing against. In college, and especially the pros, everybody is big. So you gotta be fast."

"So Bobby wouldn't have made it in the NFL if he hadn't gotten hurt?"

"Nah. He wouldn't even have been that good in college. But he'd never admit that, and don't tell him I said it."

Kenny asks me what effect my theory will have on his trial and is not happy when I tell him that right now I haven't decided how to handle it. What I don't tell him is that his life will depend on my making the right decision.

Willie and I head back home, where Laurie, Kevin, and Sam are waiting for me. Sam has spent the night and morning performing more miracles on the computer and has already placed Pollard geographically within range of the murders.

"And I'm gonna get the medical records," he says with a smile.

"When will you have them?" I ask.

"As soon as you let me get the hell out of here."

"Can't you do it from here? Adam got killed for doing just what you're doing."

He shakes his head. "Adam got killed because he called Pollard and must have mistakenly alerted him to what was going on. At the time, he probably didn't realize Pollard was the killer, but Pollard must have known he'd figure it out soon. I won't make the same mistake."

"Come on, Sam, you're going way too fast. We're not nearly that sure that Pollard is our guy."

Sam just smiles. "No harm, no foul."

He knows I'll understand his cryptic comment, and I do. It's a basketball phrase, which when twisted into this situation means that if we pursue this strategy and come up empty, what have we lost? We might as well go for it full out and see what happens. He's right.

"Okay, but can't you do all this on *my* computer?"

He snorts. "You call that thing you have a computer? You want this to take forever?"

I don't, so I let Sam leave. Kevin then brings me up-to-date on our legal situation and the few precedents that deal with the kind of predicament we are in.

None of what we are doing has in any fashion been introduced into the trial. The judge, jury, and prosecution all have no idea that Troy Preston's murder is one in a series or that Bobby Pollard is a suspect. All we have done as a defense is try to poke holes in the prosecution's case and shift suspicion onto Troy's drug connections.

What we have learned would be a bomb detonating in the courtroom, and we have to figure out how to minimize the damage our client might suffer in the explosion. After all, we could be setting up Kenny as a serial killer. Right now our only credible reason for thinking the killer is Pollard, rather than Kenny, is the fact that the imprisoned Kenny could not have killed Adam. It is possible that Quintana really did kill Adam, thinking he was me. Perhaps Adam just placed his notes in a location that the police haven't uncovered. I don't believe that scenario, but it's only important what Judge Harrison and the jury believe.

An even more immediate problem is how to get all this admitted in the first place. There is a very real possibility that Judge Harrison won't let it in. We can't even prove that the other deaths were murders; in each case the police say otherwise. Harrison could rule that none of this is relevant, and there's not an appeals court in the free world that would overturn him.

Laurie has learned from the doctor that a drug form of potassium not only can cause heart attacks when administered in an overdose but would be undetectable in an autopsy unless the coroner had a specific reason to screen for potassium poisoning. The reason it's so hard to find is that once death occurs, cells in the body break down and release potassium on their own. Potassium as an agent of homicide is very unlikely to be discovered by a coroner, especially in small-town jurisdictions.

This news points even more directly at Pollard, since as a team trainer he has substantial contact with the medical staff and the drugs that they use. He would also have access to their prescription pads.

I have a four o'clock meeting with Pollard, which had been planned to discuss his potential testimony, scheduled for sometime this week. I don't want to cancel it because I don't want to give him the slightest hint that there is anything unusual going on.

Laurie wants to come with me, no doubt because she remembers all too well what happened to Adam. I decide to go alone, for the same reason I didn't want to cancel the meeting. I don't want Bobby Pollard to have the slightest inkling that there are new developments.

We meet at the Pollards', in deference to his difficulty in getting around. I'm growing increasingly suspicious of that difficulty, but I'm not about to reveal that suspicion.

Teri Pollard greets me as warmly as she did the first time I was at their house, and I accept lemonade and home-baked cookies from the myriad of refreshments that she offers me. I can't help feeling sorry for her; she has devoted her life to Bobby Pollard, and if I'm right, and successful, it's all going to come crashing down on her.

Having been a reluctant witness herself in Dylan's case, Teri asks if I mind if she sits in on my meeting with Bobby. I tell her that's fine, and she brings me into the den, where Bobby waits in his wheelchair. I start my conversation with either Bobby Pollard an innocent paraplegic or Bobby Pollard an injury-faking serial killer.

I don't want to lie to him at this point, so I'm careful in how I phrase my comments and questions. "Character witnesses don't generally add to the facts of the case, but simply offer their high opinions of the defendant. I assume your view would be that Kenny Schilling is not the type of man that would commit murder?"

He nods. "Absolutely. I know him better than anyone."

We go through these platitudes for about ten minutes, at which point I switch to questions that Dylan might ask him, so as to prepare him. I don't make the questions too difficult, since Dylan would have no reason to attack him.

Once we're finished, we chat in more general terms about football and the Giants' prospects without Kenny. His hope is to have Kenny back in a couple of weeks, which would be ample time for a play-off run.

I tell Bobby that I'll give him at least twenty-four hours' notice before he testifies. I leave out the part about ripping him apart on the stand and about making sure he spends the rest of his life in a seven-by-ten-foot cell. There'll be time to tell him that later.

I head home and prepare for my meeting with Dominic Petrone. His people pick me up at eight P.M. sharp. Except for shrinks, mobsters are the most punctual people I know. The driver tells me to sit in the passenger seat, and I notice when I do that his partner is stationed directly behind me. I feel like Paulie being driven by Clemenza into the city to find apartments where the button men can go to the "mattresses." This driver doesn't have any cannoli, but if he pulls over to get out and take a piss, I'm outta here.

They drive me to the back entrance of Vico's, an Italian

restaurant in Totowa. It has always been considered a mob hangout, a rumor that I can now officially confirm.

The driver tells me to walk in through the back door, which I do. I'm met by an enormous man who frisks me and brings me into a private room where Dominic Petrone is waiting.

Petrone is a rather charming man, early sixties, salt-and-pepper hair, with a dignified manner that one would expect of a successful head of a large business. He's a typical CEO of a company where the "E" stands for "executions." He greets me graciously, as he might an old but not terribly close friend, and suggests I sit down. I find it a smart thing to do what Petrone suggests, so I take a seat opposite him.

The table is set for dinner for one, and in fact Petrone is already eating his bruschetta appetizer. I've got a hunch I'm not invited for dinner. "What can I do for you?" he asks.

"I may be able to give you Cesar Quintana," I say.

"Give him to me for what purpose?"

"That's up to you," I say. "Whatever you decide, all that I care about is that he no longer wants to kill me."

"You say you 'may' be able to give him to me?"

I nod. "I'm pretty sure I can, but I haven't decided yet if I want to. I won't know that until I'm in the moment."

I proceed to tell him my plan, the bottom line being that I will place a call to him if I'm going to give him Quintana. If I do, he'll have to be ready to move immediately, though I'm not yet telling him where this will take place.

He nods, as if it all makes perfect sense, though I'm sure he considers this the most ridiculous plan he's ever heard. It's also got to be, from his perspective, almost too good to be true. "Is there something else you want from me, something you haven't yet mentioned?"

"Just one thing," I say. "Can you cash a check?"

• • • • •

TODAY MIGHT BE the weirdest midtrial Sunday I've ever spent. I have witnesses scheduled for to-morrow, but they're part of a strategy that I've decided to abandon, so there's no reason for me to call them.

All I can do is wait to see if Sam can come up with enough information to make my new strategy viable, and if he does, I'll have to figure out how to convince Judge Harrison to let me use it.

The first thing I do is call Willie Miller and tell him that Petrone has agreed to my terms and that he should tell Marcus to move forward on our plan. I haven't brought Laurie into this operation because it's both dangerous and illegal. She would try to stop me, or perhaps get involved herself, and neither of those options is acceptable to me.

With that call accomplished, I have to fill the rest of the day. I would take Tara out for a long walk, to clear my head and enjoy the autumn air, except for the fact that a Mexican drug lord is sworn to kill me. I'm trying to deal with that, but for now the idea of bullets flying through that autumn air puts a damper on things.

With no other viable alternatives, I am forced to sit with Tara and watch NFL football all day. I have seen less football so far this season than in any other in recent memory, and I can't make up for that in one day, but I'm going to try.

The Giants game is particularly interesting to me. On the field their running game looks as if it's mired in quicksand, and on the sidelines I catch occasional glimpses of Bobby Pollard, taping ankles and generally performing his job as trainer. If I do my job right, both the on- and off-field situations are about to change dramatically.

Laurie plays her "little woman" role perfectly, bringing Tara and me whatever chips, beer, biscuits, and water we might need. I haven't thought about Laurie leaving in a while, and when I do, it is with increasing confidence that she won't. How could she give up this much fun?

Sam and Kevin come over at seven. Sam has tracked down some of Pollard's medical records and vows he will get the rest. The fact that some of it originated in Europe makes things a little more complicated, but Sam has total confidence.

Kevin and I kick around our legal strategy to introduce this new slant on matters. The decision will completely rest with Judge Harrison, and Dylan will be crazed by the prospect of it. We agree that we will ask for a meeting in chambers before the start of court tomorrow, and we'll take our best shot.

I wake up early and call Rita Gordon, the court clerk, and tell her of our desire to hold the meeting in the judge's chambers, thereby delaying the start of court. I tell Rita that it is an urgent matter, because I want the judge to fully expect to be dealing with a very important issue.

Kevin and I arrive before Dylan, and we informally chat with the judge for the five minutes until he does. We are prohibited from talking about the case, and because of the occupation of the defendant, we can't even do what would come naturally and talk about football.

When Dylan does arrive, I get right to it. "Judge Harrison," I say, "there has been a very significant new development which causes us to ask for a continuance."

Continuances are not something Judge Harrison willingly dispenses, and he peers down his glasses at me. "I would suggest you'll have to be slightly more specific than that" is his understatement.

I want to dole out as little information as possible, but I'm fully aware that I'm going to have to be forthcoming. I tell him about the high school all-American weekend and the fact that the majority of the young men on the offensive team have died.

His interest is obviously piqued. "They were murdered?"

"The police in those jurisdictions did not think so, but I believe that since there was no way they could have been aware of the connections, they came to the wrong conclusion."

"Why couldn't they have made the connections? You did."

I nod. "That's because we were looking for it, and we were still lucky to find it. The police in these areas couldn't have known where to look. These young men for the most part did not know each other, and the all-American team for this magazine was obscure. Besides, many publications pick all-American teams; there would have been no reason to focus on this one."

"And your client has an alibi for these other deaths?" he asks.

"At this point he does not, Your Honor. In fact, he was geographically close enough to each one to have committed them."

Judge Harrison interrupts. "Let me see if I understand this. You are abandoning your view that the murder in this case was drug-related, and you have developed a new strategy, which is to tell the jury that while your client is on trial for one murder, he may well be a serial killer?"

I'm nervous as hell, but I can't help smiling at how he puts it. "You find that unconventional, Your Honor?"

"That's not quite the word I would use."

"Your Honor, in the interests of justice, I want the jury to see the entire truth. I believe that this truth will also enable me to create a reasonable doubt as to my client's guilt."

Harrison turns to Dylan, who seems stunned by the direction this session has taken. "Mr. Campbell?"

Dylan is in a quandary. On the one hand, he would be thrilled to see the specter of Quintana and drugs out of the picture; on the other hand, he totally doesn't trust me. This seems perfect for him, but he's smart enough to know that if I want something, he shouldn't.

Conflicted as he is, he decides on the one surefire approach: No matter what I want to do, he doesn't want to give me the time to do it. "Your Honor, Mr. Carpenter is entitled to present whatever defense he wishes, but I see no reason for the trial to be delayed so that he can go on a fishing expedition to support a new strategy. Having said that, I assume his new witnesses would not be on the current witness list. Therefore, the state would reserve the right to request our own continuance, should we need time to prepare for our cross-examinations."

Harrison turns to me. "How long a continuance are you requesting?"

Earlier in this session I used the words "in the interests of justice" because Judge Harrison is obliged to rule according to those interests, even if those rulings aren't necessarily based on accepted court procedure. In a death penalty case the "interests of justice" principle becomes even more crucial. "To properly further the interests of justice, Your Honor, I would request one week."

Dylan almost chokes. "Your Honor, we have a jury out there, and—"

Harrison cuts him off. "The trial is continued for two days. Court will resume at nine o'clock on Wednesday."

I'm a little disappointed in the ruling; I was hoping for three days. But it should be enough time if we don't waste any of it. I ask Judge Harrison to seal this proceeding for the time being, and for him to order that neither Dylan nor I reveal the substance of it, at least for now. Dylan argues, but I throw in another "interests of justice" argument, and Harrison agrees.

I head to a meeting in my office to finalize our plans, and if the radio news reports I hear on the way are a true indication, the media are going crazy over the just announced continuance. All that Judge Harrison has revealed is that it was requested by the defense, and as I near my office, I can see the media hordes outside waiting for me.

I call ahead and switch the meeting to my house, since I can more easily get in and out without having to deal with the press. They are there in force, but I come in the back way and then hold a thirty-second press conference on the porch.

"As you know, Judge Harrison has issued a gag order," I say. "Gagged people by definition have no comment."

Not being gagged themselves, reporters continue to bombard me with questions, but I briefly and disingenuously profess frustration at not being able to answer, and head back inside. Before long Kevin, Laurie, Sam, and Willie have made it through and join me in the den.

Willie calls me aside and tells me that Marcus has set things up as scheduled, and it gives me a pit in my stomach the size of Norway. To put it out of my mind and focus on the matter at hand takes a mental discipline that I'm not sure I have.

I can feel the different dynamic in this meeting compared to our previous ones. Until now we've been floundering, unsure where to go and how to get there. Now we have a viable plan, and our task is simply to execute it.

Kevin and I go over the meetings we need to have tomorrow with our witnesses, and Sam reassures me that he has recruited a friend highly competent and capable of setting our trap for Pollard.

To that end I call the Pollards, and Teri answers. I ask her to have Bobby pick up the other line. Laurie, Kevin, and Sam sit silently in the room as I wait, knowing that this conversation must go well for us to have a chance.

Bobby picks up, and I tell him that he is to testify Wednesday, though I'm not sure at what time. I'll want him at the courthouse at nine A.M.

"No problem," he says. "How come the trial was delayed?"

"The judge won't let us talk about it, but it's nothing for you to be concerned about," I lie. "Your testimony will go forward as scheduled."

"It's nothing bad for Kenny?" Teri asks.

"Definitely not. It could even turn out to be good."

"Great," she says.

I take a deep breath; here comes the hard part. "Teri, with the way the media are all over everything that happens, this trial is as much about public relations as anything else. Maybe more."

"I couldn't agree more," she says. "The things they say about Kenny, it makes my blood boil."

"Me too," I say. "That's why I want you in a TV studio on Wednesday doing interviews when Bobby finishes testifying. The other side is going to have people out there saying Bobby is wrong; we need you saying he's right."

"Whatever you need, but I was hoping to be there to support Bobby."

I hate manipulating her, but I have no choice. I can't have her at the courthouse, able to tell Bobby about the witnesses preceding his own testimony. "I'm sure Bobby wants you where you can most help Kenny. Isn't that right, Bobby?"

"Absolutely," he says, and she agrees.

"Bobby, do you need me to send someone to pick you up, or can you make it to court by yourself? I can get you through the back entrance, so you won't have to go through any of the crowds."

"I can drive," he says, and the trap is set.

● ● ● ● ●

HINCHLIFFE STADIUM is an impressive relic, a former minor-league football and baseball stadium that sits overlooking the Passaic Falls. If I remember my Paterson history correctly, these falls, third largest in the country, were discovered by either Alexander Hamilton or George Hamilton.

The stadium now goes unused and is often rumored to be coming down. The old boy is about to have some excitement tonight. I'm standing near what used to be home plate, holding a briefcase and waiting. Within twenty minutes the shit might well be hitting the fan.

I thought I had planned for all eventualities, yet I now realize I should have planned for the fact that there would be no lights here. Fortunately, it is a clear night, and there is a substantial amount of moonlight. Visibility will not be a big problem. But what else have I forgotten?

I look at my watch and see that it's ten P.M. I know what is happening at this moment. Marcus is picking up Quintana at a designated meeting place. He will determine to his satisfaction that Quintana is not armed, and they will start driving here to see me. Quintana does not know where I am, and he has promised to come alone.

Willie Miller is nearby in his own car. He is watching to see if any of Quintana's men follow Marcus's car. If they do not, all is fine. If they do, then Quintana is breaking our pact and planning to kill me.

In my briefcase is four hundred thousand dollars in cash. It is much lighter and takes up much less space than I expected. But it is a great deal of money, and it represents an amount I am willing to put at risk to ease my conscience and not feel like a murderer.

The message was sent to Quintana that I wanted to see him personally, and I would be willing to provide the four hundred thousand he lost the night Troy Preston was killed. If he comes alone and promises not to come after me anymore, he can have the money and our relationship comes to a less-than-poignant end. If he tries to take the money and still attempts to kill me, then when I have him killed, I will consider it self-defense.

My cell phone rings, and in the empty stadium it sounds like about two million decibels. I answer with "Yes?" and hear Willie's voice on the other end. "They're being followed," he says.

"Are you sure?" I ask, though I know the answer.

"I'm sure," Willie says.

I hang up the phone and call a number Petrone had given me. His designated person answers it, and I say, "Hinchliffe Stadium."

His answer is a simple "We'll be there."

The next twenty-five minutes are the longest I have ever spent. Finally, I hear Marcus and Quintana coming from under the stands, walking toward me.

Quintana is tall and fairly well built, though standing

next to Marcus, he looks like a toothpick seedling. He has a sneer on his face, probably perpetually, and it tells me that he believes he is in control. He's not.

The first thing Quintana says is, "Show me the money." Despite the seriousness of the moment, it strikes me as funny, as if Quintana is playing the movie version of the song-talking that Sam Willis does.

I'm tempted to respond, "I'll make you an offer you can't refuse," but instead, I open the briefcase and show it to him.

"Did you come alone?" I ask.

"Yeah." This guy is not much of a conversationalist.

"So you'll take this money and we're even?" I ask. "You won't come after me anymore?"

"That's what I said."

I know he's lying, but I hand him the briefcase. He puts it under his arm and yells out something in Spanish, to the men he knows are outside the stadium. I am not supposed to know that those men are there and that their function will be to come in and kill Marcus and me. Marcus just watches all this impassively, betraying almost no interest at all.

Suddenly, there is the sound of gunfire, the noise rattling the old stadium. Quintana reacts with surprise and concern, looking around to see what could be happening.

"You lied to me," I say, my voice cracking slightly with nervousness. "Your men followed you so that you could have me killed. I called for some support, which was purely an act of self-defense. I'm sorry it worked out this way, but you left me no choice."

Off to our left, Petrone's men are entering the stadium. Quintana displays amazing quickness for a man his size, and I display amazing stupidity for a man any size. He grabs me before I can get out of the way and holds me in front of him so that my body is between him and the advancing gunmen.

I'm gripped by panic; I can't imagine Petrone's men backing off simply because their bullets will have to pass through my body to get to Quintana. I have no doubt that Petrone has warned them that Quintana is not to escape alive, and even less doubt that they would not be willing to go back and say, "Sorry, Godfather, but we didn't kill him. The lawyer was in the way."

Suddenly, a sequoia tree in the form of Marcus's forearm lands on Quintana's head. He goes down as if shot, and I get a quick and nauseating glimpse of the crushed side of his head and face.

Marcus picks up the briefcase and hands it to me. "Let's go," he says, and we walk past Petrone's men and out of the stadium, leaving them to attend to Quintana. Based on how he looked, and how hard Marcus hit him, they will not need their guns.

All they'll need is a shovel.

• • • • •

JUDGE HARRISON calls court to order at nine A.M. sharp. He's usually a few minutes late, but it's as if this time he's showing his determination not to allow the continuance to go on one minute longer than he had authorized.

I'm still more than a little shaken by last night. It did not have to result in any killing; Quintana could have walked off with the money. And as it played out, I can justify in my mind that it was self-defense; had I not called Petrone's people, I would have been killed myself.

But the truth is that I set a process in motion knowing it could result in Quintana's murder. Had I not done that, he would still be alive, as unpleasant as that might be for me. I'm compounding that by not revealing to the police what I know about the murders that took place at the stadium last night. As an officer of the court this has not been my finest moment.

There is no mention of those murders in the media, and Petrone may have chosen to keep them secret. It's okay with me.

Things leading up to this crucial court day have progressed as well as I could have hoped. Pollard is in an anteroom with Kevin, ostensibly to discuss his testimony, but really to keep him from hearing anything about the witnesses before him. Laurie is with Teri at a TV studio that we have rented, though she is not likely to want to do any interviews after she discovers what happened to her husband. Laurie feels as guilty about this part of it as I do, but there was no other way to handle it. We simply could not have her drive Bobby to the hearing.

I will need to get the witnesses that precede Pollard on and off in a hurry, to reduce any chance that he will get wind of what is going on. My first witness is George Karas, whom I need to set the scene. I have him testify as to the facts surrounding the high school all-American weekend. I submit the subsequent death certificates of the various athletes as evidence, so as to support him.

Dylan has little to do with him on cross-examination, since the facts testified to are indisputable. Additionally, Dylan has no idea where I'm going with this, so he doesn't want to inadvertently help me. The safest and correct thing for him to do is say very little for now, which is what he does.

Next up is Simon Barkley, a retired vice president at Hamilton Life Insurance, who ran that company's actuarial department for seventeen years. He is also a part-time mathematics professor at Fairleigh Dickinson University in Teaneck, where he teaches a course in mathematical probabilities.

Once I quickly have his credentials established, I go right to the heart of his testimony. "Professor Barkley, did we meet at my home yesterday?"

"Yes."

"Did I give you the information that Mr. Karas just gave this jury concerning the deaths of these eight young football players?"

"Yes, you did."

"What did I ask you to do?" I ask.

"To calculate the probability that these deaths could have been coincidental; that is to say, they could have happened by chance, without some common factor or cause among them."

"And did you do so?"

"Yes. Would you like to hear my conclusions?"

I smile and spread my arms to include the judge, jury, and gallery. "I think we all would."

"Well, let me say that the key assumption under which I was operating is that these young men had little or no connection to each other in the years after this weekend. For instance, had all eight been riding in the same car and that car plunged off a mountain, clearly the fact that they all died would not be a surprise to anyone. Or if they all belonged to the same army unit and went into battle together, these multiple deaths could be explainable as well. A third such example would be if they were together when exposed to a deadly bacterium."

"I understand," I say.

"Obviously, none of those things, or any circumstances like them, are applicable here."

"So what are the chances that eight out of eleven men of this young age, athletes, would die in the past seven years, without there being a single factor causing all of the deaths?" I press the point. "What are the chances it is just a terrible coincidence?"

"Approximately one in seventy-eight billion."

I hear a gasp from the gallery, and I pause to let the answer sink in. We're talking DNA-like numbers here. "Just so I understand this, are you saying that the chance of these deaths being unrelated, that the members of this all-American team were just the victims of horrible coincidence, is one in seventy-eight billion? Billion with a 'b'?"

He confirms that, and I turn him over to Dylan, who once again has no idea which way he should go. So far I've been setting up evidence of serial killings, and the only suspect in those killings until now is Kenny Schilling. Dylan has no reason or inclination to screw that up.

Once Barkley is off the stand, I ask for a sidebar conference with Judge Harrison and Dylan. As soon as we're out of earshot of everyone, I inform the judge that Bobby Pollard will be called next and that I would like to have him declared as a "hostile" witness. As such I would be able to ask tough, leading questions, as if it were a cross-examination.

"On what grounds?" Harrison asks. "What would prompt his hostility?"

"I'm going to expose him as a fake and possible murderer."

Dylan almost leaps in the air. "Your Honor, I really have to object to this. There has been absolutely no showing made to link Mr. Pollard to these crimes."

Harrison looks at me, and I say, "There's going to be plenty of showing once I get him on the stand, Your Honor."

Harrison has little choice but to grant my request, though he will certainly come down on me if I don't deliver. He allows me to treat Pollard as a hostile witness, though Dylan reiterates his futile objection.

"The defense calls Bobby Pollard," I say, and within moments the door to the courtroom opens. Kevin pushes Pollard's wheelchair to the stand, and Pollard pulls himself up

out of the chair and into the witness chair with his powerful arms.

He looks confident and unworried, which means he has
no idea what has preceded his testimony this morning. I
start off with gentle questions about the background of his
relationship with Kenny, including a brief mention of the all-
star weekend. I then have him describe the nature of his injury and the circumstances in which it took place.

"So you have no use of your legs at all?" I ask.

He nods sadly. "That's correct."

"That's amazing," I say. "Yet you hold a job . . . live a full
life. How do you get around?"

He credits his wife, Teri, with being a big help in that re-
gard, and under prodding describes some of his daily rou-
tine, including his ability to drive a specially equipped car
with hand gas and brake controls.

Since he believes he is here to say good things about
Kenny, I ask questions that let him do so. Once he finishes,
I hand him the list of the offensive players on the high
school all-American team. "Do you recognize these names?"

He looks at them. I'm surprised that he's as cool as he is;
I would have expected the list to make him look worried. "I
know a few of the names. Obviously Kenny and Troy and
myself."

"Are you aware that eight of the people on that list are
dead?"

His head snaps up from the list. "Dead?"

"Dead."

He shakes his head. "No, I didn't . . . I have no idea what
you're talking about."

I have no inclination to tell him what I'm talking about,
so instead, I give him a group of copied pages that Sam has
gotten from hacking into computers. "Please look through

these pages and tell me if they are copies of your credit card bills."

He looks, though not too carefully. His mind must be racing, trying to figure out a way out of the trap that he's just "wheeled" himself into. "Yes . . . they look like mine. Sure."

"You can take some time to confirm this, but I will now tell you that based on your credit card receipts, you were within two hours' drive of every one of those deaths at the time they happened. Yet you lived in New Jersey, and these deaths occurred in all different parts of the country."

"You're not saying I killed these people. Is that what you're saying?" He's showing a proper measure of confusion and outrage, an amazing job under the circumstances. But for someone who can fake paralysis for years, this bullshit must be a piece of cake.

"So you did not kill them? You did not kill any of them? Including the victim in this case?"

"I have never killed anyone in my life."

"And everything you've said in court today is truthful?"

"Totally."

"Equally truthful? None of your statements were less true than others?"

"Every single word has been the truth."

"How did you get to court today, Mr. Pollard?"

Finally, a crack in his armor, the kind of crack that the Iraqi army left on the way to Baghdad. First his eyes flash panic, then anger. "You son of a bitch," he says.

Harrison admonishes him for his answer, and I ask the question again. "How did you get to court today, Mr. Pollard?"

His voice is soft, his teeth clenched. "I drove."

"Using the set of hand controls you described earlier?"

"Yes." He has the look of a man being dragged closer

and closer to a cliff. All the while his mind must be racing, trying to figure out if I can prove that he's lying. If I can prove it, he'll stop lying and try to lessen the damage. If I can't, there's no reason for him to stop.

"And that statement is as truthful as every other one you've made today?"

"Yes."

I let him off the stand, asking that he remain in the court, subject to recall. Harrison grants the request, and Dylan doesn't object. Dylan looks like he's planning to follow Pollard over the cliff.

Pollard takes a seat near the back of the room, and I call Lester Mankiewicz, a client of Sam's. Mankiewicz was a computer technician for the Ford Motor Company at their Mahwah, New Jersey, plant. He worked there for eleven years, installing and operating the computers that exist in every car made today.

Lester agreed to Sam's request for help in this case because it sounded like fun, and Sam says there's pretty much nothing that Lester won't do for fun. I had explained to Lester that what he would be doing was technically illegal, but that I could guarantee that he would not be charged with a crime. Once I told him what we wanted him to do, I think he would have paid us for the opportunity.

I have a television and VCR brought into the courtroom and take Lester through his story. He and Sam taped every aspect of it, so his words are like televised voice-over.

"Last night at three A.M. I entered Bobby Pollard's unlocked vehicle, which was parked on the street in front of his neighbor's house. I installed a device that is technically a small computer chip but really operates like an alarm clock. In this case it was set to go off five minutes after the car was started."

"What would happen when it went off?" I ask.

"It would disable the hand controls . . . neither the brakes nor gas would work, other than by using the foot pedals."

He continues to describe the rest of the operation. He installed another device to measure pressure on the foot pedals, and both devices could be monitored at a remote location.

"Please take us through what happened when Mr. Pollard started driving," I say.

His presentation is devastating. I expected that when the hand controls lost power, Pollard would be forced to use his legs to control and drive the car, secure that no one would ever know the difference, since he was alone. Amazingly, Pollard never used the hand controls at all, using the foot pedals the entire time. Every bit of this is measured by computer.

I let Lester off the stand and try to introduce copies of Pollard's medical records. They show that he was in fact in an accident in Spain but that it was relatively minor. The accident left him paralyzed, but the attending physician found no medical explanation for it.

Dylan objects to the introduction of the medical records, on the grounds that there is no one in the court qualified to authenticate them. Harrison agrees, as I figured he would, and we don't get to use them.

Next up is Carlotta Abbruzze, a shrink I went to for a while when my marriage was breaking up. I decided I didn't want to be shrunk, and my marriage broke up, but Carlotta and I remained friends. She has more Ph.D.'s than anyone I know, and she is easily qualified to testify in this case.

I ask Carlotta to explain psychosomatic paralysis. In layman's terms she explains that while there is no physical reason for it, the paralysis itself is real. She also describes how the human mind, if it leans toward such a syndrome, can be incredibly opportunistic. A minor car accident such as Pollard had could have triggered the immediate mental response to develop the syndrome.

"How long might it last?" I ask.

"Anywhere from a few minutes to a lifetime. When it disappears, the patient might intentionally continue to fake the paralysis, if it is providing some mental comfort for him."

"Just hypothetically, if a young man whose entire life was dedicated to football came to believe that he was not good enough to make it in the NFL, might even that subconscious realization bring on the syndrome?"

"It's certainly possible," Carlotta says.

Dylan's cross-examination is relatively effective, getting Carlotta to admit that she has never examined Pollard and that she can't be sure that he has ever suffered from this syndrome. I'm ultimately satisfied with her testimony; the jury understands this is a possible explanation for Pollard's situation.

To cap off an extraordinary day, I call a devastated Bobby Pollard back to the stand. "Mr. Pollard," I ask, "were all of your previous answers to my questions truthful?"

His reply is terse. "I take the Fifth."

"Have you been lying about your medical condition?"

"I take the Fifth."

"Did you kill members of the high school all-American team that you were chosen to be on?"

"No."

I let Bobby go and call Pete Stanton. He testifies about Adam's murder, including the fact that Adam's computer showed that he had been investigating the high school all-American team. He also confirms that the phone bill from the phone Adam used in my office shows two calls to Bobby Pollard the day he was murdered.

"And where was Kenny Schilling on that day, the day Adam Strickland was murdered?" I ask.

"In County Jail," Pete says.

Dylan's cross-examination is quick, as if he doesn't want to concede Pete has had anything important to say. "Lieutenant Stanton, have you arrested Bobby Pollard for the murder of Adam Strickland?"

"No."

"Have you decided to?"

"Not at this moment."

Dylan nods; his point is made. "But you did arrest someone for this murder?"

"Cesar Quintana, but he was released for lack of evidence."

"And you believed that he was the killer and that the murder was a case of mistaken identity? Is that not true?"

"I believed it then, but I've learned a lot since then."

"But again, you haven't learned quite enough to make another arrest?"

"It won't be long now," Pete says.

Dylan smiles. "I can hardly wait."

Pete leaves the stand, and I call Dr. Stanley Robbins, my last witness of the day. He testifies as to the properties of potassium and its ability to cause fatal heart attacks while being very difficult to discover.

Dylan's cross-examination is brief, and a very eventful court day is over. As I'm leaving, Laurie arrives, looking somewhat shaken from her experience at the TV studio with Teri Pollard.

"It was horrible," Laurie says. "Before she knew what we were doing, she was confiding in me, talking about how difficult their life has been since Bobby's injury. Then, when she realized what was going on today, and that Bobby was faking that injury . . . I don't think she had any idea, Andy."

Laurie is feeling guilty about having deceived her, and I am as well, but I don't know how it could have been helped.

I do know one thing . . . I'm glad I'm not there to hear the conversation in the Pollard house tonight.

• • • • •

TONIGHT'S MEETING is to make the

most important decision a defense attorney has to make in every trial: whether or not to let the defendant testify in his own defense. Usually, that important decision is a no-brainer, and my clients would have to walk over my dead body to reach the witness stand. Of course, most of them would prefer it that way.

This case is different, mainly because Kenny is the only person who can testify to a crucial fact: the subject of the "team meeting" the high school kids held in that restaurant those many years ago. Only three people are left alive who were there and know about the pact to share their NFL riches with each other. One is Kenny, one is Pollard, and the other is Devan Bryant, who is currently serving in the United States Army, stationed fifty miles outside of Kabul, Afghanistan. Bryant is unavailable to us, and Pollard seems likely not to aid in his own demise, so that leaves only Kenny.

Kenny wants to testify, which is typical of most defendants. In his view he will tell his story, and everyone will then believe him, and he can go home. This fantasy is greater in

celebrities than mere mortals; they are used to their fans hanging on their every word. The problem is, Dylan is not a fan.

Laurie and Kevin are divided on the issue. Laurie thinks
that Kenny should testify, that without the story of that pact
the players took, there is not a strong enough basis for anyone to accept the serial killing connection. She doesn't think
the statistical-probability evidence, while unequivocal, got
through to the jury.

Kevin, with proper lawyer's caution, is opposed to Kenny
testifying. He has seen too many people, many innocent, self-
destruct under a wilting cross-examination. Dylan is good.
Kevin knows it and doesn't want to take the chance.

This is a decision I always make myself, with equal
amounts logic and gut instinct. Both are telling me that Kenny
should not go near that stand, that the benefits of the "pact"
story and Kenny's appealing demeanor will be outweighed by
the negative of cross-examination. I don't want to give Dylan
a chance to take Kenny through the facts of this case, most of
which are incriminating. And I sure don't want Kenny up
there talking about how he held off the police at gunpoint
while Troy Preston's body was stuffed in his bedroom closet.

Kevin leaves, and I start thinking about my closing statement. Like my opening statement, I don't write it out, rarely
even take notes, because I want it to be as spontaneous as
possible. But there are points I want to be sure I cover, so I
start mentally ticking them off.

Laurie comes into the den and asks if I want something to
eat. I don't, and I'm about to tell her so when the phone rings.
She picks it up. "Hello."

She listens for a few seconds and then says a tentative
"Hi." Since the initial "Hello" should have covered the greeting part of her conversation, and since I can hear a tension in

her voice, I immediately know that this is a charged phone call.

The rest of the call is peppered with clever Laurie-phrases like "I see," "I will," and "Of course." Laurie sneaks glances over at me to see if I'm paying attention to her, so I try to pretend that I'm not, though of course she knows I am.

She throws in a final "I will," and then hangs up. She looks over at me, and I say, "Wrong number?"

She smiles slightly, as if caught, and says, "That was Sandy. They're pressuring him to pressure me for an answer."

"You said 'I will' twice. Was that as in 'I will move back to Findlay,' or as in 'I will never leave the love of my life, Andy Carpenter'?" I'm trying to make my tone sound flip, which is tough considering I'm so nervous I can't unclench my teeth.

"It was as in 'I will have an answer by next week,'" she says.

"You don't know what you're going to do yet?" I ask.

"Andy, you will know the moment I do." She comes over and sits next to me, putting her hand on my knee. "And I'm sorry to put you through this . . . it's just very hard for me. I'm finding this so terribly difficult."

"Join the club," I say.

Laurie leaves me to work on my closing statement, not the easiest thing to do under these circumstances. Tara lays her head on my knee, in the same place where Laurie's hand had just been. "You're going to stay with me, right?" I say to her. "I'm prepared to guarantee you biscuits for life if you do."

She snuggles against me. Just what I like, a woman who can be bought.

• • • • •

THE MOMENT COURT is called to
order, I announce that we are resting our case. Harrison asks
Dylan if he would like to adjourn until after lunch to prepare
his closing argument, but Dylan's preference is not to wait. He
clearly had correctly predicted I would not let Kenny take the
stand, and is fully prepared.

"Ladies and gentlemen," Dylan begins, "when I stood before you at the start of this trial, I told you that Mr. Carpenter
would invent theories and attempt to confuse you with irrel-
evancies. I told you that you should keep your eyes on the
evidence and not let his sleight of hand fool you. But I've got
to be honest, I had no idea how far he would go with it.

"Think about it. None of it had anything to do with the
facts. Those facts haven't changed, haven't even been challenged. Kenny Schilling was seen leaving the bar with Troy
Preston shortly before he was killed. Mr. Preston's blood was
found in Schilling's abandoned car. His *body* was found in a
closet in Schilling's *house*.

"But we hear that Mr. Schilling was somehow framed; that
he's innocent, pure as the driven snow. So how did this in-

nocent man act when the police arrived? He shot at them and barricaded himself in his house." Dylan shakes his head sadly. "Amazing.

"Now, Mr. Carpenter is a very clever lawyer, but when confronted with these facts, he acted like a man in a trap. First he tried to get out of that trap by claiming a Mexican drug gang did it, though he neglects to say why. Then, when he realized that exit was closed off, he tried to escape the trap by completely reversing direction, claiming it was part of a se-rial killing and the trainer did it." Dylan chuckles slightly to himself and shakes his head at the absurdity of it.

"I don't know how those poor young men died, but I do know the police in each case did not consider them mur-ders . . . not even suspicious. And I also know that those deaths bear no resemblance whatsoever to the kind of death Troy Preston suffered: dumped in a closet and shot in the chest.

"I also don't know what drives a man like Bobby Pollard to fake such a serious injury. And I don't know how cell phones work, or what keeps airplanes in the air, or how we landed a man on the moon. And all of those things that I don't know have nothing to do with this case.

"I do know that Troy Preston is dead," he says, and points to Kenny, "and that this man killed him. And I am confident that you know it as well and that you will find him guilty as charged."

Dylan has outdone himself; I have never heard him bet-ter. I feel a momentary panic that, while I've been focused so much on the deaths of all those football players, the jury might well see them as irrelevant.

I stand and walk slowly toward the jury. "On a December weekend almost eight years ago eleven teenagers were brought together. They came from Iowa, and Wisconsin, and

Alabama, and Texas, and California, and Pennsylvania, and Nebraska, and Ohio, and North Carolina, and two from right here in New Jersey.

"Except for the two men from New Jersey, Kenny Schilling and Bobby Pollard, they were all meeting for the first time. So they spent the weekend together, and they talked. In fact, one of their talks was so secret that they asked the only adult in the room to leave so he wouldn't hear them.

"And then the weekend ended, and they went home, and one after another they died.

"There is simply no chance that this is a coincidence. You did not hear me arguing against the DNA evidence, because that was simply a matter of mathematics, and numbers don't lie. Well, you heard an expert tell you that the odds of these deaths being a coincidence are one in seventy-eight billion, and those numbers don't lie either.

"But if you're shaky on those numbers, just add in the fact that Bobby Pollard and Kenny Schilling were both geographically available to have committed every one of those murders. I should have asked the mathematics professor what the odds would be against that. I probably can't count that high.

"So it is reasonable for you to assume that either Bobby Pollard or Kenny Schilling killed these people. That alone should tell you, after you listen to Judge Harrison's charge, that you should vote to acquit Mr. Schilling. If it could have been either one of them, then by definition there is more than a reasonable doubt that it was Mr. Schilling.

"But that's not all you know. You know that Adam Strickland, who was in the process of investigating Bobby Pollard, was suddenly and brutally murdered to cover up what he learned. You also know that Mr. Schilling was in jail, was living through this trial, at the time. Even the prosecution would admit that Kenny Schilling did not murder Adam Strickland.

"And most important, you know that Bobby Pollard is a liar. A liar under oath. A liar of mega-proportions. To believe that Kenny Schilling is the murderer, you must believe Bobby Pollard. I submit that no one should believe Bobby Pollard.

"Kenny Schilling had a very difficult upbringing, the kind of childhood that destroys far too many lives. It takes a very strong person to overcome it, but Kenny did more than just overcome bad luck. He went on to become an exemplary citizen, a good guy in an era and an occupation in which bad guys are all too prevalent.

"There is nothing that Kenny Schilling has ever done, not even anything he's ever said, that would give the slightest credence to the view that he could have suddenly committed a heinous crime like this. And he did not commit this crime, nor any of the others you've heard about.

"Do not end another life, one that is really just beginning, and one that is filled with such promise." I point to Kenny. "This man deserves his life back. Thank you."

I have never given a closing statement without being positive I screwed it up, and comments to the contrary from Kevin, Laurie, and Kenny don't come close to penetrating that pessimism. My guess is that I feel this way because it was my last chance to influence the jury, and matters are now totally out of my hands.

Harrison has decided to sequester the jury for the duration of their deliberations, and after charging them he sends them off to begin. I am now waiting helplessly for twelve citizens to decide the fate of a man I consider innocent. I am also waiting, just as helplessly, for Laurie to decide whether she will exit my life.

Suffice it to say, I am not a happy camper.

• • • • •

EACH PERSON REACTS differently to the stress of waiting for a jury verdict. I become cranky and obnoxious, snapping at anyone who asks anything about the trial. I also become intensely and uncharacteristically superstitious, living according to a long-held list of idiotic behaviors that would make life intolerable if I attempted it on a permanent basis. For instance, for fear of pissing off the justice system god, I won't do anything remotely illegal. I won't drive one mile over the speed limit, I won't jaywalk, I won't even play loud music on my car radio.

My other trait during these times ties in well with the first two. I also become a hermit, and anyone who has suffered through any time with me while waiting for a verdict thinks my reclusiveness is a good thing.

"Verdict stress" brings out Kevin's hypochondriac tendencies even further, which is no small statement. This time it happens more quickly than most: When Judge Harrison sends the jury off to deliberate, Kevin literally can't get up with the rest of us to leave the courtroom. He decides that something called his L4-L5 disk has degenerated, apparently overnight, and he needs a spinal fusion. What he really needs is a head transplant, but Laurie and I are obliged to almost carry him to his car.

Making matters worse is that my pessimism is shared by the large majority of television pundits covering the trial. In fact, I would say that three out of every five people in America are serving in the role of television pundit on this case. The majority view is that the defense is hoping for a hung jury, since not only would it obviously not be a loss but it would give us more time to investigate Bobby Pollard.

I actually have Laurie and Sam continuing to look into Bobby, in the likely event that we should lose and have to appeal. The unfortunate fact is that even a victorious appeal would take years and would destroy Kenny's football career in the process.

Laurie has spoken to three members of the defensive half of the *Inside Football* all-American team, all of whom were in the restaurant that night, but not with the offensive team when the pact was discussed. One of them remembers Bobby telling him about it, and his surprise that Bobby seemed to take it so seriously. That person should be a solid witness at what I hope will be Bobby's eventual trial.

It is an irresistible impulse to try to gauge the jury, to try to guess what they must be thinking. I never do so out loud, since that's one of my superstitions, but it certainly rattles around in my head enough.

In this case I'm hoping for a long deliberation. Our defense of the serial killings came out of left field, something the jury didn't expect, and without a necessarily clear connection to the offense charged. If the jury gives it serious consideration, it should take time for them to examine and debate. If they reject it out of hand, certainly a possibility, then there's really nothing to ponder; all the other evidence favors the prosecution.

I'm at home obsessing when the phone rings, always a traumatic event during a verdict wait. It's Rita Gordon, the court clerk, calling. Since it's only the morning of the second day of deliberation, if there's a verdict we're finished.

"I hope you're just calling to say hello," I say.

"Hoping for a long one?" she says. Knowing how anxious I am, she doesn't wait for an answer. "No verdict yet. The jury has a question."

The TV is on, and I see the "Breaking News" banner, "Schilling Jury Has Question," at the same moment Rita is telling me this. Rita says the judge wants us there in an hour, so I call Kevin and trudge down to the court.

On the way to the courthouse I hear that Quintana's body has finally been discovered in a field near the New Jersey Turnpike. I had been thinking that Petrone had sent him to the bottom of the ocean, but apparently, he wanted to use this killing to send a message to others stupid enough to mess with his territory.

I arrive at the courthouse having not even thought what the jury's question might be, since requests from juries are rarely revealing. They usually focus on a specific piece of evidence, but that in itself reveals nothing. They could be looking at the evidence because they are skeptical of it or because they give it real credibility and importance to the case.

This situation is slightly different. The jury wants to know if they can see police reports related to the other deaths of the young football players. Judge Harrison tells them they cannot, that only evidence introduced at trial is to be considered, and these reports were not part of the trial record. He says this patiently, even though he had made the point in his charge to the jury just before they went out. They essentially dragged us down here to answer a question that has already been answered.

I'm encouraged, though, because at least they're paying attention to our defense and not rejecting it out of hand. It's a small sign of hope, and I'm quite willing to shed a tiny bit of my pessimism and grab on to it.

Even during my self-imposed isolation during a verdict wait, I quite willingly have Laurie sleep over on our regular nights. I might be a hermit, but I'm not a crazed hermit. She is also quiet and reserved, and between us we're not a terribly fun couple.

I know she's finalizing her decision, but I'm past dwelling on it by now. I'm actually starting to get a little annoyed; it probably didn't take Truman as long to decide to drop the A-bomb.

I meet every day with Kenny Schilling, who acts as stoic as he can. The strain is starting to line his face to the point where he's looking like a paint-by-numbers drawing. I also talk on the phone each day with his wife, Tanya, who is better at verbalizing just how agonizing this process is. I am not able to give either of them any indication of how things will go or when.

Bobby Pollard has stayed out of the public eye, and I assume and hope that the authorities are digging into the nuts and bolts of the case we presented. Teri, ever the amazingly supportive wife, has made a public statement supporting her husband and declaring him innocent, but I can't imagine that she isn't feeling horribly betrayed.

The call comes from Rita Gordon on the morning of day six. "It's showtime, Andy," she says. "The judge wants all parties here at eleven A.M."

"Okay" is the cleverest response I can come up with.

● ● ● ● ●

I'M TOLD THAT a heavyweight championship fight has the most "electricity" of any live event, but I can't imagine how it could be more charged than this courtroom. The entire country has followed this case, hanging on every word, analyzing every nuance, and it has all come down to this. A young athlete, a member of the "celebrity class," is going to learn whether he's heading for death row or back to the locker room.

Just before Judge Harrison comes into the room, I walk over to Tanya Schilling to shake her hand. I have a million things I could say, and I'm sure she does as well, but neither of us says a word.

As I head back to my seat at the defense table, I see that a bunch of Kenny's teammates, as well as Walter Simmons, have managed to get seats. I briefly wonder whether they got them from scalpers; I can imagine these seats would go for a lot of money.

Kenny is brought in and takes his seat. As Judge Harrison comes in, Kenny takes a deep breath, and I can see him trying to steady himself. He has handled himself with dignity throughout the trial, and he's not about to stop now.

The jury is led in, looking at neither the prosecution nor the defense. They haven't been able to take their eyes off Kenny since jury selection, and now they're looking away. If I were rating signs, this would not be a good one.

Judge Harrison asks the foreman if his jury has reached a verdict, and I find myself hoping he'll say no. He doesn't, and Harrison directs the clerk to retrieve the verdict slip from him. The clerk does so and hands it to Harrison.

Harrison reads it, his face impassive, then hands it back to the clerk. He asks Kenny to stand, and Kenny, Kevin, and I stand as one. I have my hand on his left shoulder, and Kevin has his hand on his right. Kenny turns to Tanya and actually smiles, a gesture of immense strength and generosity.

I can almost feel the gallery behind me, inching forward, as if that will let them hear the verdict sooner.

The clerk starts to read. "In the matter of *The State of New Jersey v. Kenneth Schilling,* we the jury find the defendant, Kenneth Schilling, not guilty of murder in the first degree."

Kenny whirls as if avoiding a tackle and reaches for Tanya. Their hug is so hard it looks like one of them is going to break. He outweighs her by over a hundred pounds, but I'm not sure which one I'd bet on.

After a short while Kenny spreads his arms to include Kevin and me in the embrace. As group hugs go, it's a good one. Kenny and Tanya are crying, while Kevin and I are laughing. But we're all making the same point in our own way . . . it doesn't get much better than this.

Judge Harrison gets order in his courtroom and officially releases Kenny, who's got to do some paperwork. Tanya waits for him while Kevin and I go outside to answer a few questions from the assembled media.

When we get to the area set up for the press briefing, we see something unusual going on. Rather than waiting for us to arrive, the press is gathered around a TV monitor, watching a cable news station. They are watching the news, when they're supposed to be covering it.

"What's going on?" I say, a little miffed that nobody is paying much attention to me. One of the reporters answers, "Bobby Pollard is threatening to kill his wife."

I start walking toward the television monitor when a uniformed officer comes over to me and grabs my arm. "Mr. Carpenter, Lieutenant Stanton asks that you come with me immediately."

He quickly starts leading me away, and when I look back, I see that Kevin is lost in the crowd. Within moments we're in a police car, heading toward Fair Lawn, and I ask the officer to bring me up-to-date.

"Pollard's wife called 911. He's in their house with a gun, and she said he's going crazy, threatening to kill everyone."

"Why does Pete want me there?" I ask, but he shrugs and says he has no idea.

We arrive near the Pollard house in a few minutes, and the scene is a middle-class version of the standoff at Kenny Schilling's house. This case has ironically come full circle, except this time there is no way I'm going in.

I see Pete, who is second-in-command to his captain. It turns out that I have no real function here; Pete tells me that they figured that since I know the players, they might have some questions I could answer. I'm told to stay in the police command van and wait, which I'm more than happy to do.

In the van one of the sergeants plays back a copy of the 911 call. Teri Pollard's voice is the sound of pure panic. "This is Teri Pollard. My husband has a gun. I'm afraid he's going to—it's okay, honey, I'm just calling to get you some help, that's all . . . just some help." I can't hear Bobby's voice through the tape, but it's obvious she's talking to him.

She continues. "Please. He left the room. Send officers quickly . . . please!"

The dispatcher asks for her address and, after she gives it, asks if there is anyone else in the house. Teri says no, that their son is staying at her mother's in Connecticut. The call is then cut off, suddenly and with no explanation.

"Has there been any contact with her or Bobby since?" I ask.

"No," he says. "We've been calling in, but nobody answers the phone. But no gunshots either."

Then, in literally a sudden blast of irony, a gunshot rings out, seemingly from inside the house. I hear a policeman from the forward lines near the house yell, "Move!" and I see a SWAT team head toward the house and break in from all sides in a beautifully coordinated movement.

Maybe thirty seconds pass, though they seem like three hours, and a voice yells out, "Clear!" Pete and a bunch of other officers head for the house and enter. The sergeant I am with does so as well, so I tag along with him. I'm not sure if he even notices me, but he doesn't tell me to stay back.

There are at least a dozen officers in the house, all talking, but above the din I can hear a woman crying, a frighteningly pained sound. I move toward the den, which is where the sound is coming from. It's the room in which I talked to the Pollards on two previous occasions.

Teri Pollard is on the couch, hysterical, while Bobby is dead on the floor, against the wall, his head a bloody mess. Next to his outstretched hand lies a gun, more effective than a thousand justice systems.

• • • • •

LAURIE AND TARA are waiting for me

when I get home. My two favorite ladies.

We all go for a walk around the neighborhood. I haven't been spending nearly enough time with Tara, and I want to change that now. She seems to be getting more white in her face each day, a sign of advancing age in golden retrievers. In Tara's case it's less significant than in other goldens, because Tara is going to live forever.

The scene at the Pollards' and the lingering depression over Adam's death have really taken their toll on me, and I'm feeling little of the euphoria that I would ordinarily feel after a victory like the one in court today. For that reason I didn't schedule the party we have at Charlie's after every positive jury verdict.

"You were brilliant, Andy," Laurie says. "I don't know that there's another lawyer in the country that could have gotten Kenny acquitted with the evidence they had."

"Adam did it. I was nowhere until Adam came up with the answer."

"He helped, but you led the team, and you got it done. Don't take that away from yourself."

"It was awful at the Pollards' house today," I say. "I'm just so tired of all this death and pain. And I keep saying that, and yet I don't change anything."

"You're doing what you were meant to do, in the place you were meant to do it. And I think that down deep you know that."

I shake my head. "Not right now I don't."

"If not for you, Kenny Schilling's life would be over, and Bobby Pollard would still be out there killing. The death and pain would be much worse."

"But I wouldn't have to look at it."

We walk for a while longer, and I say, "What Teri Pollard went through is beyond awful. This man she devoted herself to, every day of her life, completely betrayed her. And then, after she stayed, after she forgave him, he left her to deal with everything alone."

"She's a strong woman," Laurie says. "She'll rely on the core of that strength, and she'll get through it."

"You're a more optimistic person than I am."

"I don't think so," she says. "You're just more honest about it. I have as many doubts as anyone, but I learned a long time ago that it doesn't help to give in to them. That we have to do what we think is best and deal with the consequences."

We walk another block in silence, and I say, "You're leaving." It's a statement, not a question, that comes from some hidden place of certainty and dread.

"Yes, Andy. I am."

I feel like a house is sitting on top of me, but it hasn't been dropped suddenly. It's more like it's been lowered on me. I've seen it coming for a while, but even though it was huge and obvious, I just couldn't seem to get out of the way.

I don't say anything, I can't say anything, so she continues. "I wish more than anything in the world that you would come with me, but I know you won't, and I'm not sure that you should. But I will always love you."

I want to tell Laurie that I love her, and that I hate her, and that I don't want her to go, and that I want her to get the hell out of my life this very instant.

What I say is, "Have a nice life."

And then Laurie keeps walking, but Tara and I turn and walk back home.

• • • • •

PEOPLE TELL ME that the intense pain is going to wear off. They say that it will gradually become a dull ache and eventually disappear. I hope they're right, because a dull ache sounds pretty good right now.

Of course, my circle of friends is not renowned for their sensitivity and depth of human emotion, so they could be wrong. The agony I currently feel over losing Laurie could stay with me, which right now would seem to be more than I can stand.

I tell myself to apply logic. If she left me, she doesn't love me. If she doesn't love me, then I haven't lost that much by her leaving. If I haven't lost that much, it shouldn't hurt like this. But it does, and logic loses out. I can count the times that logic has lost out in my mind on very few fingers.

Even gambling on sports doesn't help. In normal times a Sunday spent gambling on televised games allows me to escape from anything, but Laurie's leaving is the Alcatraz of emotional problems. I can't get away from it, no matter what I do.

I spend half of my time waiting for the phone to ring, hoping that Laurie is calling to change her mind and beg my forgiveness. The other half of my time I spend considering whether to call and tell her I'll be on the first plane to Findlay. But she won't call, and neither will I, not now, not ever.

Tonight Pete, Kevin, Vince, and Sam have taken me to Charlie's to watch *Monday Night Football*. The Giants are playing the Eagles, which would be a big deal if I gave a shit about it. I don't.

Halftime has apparently been designated as the time to convince me to get on with my life. They've got women to fix me up with, vacations I should take, and cases I should start working on. None of those things have any appeal, and I tell them so. The chance of my going on a blind date, or taking on a new case, is about equal in likelihood to my setting fire to myself. Maybe less.

Sam drives me home and is sensitive enough not to song-talk, though he would have no shortage of sad tunes to pick from. Instead, he thanks me for the opportunity I gave him to work on the case; it's something he loves and would like to do more of in the future.

I remind him that both Barry Leiter and Adam have died in the last couple of years doing the same kind of work. "Why don't you do something safer, like become a fighter pilot or work for the bomb squad?" I ask.

Sam drops me off at home, and I open the door to a tail-wagging Tara. I believe she knows I need more love and support than usual, and she's trying to provide it. I appreciate it, but this may be that rare job bigger than Tara.

I get into bed and take a few minutes to convince myself that tomorrow will be a better day. I mean, the fact is that Laurie was my *girlfriend*. Nothing more, nothing less.

It's just not that big a deal. Who's going to feel sorry for you just because you and your *girlfriend* broke up? It's not exactly high up on the list of personal tragedies. In fact, if somebody hears you say it, the question they would be expected to ask is something like, "Well, then, who are you going to take to the prom?"

With that self-administered pep talk having failed once again to get through to me, I remember that I had set up a therapy session with Carlotta Abbruzze tomorrow, hoping that she could help me deal with Laurie's leaving. My view now is that the only way Carlotta can help me is if she calls Laurie and talks her into coming back.

In the morning I take Tara for a walk, and we're halfway through it when I realize I had scheduled a meeting with Kenny Schilling at his house at ten. After every case I wait a while and then meet with the client. It's to go over my final bill, but, more important, to find out how the client is adjusting and to answer any remaining questions he or she has. It's always nice when that meeting is not in prison.

Kenny and Tanya graciously welcome me into their home, and Tanya goes off to get coffee. Kenny's wearing a sweat suit, aptly named because it's drenched with sweat.

"Sorry I didn't get dressed all fancy for my lawyer," he says with a smile, "but I've got to get in shape."

"I won't keep you long," I say, and we quickly go over my bill, which despite its large size draws no objection from him. It's actually less than the estimate I had given him at the start of the trial.

"I still can't believe Bobby killed all those people," Kenny says.

"Could you believe he wasn't paralyzed?" I ask.

"No, that just blew me away."

Kenny and Tanya have very few questions; they're still flushed with relief that their lives haven't been permanently derailed. I finish my coffee and get up to leave.

"Man, can't you stay another couple of hours? I need an excuse not to work out."

"That's probably the only athletic thing we have in common. Hey, let me ask you a question," I say, and then describe in detail my plan to become a placekicker for the Giants.

"That sounds pretty good," he says.

"You think it could work?"

"Not a chance in hell," he says, and laughs.

He's challenging my manhood. "Be careful or I'll be on that field before you will," I say.

He shakes his head. "I don't think so. They're looking to activate me next week in time for the game at Cincinnati."

Tanya stands to pick up the coffee cups. "Don't remind me," she says, smiling.

The comment surprises me. "You don't want him to play?"

"Not in Cincinnati. I've got bad memories of that. But this time I'm going . . . Watching it on television was horrible."

Kenny explains. "I got my bell rung in the fourth quarter when we were out there two years ago. I was out cold. Late hit."

I nod. "I think I remember that."

"Only time that ever happened to me. Man, that was scary as hell. Next thing I knew it was four hours later in the hospital. I didn't even know who won. Bobby had to tell me." He shakes his head sadly, probably at the aware-

ness that Bobby won't be there to tell him anything anymore.

I head out to the car, and I'm three blocks away when
it hits me. I drive the three blocks back to the house about
twice as fast, then jump out and pop open the trunk. I've
brought a lot of my case files with me, in case I needed to
refer to them to answer any questions about my bill, and
now I pore through them until I find the piece of information I need.

Tanya Schilling is surprised to find me standing there
when she answers the doorbell. "Sorry, but I need to talk
to Kenny."

"Sure, come on in," she says. "He's still in the den
goofing off."

She goes into the kitchen while I go back into the den.
Kenny is also surprised by my reappearance. "Hey, you
forget something?"

"Are you positive that Bobby was with you in the hospital in Cincinnati?" I ask.

"Absolutely. And not just because he was my friend.
He was my trainer . . . it was his job to be there."

"Kenny, I'm going to ask you something I've asked you
before. Last time you wouldn't answer; this time you've
got to."

"What is it?"

"The night you dropped Troy off at his house . . . the
night he died . . . who was the woman you were arguing
about?"

"I told you, I don't remember," he says. He can see by
my face that I'm not going to drop it, so he changes his
approach. "She's got nothing to do with this."

"I think she's got everything to do with it," I say.

"Tell him, Kenny." It's Tanya, standing in the doorway.

Kenny looks like the classic deer in the headlights. "Tell him what?" he asks, but it's clear he knows what. And he now knows that she knows.

Her voice is firm. "You tell him or I will."

I press him. "Who were you arguing about that night, Kenny?"

He nods in resignation. "Teri Pollard. Bobby's wife."

I already knew the answer to that question, and I can make a good guess at the answer to the next one. "Why were you arguing?"

Kenny looks at Tanya, gets no help, and turns back to me. "Troy was fooling around with her."

"Why did you care?"

"Bobby was my friend. They had a good marriage . . . they had a son . . . I didn't want him breaking them up."

"There's more to it than that," I say.

"No," Kenny says, "that's it."

I turn to Tanya. "Can you tell me?"

She nods. "Yes, I'll tell you. Jason Pollard is Kenny's son."

Kenny whirls in surprise. "How did you know that?"

"Because I know you. Because I live with you. Because I understand you. You think I could watch you for all these years and not know what was going on? How stupid do you think I am?"

With no need to keep the secret from Tanya anymore, the story pours out. Kenny had a brief affair with Teri back when they were graduating high school; he thinks it was not long after the all-American weekend, but he can't be sure. Teri was planning to marry Bobby at the time and went ahead with it.

"When did she tell you that you were the father?" I ask.

"Maybe six months after Bobby's accident. I had just

met Tanya. I've helped support Jason ever since." He looks at Tanya. "Teri insisted that I keep it a secret, or she would cut me off from Jason. I didn't want that to happen. I'm so sorry."

"Did Teri want to leave Bobby for you?"

He nods. "Yeah, at first. But that was years ago. Why do you need to know all this?"

"Unless I'm very wrong, Teri Pollard killed Troy Preston. She killed her husband. She killed all of them."

• • • • •

SHE ASKED ME TO come over tomorrow night." It's the first sentence Kenny can manage to say after he processes what I've just told him.

"Why?" I ask.

"She said she was going through Bobby's stuff, and she needed some help, and that there might be some things I'd want to keep for myself. I told her I'd be there at eight."

"You're not going," Tanya says.

Kenny looks to me for guidance. "Don't say anything to Teri right now," I say. "Let me think about this for a while. We have until tomorrow night."

I promise to get back to them later today. I leave to be on time for my twelve-fifteen session with Carlotta, which has just changed in content and increased in importance.

Carlotta's door opens at exactly twelve-fifteen, not one minute sooner or later. This would be true if we were sitting just below an erupting volcano, with hot lava raining down on us, or if we were in Baghdad dodging cruise missiles. I suspect that punctuality is a trait common to all shrinks, but it is nonetheless amazing.

Once I'm seated in the chair opposite her, Carlotta asks, "So, Andy, why are you here?"

"Laurie left and I'm in such pain that sometimes I think I can't breathe," I say. "But that's not what I want to talk to you about."

She laughs. "Of course not. Why would it be?"

She's familiar with the case, having testified, but I proceed to tell her everything that I have just learned about Teri Pollard and Kenny Schilling, stopping frequently to answer her questions. Finally, I say, "I know it's hard for you to judge people from a distance, but if you can enlighten me at all, I'd appreciate it."

"Well," she says, "assuming Teri is the murderer, we can also assume two other things. One is that she is terribly unstable, in layman's terms a wacko. Such people only flirt with rationality, and it's not always helpful to try and predict their actions using logic. Two is that she took the pact that those young men made that weekend very seriously, maybe even more seriously than her husband did. When he had his accident, she thought she could rely on that pact, that the others would support her husband, and by extension her, in the manner in which they had promised. When they didn't, she exacted her revenge. She was possibly taking out on them her anger at her husband for failing her."

"But why commit the other killings in secret and Preston's so publicly? And why frame Kenny? Why not kill him also?"

"I think she would have felt that Kenny deserved a special kind of demise, of torture, compared to the others. He loved her, at least in a physical sense, and then abandoned her and her child. Plus, he succeeded dramatically in the

NFL, which in her eyes made him the most guilty of non-support."

"But he provided support," I say. "He made sure her husband was employed, and gave her money to raise the child."

Carlotta shakes her head. "Not enough. In her eyes not nearly enough. She wanted to be married to a star, and instead in her eyes she thought she was living with a cripple."

"Why now? Why would she wait and then choose to go after Kenny now?"

She shrugs. "That's beyond my range of knowledge. Did anything significant happen in Kenny's football career recently? Any special achievement?"

There it is; I can't believe I hadn't seen it. "He just signed a fourteen-million-dollar, three-year deal, plus incentives."

She smiles. "That might be rather significant, don't you think?"

I nod. "What is she likely to do next?"

"It's hard to say. She could continue to try to exact her revenge on Kenny, and that desire could be increased by her husband's death, even if she is the one that killed him. Or she could try to win him over, in the misguided notion that her husband stood between them. She might think that Kenny will now love her and they can ride off into the sunset together. One thing you can be sure of, though: She will do something. This doesn't end here."

On that ominous note I head down to the police station to meet with Pete Stanton. He is a very good friend of Laurie's, and I have to resist a strong temptation to ask if he's heard from her. Instead, I repeat the saga of Teri Pollard.

Since he's a good cop, his first reaction is skepticism that someone like Teri Pollard could have pulled off all these killings.

"Think about it," I say. "Most of them were heart attacks,

and I'll bet she used potassium, or something just like it. As a nurse she would have had even greater access to it than Bobby. As for the other deaths, Kenny told me she grew up in Kentucky and as a girl went hunting with her father, so she could handle a rifle. And a hit-and-run, anybody could do that."

"Have you established that she was present in the cities where the deaths took place?" he asks.

I shake my head. "Not yet. But Bobby said she went on all the road trips with him. That's why she couldn't hold down a full-time nursing job. She had the same access he did."

He's looking doubtful, so I add, "And there was evidence that a woman called a taxi from the convenience store near where Kenny's car was found. No one made the connection until now."

"What about her husband's suicide?" Pete asks. "He fired the weapon that killed him; there was gun residue all over his hands."

"I'd be willing to bet she had given him a drug to knock him out . . . probably potassium as well. She held the gun to his head with his own hand."

He still doesn't fully believe me but is cautious enough to be alarmed by Kenny's plan to visit her tomorrow night. He also knows that if I'm right, then Kenny's canceling the visit is not going to solve the problem. She'd keep coming after him.

We come up with a plan, but one that requires Kenny's participation. Pete comes with me to Kenny's house to present it, and Tanya joins us as we do so. Basically, we want Kenny to go to Teri's wearing a wire, and with a contingent of police secretly stationed right outside the house. If she makes a threatening or incriminating move, they will rush in and arrest her.

It's obviously dangerous, and Tanya predictably is against it. "If you're so sure she's the one, why don't you just arrest her now?" she asks.

"Because there's not enough evidence to make it stick," I say, and Pete voices his agreement. I go on, "Tanya, if we're right, she's going to keep coming after Kenny. We can either wait for her to do it on her terms or get her to do it on ours, when we're ready."

Kenny, who has been silent, considering this is his life we've been talking about, nods. "Let's do it. I want this over with."

• • • • •

PETE ALLOWS ME TO sit in the police communications van, situated just around the corner from Teri's house. Small cameras and microphones have been surreptitiously placed to monitor everything that goes on inside, and it's all in front of us on screens.

In the van are two technicians, plus Pete and I. The armed units are stationed near the house, out of sight from the street because, although it's seven-forty-five, Teri isn't home yet. Kenny is due in fifteen minutes, and we've told him to be right on time.

I'm vaguely uncomfortable with Teri's late arrival. If we're right, and she's going to make an attempt on Kenny's life, it's the type of thing you'd think she'd want to prepare for. You wouldn't expect her to be somewhere looking at her watch and thinking to herself, "Gee, I'm running late. I'm supposed to be killing Kenny Schilling in fifteen minutes."

"She might have made us somehow," Pete says. "She may know we're here. Or maybe something happened with her kid."

"She told Kenny that the son was at his grandmother's and wasn't coming back until next week." I don't mention that the boy is Kenny's biological son; it's not something that Pete needs to know.

At eight o'clock sharp, Kenny arrives. He rings the bell and gets no answer, then seems confused as to what to do. He looks around at the street, possibly hoping that we'll show up and tell him what the hell is going on, but of course we can't do so, since Teri might arrive at any time. Kenny does the proper thing: He sits on the porch and waits.

Another five minutes go by, and still no Teri. Kenny just sits there on the porch, completely and rightfully confused. Pete says, "Poor guy is getting stood up by the person supposed to kill him. You can't get much lower than that."

One of the technicians laughs and says, "Maybe she changed her mind and wants to date him. My dates stand me up all the time."

I don't share in the laughter, because what he has just said triggers a recollection of Carlotta saying that Teri might no longer want to kill Kenny, that with Bobby out of the way, she might want to win Kenny back. And that recollection sends a cold chill down my spine.

"Come on!" I yell. I open the door and jump out of the van. Pete is behind me, asking what the hell is going on. I rush to his car and say, "Hurry up! I'll tell you on the way!"

I tell him how to get to Kenny's house and that he should get backup to follow us. Once he's done so, I say, "Teri invited Kenny over to get him out of the house. Tanya's the target."

"Why?"

"To get her out of the way. Teri's nuts enough to think that Tanya is the only reason she can't have Kenny to herself. If she gets Tanya out of the way, she would think the coast is clear."

"Shit," Pete says, a sentiment I share completely.

We're a block away from the Schilling house when I see Teri's car.

Pete pulls up in front of the house, and I'm out of the car before he is. I run to the front door, which is fortunately but ominously open. I rush in, Pete right behind me.

We hear a woman's voice, a frightening sound somewhere between a scream and a plea. It's a large house, and impossible to be sure where the noise is coming from, but I realize where it must be.

"Pete!" I call out, hoping he can hear me but Teri can't. I run for the room I was in months ago, the room where Troy Preston's body was in the closet. I push open the door, and Tanya is huddled in a corner. Teri faces her, holding a handgun, but turns to me when she hears me coming in. Unfortunately, the gun turns along with her. "How nice you could join us," she says.

I raise my hands, even though I haven't been told to, and she motions me to stand near Tanya. I know Pete is out there in the hall, but he would have to get well into the room before having a clear shot at Teri. Teri could easily hear him coming and kill one of us before he could intervene.

I have no idea what to say to get out of this. Things that come to mind, like "You'll never get away with this" and "There's no reason anyone should get hurt," seem like pathetically ineffective clichés.

Instead, I try to surprise her, to make her think. "Why did you kill those young men?" I ask.

"You know about that?" she asks, her voice and half-smile reflecting pride in her own accomplishments. "Bobby said you were smart."

"Is it because they broke the pact? They didn't take care of Bobby?" As I say it, I'm watching the small corridor between the doorway and the main part of the room, hoping Pete can get in here without her noticing him.

"He would have taken care of *them*. If he had his legs, he would have been a star, and he would have taken care of every one of them. They took an oath. A goddamn blood oath."

Bobby did have his legs, but I don't think I'll remind her of that fact right now. I think I see a slight shadow in the corridor, and right now all I can do is hope the shadow is who I think it is.

The panicked Tanya seems to move slightly, causing Teri to yell and point the gun at her. I'm afraid she's going to shoot, but she doesn't. "Look at her," Teri says to me, indicating Tanya. "This is who Kenny thanked on television, for making him a star. Doesn't that make you sick?"

I see the shadow in the corridor move, so I look in the other direction, the direction of the window, and yell, "Pete!"

Teri turns toward the window, just for a split second, and it's enough time for Pete to get into the room. He yells, "Drop the gun!"

But Teri doesn't drop the gun, instead turns with it, and Pete has no choice but to shoot. The bullet hits her full force in the shoulder, sending her flying back into the wall as her gun falls harmlessly to the floor.

I grab Tanya and hold on to her, and it feels like within moments the room is filled with every cop and paramedic in the United States, as well as one running back for the Giants.

• • • • •

THIS SESSION WITH Carlotta is going to be about me, and as I sit in her waiting room at eight o'clock in the morning, I'm looking forward to it. She's seeing me on an emergency basis, since I called her and told her I was in a lot of pain.

"Emotional pain?" she had asked.

"Emotional pain," I had confirmed. "I've got things I need to talk about."

Carlotta opens her door and lets me in precisely at eight. I mutter a greeting, head straight for the couch, and lie down. "I don't think I can deal with Laurie being gone" is what I think. "Do you think Teri Pollard is sane enough to stand trial?" is what I actually say.

"This is the source of your emotional pain?" Carlotta asks.

"Not exactly."

"Then perhaps we should talk about the source of that pain."

I sit up and shake my head. "It's too painful."

We go on to talk about Teri, and I tell Carlotta what Pete Stanton has told me about his interrogation of her. Teri has openly admitted—in fact, bragged about—how she looked up each player who had verbally signed on to the "pact," all those years before. The first young man had laughed at her, ridiculing the idea that anyone could have taken it seriously.

Carlotta nods. "That would have set her off. And once she killed him, there was no turning back."

"But according to Pete, she was very calculating about it all. She took her time, didn't make them at all suspicious. She just slipped the potassium in their drink, and that was that."

"And her husband had no idea what she was doing?"

"It doesn't seem so. Bobby apparently didn't take the pact as seriously as she did, although she could only have heard about it through him. She wasn't there that weekend."

"The insecurity that would have driven Bobby to his psychosomatic injury would have made him build up the importance of the pact when he first related it to his wife," Carlotta says. "He was afraid he wasn't good enough to achieve success, so he was telling her that they'd be taken care of even if he failed."

"And she bought into it," I say.

Carlotta nods. "So strongly that she couldn't rationally deal with the disappointment when it turned out to be an illusion."

We talk about it some more, and even though there are twenty minutes left in my session, I stand up to leave.

"Andy, why don't you talk to me about what's bothering you?"

"I find it harder to deny things if I admit them first."

"It might help," she says.

"I'm not ready."

"When you are, I'll be here."

I nod. "I'll call you as soon as I am. Figure about four years from Wednesday."

• • • • •

I'M NOT GOING TO make it as a place-kicker. I know that now. I got a book to study the technique, and I've been trying it in the park for an hour a day, each of the last two days. I've been kicking off a tee, while Willie fields the kicks and Tara and Cash watch. All of them knew I was going to fail long before I did, as they watched my kickoffs bounce pathetically along the ground.

I do have another plan to reach the NFL, though. I'm going to be a coach. But I don't want to be like those other crazed coaches who stay up until three o'clock in the morning watching opponents' tapes. I'm going to be a placekicking coach. The hours shouldn't be too long, and the placekicking book I got gives me a head start.

I have already taken on another case. I'm representing Kenny and Tanya Schilling in proceedings to let them adopt Jason Pollard. Since he's Kenny's natural son, and they are an upstanding family with sufficient financial resources, it will be an easy win. Especially since there is no doubt that Teri will be confined for the rest of her life.

I've now added "breaking and entering" to the personal

criminal history I began when I instigated Quintana's murder. I made the assumption that Teri Pollard had taken the four hundred thousand dollars of Quintana's money from Troy Preston the night she killed him, and on Tuesday I climbed through a window of the Pollard house to look for it.

It took about an hour, but I found it buried under a mountain of toys in Jason's closet. I sent it, in the form of a check, to Adam's parents, with an accompanying note telling them that it was money he had earned. I also mentioned that he had talked about buying them a house, but that they should certainly do what they wish with the money.

Laurie sent me a letter. I got it last Wednesday, a couple of days after I talked to Carlotta. The envelope is pretty thick, so it's probably a few pages. Someday, maybe in the next couple of years, I'm going to open it. And then, a few years after that, I'll probably read it. If she wanted to come back, she'd call. This is probably a rehash of her reasons for leaving, and I just can't let myself think about it right now.

I read in this morning's paper that there's an eclipse coming up early next month. It upsets me that I have no one to whom I can say, "I told you so, the whole thing is a scam."

The truth is, there's a lot of things I want to say, but there's no one around that I want to hear them.

Laurie is the only person I really love in this world, and I hate her.